THE
OSLO
CONSPIRACY

THE OSLO CONSPIRACY

ASLE SKREDDERBERGET

Translated from the Norwegian by Paul Norlen

Thomas Dunne Books
St. Martin's Press
New York

This is a work of fiction. All of the characters, organizations, and events portrayed in this novel are either products of the author's imagination or are used fictitiously.

THOMAS DUNNE BOOKS.
An imprint of St. Martin's Press.

www.thomasdunnebooks.com
www.stmartins.com

Library of Congress Cataloging-in-Publication Data

Names: Skredderberget, Asle, 1972– author. | Norlen, Paul R., translator.
Title: The Oslo conspiracy: a thriller / Asle Skredderberget; translated by
   Paul Norlen.
Other titles: Smertehimmel. English
Description: First U.S. edition. | New York : Thomas Dunne Books, 2016. |
   "First published in Norway as Smertehimmel by Gylendal" [2013] — Verso
   title page. | Includes bibliographical references.
Identifiers: LCCN 2016007863| ISBN 9781250049612 (hardcover) | ISBN
   9781466850583 (e-book)
Subjects: LCSH: Private investigators—Fiction. | Women scientists—Fiction. |
   Murder—Investigation—Fiction. | Conspiracy—Fiction. | Pharmaceutical
   industry—Fiction. | Rome (Italy)—Fiction. | Oslo (Norway)—Fiction. |
   GSAFD: Mystery fiction. | Suspense fiction.
Classification: LCC PT8952.29.K73 S6413 2016 | DDC 839.823/8—dc23
LC record available at https://lccn.loc.gov/2016007863

First published in Norway as *Smertehimmel* by Gyldendal

First U.S. Edition: October 2016

10 9 8 7 6 5 4 3 2 1

Poor man wanna be rich,
rich man wanna be king.

—BRUCE SPRINGSTEEN, "BADLANDS"

THE
OSLO
CONSPIRACY

PROLOGUE

May 23, 1977, Mediterranean Sea between Tunisia and Sicily, on board Corvette F541

He lit a cigarette and thought about her.

The five-week-long mission was into its final day. In two days they would be reunited in Rome—and start planning.

Even after a twelve-hour watch, he couldn't just go straight to bed. He was too tired to sleep. Instead he went down to his cabin and changed into civilian clothes, before climbing the stairs back up on deck and heading toward the stern.

All around him there was total darkness. At this time of day the sky and sea were one. The only deviation was the white foam from the two propellers that drove the little Minerva Class Corvette military vessel steadily closer to Sicily, and steadily farther from North Africa.

At the start of the mission the atmosphere on board had been marked by noisy expectation. The crew talked about the cities they would visit on their trip, which would take them from

Sicily to Greece, on to Turkey, Cyprus, Lebanon, Israel, Egypt, past Libya into Tunisia, before they returned to Syracuse on Sicily.

Now the mood was marked more by impatient expectation. *Expectation* to get home to their families, *impatient* because it wasn't happening fast enough. A day did not pass without him having to mediate between quarreling sailors, and the mood was also tense among the officers at times.

Somewhere far off he glimpsed a lantern. He guessed at either fishermen or smugglers. Contraband was widespread in this part of the Mediterranean, and on this trip alone they had stopped several who looked like fishermen, but whose boats were full of everything from oil barrels to cigarettes and guns.

And every time they had to board a boat, his whole body felt uneasy.

Only two days earlier they had stopped a small fishing boat, and as he and a group of three men made their way on board, he knew something didn't add up. The fact that his captain—his superior—was inclined to let the little fishing boat pass did not improve his gut feeling. They were often at odds about this. He thought they had a right and a duty to stop any boat they perceived as suspicious. Either because it sat low in the water or because it was outside a fishing zone. The captain, on the other hand, preferred to let things pass. Presumably because it saved them a lot of paperwork, which in turn gave the captain more time for his favorite occupations, drinking and poker.

As the little group from *Marina Militare*—the Italian Navy— set foot on the deck of the fishing boat, they could tell that something was wrong. There was something in the gazes they met. The blankness in the eyes of the crew, as if they had given up.

And he knew that people who had given up—who saw no way out—could be dangerous.

They quickly gathered the crew and started searching the boat. Under the deck they found several dozen kilos of heroin, probably en route to Sicily or Naples. But they also found an injured North African with an unsecured hand grenade in his hand and nothing to lose by blowing them all to pieces. Instinctively he tackled the African and squeezed the grenade to keep him from detonating it. They rolled around on the floor while they fought over the grenade, and finally he sank his teeth into the back of his hand and bit as hard as he could, until the African let go with a howl.

In a few seconds he was on his feet, running up on deck and throwing the grenade as far as he could away from the boats. It made a little splash when it hit the surface, and then a big spurt of water when it detonated.

Forty-eight hours later he could still feel the incident in his body. He could have lost his life if the North African had dropped the unsecured grenade.

But it worked out, and they were on their way home.

He took two deep drags on his cigarette before he sent it in a long arc out into the darkness. Fatigue came on slowly. He enjoyed the warm wind of early summer that gently rumpled his hair, and stood swaying with eyes closed while he held on to the railing and tried to remember the smell of her.

He just had time to register a deep shaking in the hull and a bang, then everything went black. The pressure wave that followed tore the deck to pieces as if it were made of paper, blowing loose objects—and people—into the sea.

He did not notice that he ended up in the water. He did not notice how the waves took hold of his life vest and pulled him along. And he did not notice how little time it took before the sea extinguished the fire on the boat by engulfing it and sending it and his shipmates more than a thousand meters down to the seabed.

He remained bobbing in the waves, his arms and legs hanging limply down in the water. In no condition to undertake anything at all.

Because it was not up to him if he would live or die.

MONDAY

Present Day, Rome

There are two types of people.

Those who start to panic when they know they're going to die. And those who stay calm, as if the very certainty makes their thoughts weighty.

She stood there quietly looking at him and knew it was over. Obviously she could have tried to slam the door, thrown herself toward the bed and tried to call reception. Or run out onto the little balcony and tried to make herself heard over the Rome traffic six stories below.

But she just stood there. Resigned.

For a brief moment it suddenly felt absurd to think he might be dangerous. But deep down she knew. There was something in his eyes.

He stepped soundlessly across the threshold, his body almost springy on the thick hotel carpet, and an odor of cigarettes and sweat reached her nostrils. He quickly took a firm hold around her neck, and she felt a sharp prick below her ear.

He let go, and she shoved him away and staggered toward the bathroom. She locked the door and waited for him to start pulling on it. But outside it was quiet. He had time to wait.

She felt the onset of nausea, and her heart was pounding faster. There were tears in her eyes.

She knew she did not have much time before the anesthetic took effect.

The thought that everything had been in vain cut her in the gut, and she suppressed a "the hell it is." She knew that he would take the PC, the notebook, the flash drives, the phone, and anything else that might reveal what she had been working on the past year. She knew that he was thorough.

From the hotel room she could hear him clear his throat.

She let her eyes sweep across the little bathroom and stopped at the row of medicines on the shelf beside the mirror. For a few seconds, she stood as if frozen. As if the four pill bottles were speaking to her. Quickly she went over to the shelf, pulling out one of the middle bottles. The choice was not random, but she could not count on anyone understanding. For that reason she tore off a little toilet paper and took out her mascara.

She tried to write, but the paper tore and she had to start over. Her heart was hammering as she carefully tried to write his name. It was almost illegible, but it would have to do. She thought for a moment while she tried to blink away the tears. Then she wrote one more word, before folding up the paper and putting it in the bottle.

After that she stepped up into the bathtub and threw the bottle out the air vent. She heard it hit the cobblestone in the courtyard a few seconds later.

Is anyone going to understand? she thought.

In her toiletry case she found the nail clipper and made a

few quick scratches in the joint between two of the bathroom tiles under the vent.

She sat down on the tiles and leaned against the bathtub.

The haze came slowly and could not be stopped.

Her heart was beating more slowly and her upper body slid sideways along the bathtub.

She felt no pain when her head pounded hard against the floor.

FRIDAY

1

Milo Cavalli looked out over the gathering.

Besides his fellow officers from Financial Crimes, the group in the room consisted of a unit from the police task force and detectives from the organized crime departmemt with the Oslo police authority. They listened to him attentively. Men with arms crossed and snuff under their upper lips. The detectives in jeans and T-shirts, the task force in uniforms.

Milo adjusted his tie a little, and leaned down toward the laptop. A few seconds later the presentation was up on the wall behind him. The screen showed a grainy image, obviously taken with a telephoto lens, of a dark-skinned man in a suit on his way out of NB's head office at Aker Brygge.

"This is Reeza Hamid. He is twenty-eight years old, and by using a false reference he got a job in the brokerage house NB Markets. He's worked there the past year and a half, but he is actually associated with the so-called Downtown Gang."

The pictures showed the young Pakistani man at various

places in the city. He looked fit in a well-tailored dark suit. The prototype of the well-educated, well-integrated second-generation immigrant. Milo stopped at a picture taken outside a Narvesen convenience store, where Hamid was leaning forward as he accepted a light on a cigarette from another Pakistani.

"This is the only picture we have of him together with Anzaf Mukbar, whom you know as the undisputed leader of the Downtown Gang. According to our informants, Mukbar simply calls him the 'Finance Minister,'" said Milo, looking up at the gathering.

Some of the detectives from Organized Crime nodded in recognition, and Milo continued the briefing.

"We've been doing surveillance on Hamid for about six months and, with NB's help over the past month, we can now link him to a dozen insider transactions on the stock market."

The investigation had revealed how the computer-savvy young man, from his position as an accountant in the brokerage firm, had an overview of what plans were in the works for acquisitions and transactions under the auspices of NB Markets, and how he used this information to buy shares in companies he knew would be bought, and how he knew in advance what stocks major funds run by NB planned to buy and thus push the price higher. Milo continued to explain how the investments were made through various companies.

"We're talking in part about companies that run a car wash, a construction company, and a cleaning business. These are all companies that Hamid and the rest of the Downtown Gang are behind, and that take in large amounts of cash from criminal activity. After that they plow the surplus into stock investments, sell out over time and launder millions."

Milo looked at the gathering again. Most of them were

familiar with the activity of the various criminal gangs, whether it concerned torpedo activity, narcotics or prostitution. But it struck him that they did not fully understand the scope of what he was now telling them. He straightened up and cleared his throat slightly.

"Just to emphasize: We assume that this group, which consists of a core of between ten and fifteen individuals, has earned more on illegal insider training on the Oslo Stock Exchange the past six months than they have pushing dope and ladies the past year."

The head of the task force, Daniel Guttormsen, rose and came up to the podium beside Milo. Guttormsen was short and broad with a bad haircut.

"Very good, Cavalli. Thanks very much."

Milo nodded curtly and found a vacant chair while Guttormsen proceeded to his part of the presentation. He clicked through pictures of the neighborhood, architectural drawings of the apartment and evacuation routes.

"Now we have the opportunity to crush the Downtown Gang by arresting Reeza Hamid, and we'll make short work of it, lads. We'll go in both from the main entry and the veranda. And then we'll bring him in. We're ready to move out of here as soon as it's confirmed that he's home. Probably about six thirty or seven," he concluded.

The gathering broke up and the participants slipped out of the room.

Milo stayed behind and went over to Guttormsen.

"Where do you want us?"

Guttormsen smiled and patted Milo overly hard on the shoulder.

"You've done a great job. We'll take care of this now. So all you have to do is take off for the weekend."

He packed up his briefcase and started to head for the door after the other broad-shouldered officers.

Milo walked alongside.

"Guttormsen, the reason that Hamid managed to forge the reference from the business school was that he and the gang threatened one of the employees in the school administration. They promised to beat her husband and children senseless if she didn't fix the grades for him. I only want to underscore that even if this guy has a bean counter's brain and a nice suit, he's dangerous," said Milo.

Guttormsen stopped, a broad smile on his face.

"We are too, Cavalli."

The Lorry restaurant at the far end of Hegdehaugsveien was just as noisily charming as always on a Friday afternoon, and Milo found Frikk in the bar, where he was trying in vain to impress a coed. If it had been one of the usual financial hangers-on, she would have realized from the oversize watch, outrageously expensive suit and swaggering tone of voice that this was a guy with assets she could milk. Fredrik B. Hanefjell, "Frikk" to his friends and enemies because he swallowed his words and talked at breakneck speed, was among the ten most successful stockbrokers in the city and pulled in between ten and fifteen million a year in salary.

But all she saw was one big father complex.

A guy who was a bit too short, talked way too fast, and who was faithful to only one person in the whole world: himself.

She was clearly not letting herself be dazzled, and Frikk

mostly resembled a calf trying to fight its way out of a swamp. With every movement, every bellow, he sank lower. And closer to destruction.

"Hey! Milo!" he said when he caught the eye of his former associate, giving him a firm handshake and a pat on the shoulder.

"You gotta meet Solveig. Law student."

Milo shook her hand and met her gaze. For a few seconds she measured him with her eyes, from the dark, half-length naturally curly hair, to the tailor-made Italian suit and handmade Neapolitan tie to the shiny black shoes. She sighed audibly.

"Why didn't you get here first?" she said with a little smile and a quick glance at Frikk.

Before Milo could answer, she slipped off the bar stool and left them in favor of a girlfriend who had just come into the place.

"Good that you came, Milo. Was startin' to get bored!"

With an experienced finger motion he got the attention of the Swede behind the bar, and a short time later they were each standing with a half liter. They talked absently while constantly checking their cell phones for messages and e-mail. Neither of them was quite ready to leave the workweek behind.

"Make any money today, then?" Milo asked.

Frikk snorted.

"Even in a shitty market, like now, I don't have to work too many hours before I've pulled in what corresponds to your lousy salary."

Milo smiled over the half liter and took a gulp.

"And yet you'll never be as rich as me," he said.

Milo could not contain himself, and Frikk turned sulky. Like so many of his colleagues in the financial industry, Frikk was merciless in his characterization of competitors and colleagues, but lacked self-irony. And if there was anything he didn't like, it was being reminded that others were richer than him. Because the milestone for success in the industry was the size of your fortune, and Milo knew that it was even more frustrating for Frikk not to be able to overtake an underpaid Financial Crimes investigator who lived on an endlessly growing family fortune from Italy.

"Just kidding, Frikk. Relax. You're plenty rich and smart."

"Just shut up."

They were waved over to a booth with various stockbrokers and analysts who had also strayed from the wine bars on Tjuvholmen, and Milo sat absentmindedly while he checked his cell phone regularly. It was approaching six thirty, and he could not keep from thinking about the arrest. He bitterly regretted that he hadn't insisted on going with Guttormsen and the force, and wondered whether there was still time. He signaled to Frikk that he was going out to take a call, and sent a text message to Guttormsen on his way toward the exit.

WHAT'S HAPPENING?

Outside, the sun had long since disappeared and a cold draft in the air reminded the Friday crowd that winter was on its way.

It suddenly occurred to Milo that he was only a few blocks from Reeza Hamid's apartment, and he started walking up Hegdehaugsveien. There was a beep on his phone.

THE OBJECT JUST CAME HOME. WILL HAVE HIM SOON. 5 MIN. RELAX.

Milo could picture Guttormsen sitting in the operations vehicle, guiding his force as he had done hundreds of times before. But Milo was unable to do as he'd been told.

He was unable to relax.

Not until he's in handcuffs, he thought.

If Hamid got away today and realized that he was in hot

water, he would destroy all the evidence and lay low for the next year. Months of investigations would be wasted, and the Downtown Gang would take even more precautions and be even more difficult to nail.

Milo stopped twenty meters outside the courtyard to Hamid's building, on the other side of the street, and quickly looked around. Not a task force member in sight, but that was also the point.

With his eyes fixed on the building, he suddenly became aware of something moving on the roof. He had a brief glimpse of a dark figure on a balcony, and Milo noticed that a roof window was open. A passerby bumped him without stopping and therefore did not hear the little *"scusa"* that automatically came out of Milo.

He moved closer to the building, making a rapid zigzag between young people with backpacks and shopping bags. He looked up toward the building again and had a better view now. This time there was no doubt. A man was in the process of creeping from a loft balcony over toward the roof terrace on the neighboring building.

And it was not a policeman.

Milo did not want to lose sight of him and called Guttormsen. It rang only once before going to voice mail.

Damn!

Guttormsen had declined the call.

"This is Milo, I've just seen a male on the roof in the vicinity of Hamid's apartment, and I doubt that it was one of your people. I'll follow him," an irritated Milo spoke into the phone and hung up.

He remained standing next to the building façade and followed the figure with his eyes. He had worked his way over onto the roof terrace, after which he disappeared from sight. Milo fixed his gaze on the entry, and a minute later Reeza Hamid walked out onto Hegdehaugsveien from the exit door in a building fifteen meters from his own entry.

He started walking toward the city center, and Milo did the same. Between them the trolley, scooters and taxis were racing. Milo had still not made contact with Guttormsen on the cell phone, and when he saw Hamid starting to cross the street at Parkveien, he decided.

Milo was on the other side of the street, and remained standing at the crosswalk with the phone against his ear, pretending he was talking. He looked like the perfect financial analyst, not a detective doing surveillance.

Hamid approached and looked around a little nervously, but his gait was determined. He looked strong and fit, and Milo knew that he would have to surprise him to have any chance at all of holding him until the task force arrived. He waited until Hamid was a couple of meters away.

"I'll ask a guy here, wait a moment," said Milo loudly and artificially into the phone and took a step toward Hamid, who automatically slowed down.

"Do you know if Industrigata is farther up this way?" he asked with his eyes directed at Hamid, but still with the phone to his ear.

Hamid stopped a moment.

"Uh, I think you have to go farther—"

While he spoke, Milo raised the elbow on the arm he was holding the phone with, and swung it with all his force at Hamid. His elbow struck him in the temple and pushed him off balance, but not enough to knock him to the ground. Quickly Milo threw himself against him, pulling his torso with him so that the muscled man lost his balance with his weight on only one foot. Milo made a quick leg takedown, Hamid fell to the asphalt and Milo crouched down by his side and put a control hold on his arm and wrist.

Reeza Hamid moaned in pain, but not nearly as much as Milo had expected. He realized that this body must have taken in a few ampoules of steroids, and Milo sat on his back while he maintained the control hold. He was about to fish his cell phone out again when he felt himself being seized under the arms and raised backward, ending up on his back on the asphalt. Suddenly a man was straddling him, holding his wrists while another tried to hold his legs.

In the corner of his eye he saw Hamid get up and rush off like a sprinter from the starting block.

"You don't attack people on the street like that!" the man sitting on him shouted.

He was in his thirties, dressed like a student, and Milo smelled alcohol on his breath.

"I'm a police officer!" he hissed, but instead of letting go, that seemed to irritate the other man even more.

"Fucking racist pig!" he shouted.

Milo felt the aggression explode and kicked at him, pushed him away and got on his feet. Hamid now had a head start of at least a hundred meters.

Milo caught sight of a community bike that had fallen down on the sidewalk.

"Is this yours?" he asked the man who had been sitting on him.

He got a nod in response and jumped onto the bike. Far up the street he saw Hamid round the corner and disappear down Pilestredet. Milo pedaled as fast as he could, closing the gap.

On Pilestredet he saw Hamid hail a taxi, which quickly started moving. Milo was only thirty meters behind, but the distance was increasing now. He pedaled like crazy.

The taxi drove toward Ring 1. Milo crossed the trolley tracks and sidewalk, cutting through students on their way to and from the high school. For a moment he considered stopping and calling Guttormsen, but then the taxi would be gone for good. He had one more hope left: the roadwork that was always going on in central Oslo.

And sure enough, on his way across Ring 1, after the turnoff to the Sentrum parking building, he saw how the traffic suddenly started moving more slowly, down to a snail's pace through the Vaterland Tunnel that ended up at Oslo Plaza.

He tossed aside the bike and jogged alongside the cars. There he caught sight of the taxi.

The phone vibrated.

"Milo, what the hell—"

"Entrance to Vaterland Tunnel in the direction of Plaza. I'll have him in a minute," he said and hung up.

An oncoming truck honked at him, but he paid no attention to it and crouched down while he moved toward the taxi.

He tore open the door on the left side and took hold of a perplexed Reeza Hamid. With an exertion of strength he pulled him out of the car, but then Hamid landed a kick that sent Milo over into the other lane. He heard tires squeal, and then a truck approaching too fast to be able to stop. With his left leg he kicked and tried to jump away, and avoided getting hit head-on. But he wasn't able to get clear of the side mirror. It struck him on the shoulder, and it felt like someone had hit him with a baseball bat. The collision sent him right to the pavement.

He cursed in pain and got on his feet. Ahead of him, in the

tunnel opening, he saw the outline of a limping Hamid. The adrenaline that pumped through his body kept Milo from feeling the pain he should have felt after the collision and fall, and in a leap he was after the Pakistani. The traffic had stopped, it was safer to run now and, after a few seconds, he threw himself over Hamid with all his weight. He moaned, and Milo quickly put a choke hold on him while making sure that no one approached to try to pull him off again. One of the drivers had summoned courage and got out of the taxi. Now he approached slowly.

"Don't come closer! I'm a plainclothes policeman! Call one-one-two now!" Milo shouted authoritatively, holding Hamid's neck as if in a vise.

But the words were superfluous. Suddenly he heard sirens, and shortly thereafter, two unmarked police cars stopped by the tunnel opening. Guttormsen got out of one of the cars, and three of the men from the task force picked up Hamid as Milo released his hold.

He stood there panting heavily while he tried to straighten his dirty, torn suit. His shoulder ached.

"Good, Cavalli! Someone on the inside must have tipped him off. He slipped out just in time."

"I told you he was dangerous, but forgot to emphasize that he's smart too," said Milo, trying in vain to massage his shoulder as he stood in the middle of the road.

Guttormsen stared up at him with a grin.

"Smart and dangerous. I'll be damned! Didn't matter, though. So are you."

SATURDAY

2

Milo woke up with a start, pain shooting through his shoulder, arms and torso. He rolled up into a sitting position on the bed, and looked at the blue and red marks on his body.

Eight o'clock was too early to get up on a Saturday morning, but he needed a shower. He padded toward the bathroom while he stretched his arms and carefully tried to warm up his muscles a little.

Twenty minutes later he went downstairs to the kitchen and made a rejuvenating espresso.

Outside the Briskeby trolley clunked past. Oslo was, little by little, coming to life. The wind blew leaves and raindrops against the window. He went over to the thermostat and turned the heat up a few more degrees in the kitchen, living room and library. The loft level with the bedrooms, office and guestroom that he used for exercise he left alone. He liked it a little cooler there.

He turned on his cell phone and sat and browsed the weekend edition of *Dagens Næringsliv* while he had a bowl of cereal. He had no plans other than resting after several months of intense work. Maybe dinner with some friends, but he had accepted with a clear reservation in case something unforeseen turned up.

The cell phone let out a *beep*. There was a new message in voice mail. It was from Sørensen, chief inspector at the Oslo police agency.

"Milo, it's Sørensen. Call me," was all he said.

The message had been left just before eight o'clock that morning. Milo returned his call.

"Hi, Milo, thanks for calling me back. Am I disturbing your weekend?" Sørensen asked.

"No, I'm up. Having a coffee and skimming through the newspaper."

"Probably one of those teeny-tiny finger bowls, that you finish in one gulp. Lasts long enough to read one headline before your cup is empty."

"Quality ahead of quantity," Milo countered and could hear Sørensen coughing out a cloud of smoke on the other end.

They had not seen each other for a few months, and Milo had missed the bald, blustering chief inspector.

"Nice, Milo. Enjoy your quality. But what are you doing later?"

"No plans."

"Fine, I need your help. Come down to the police station when you're done with breakfast, please."

"All right," Milo replied.

It would not occur to him not to show up when the man who had saved his life six months earlier asked him to.

•   •   •

The black Abarth model of the popular Fiat 500 series purred out of the garage. The quiet Saturday streets meant that he could park outside the police station on Grønland seven minutes later.

Shortly after the guard let him in, Sørensen came tottering toward him. The suit was the same worn one, the tie poorly knotted and his head just as shiny.

"Thanks for coming so quickly," he said.

"No problem. What's going on?"

"Come on up. I'll explain."

They walked toward the elevator, where Sørensen fished out his snuffbox and shoved two pouches under his upper lip. On the sixth floor they got off and made their way to Sørensen's office. A desk was pushed in against an overfilled bookcase in front of which were two chairs. Sørensen pointed toward one of them and sat down behind the desk. The desktop was covered with papers and coffee cups, and on the surrounding workstations the screensavers on the PCs were the only signs of life. Saturday morning was not exactly the busiest time at the police station.

Sørensen ran one hand over his head and tilted his chair back a little.

"Damned touchy case, Milo. Damned touchy."

He had dark rings under his eyes, as if he hadn't slept the past few nights. There was a touch of sadness in his eyes as he twirled a snuffbox in his hand.

"Tell me."

"You can read this quickly," Sørensen answered, giving him a file folder.

Milo leaned back in the chair and suppressed a moan as it pressed against his battered back muscles. The content of the folder was sparse. Four sheets with two pictures on each of them, a report from the homicide section at the Oslo police department only a page and a half long and a letter from what must be the corresponding department at the Rome police.

Milo held up the sheet with *Polizia di Stato* at the top of the letterhead and the signature of a *Commissario* A. Benedetti at the bottom, and aimed an inquisitive glance at Sørensen.

"Read the report first. Look at the pictures. I'll explain later," the chief inspector said, brushing him aside.

Milo looked at the pictures. They showed a woman lying on a made-up double bed. Her arms were lying limply at her sides, while one leg was extended over the edge of the bed. The tip of her foot pointed down toward the light gray carpet. He estimated her age at about thirty. The light hair was spread in a semicircle around her head, as if she was drifting in calm water.

The woman was dead, and the red marks around her throat revealed that it had probably happened from someone putting both hands around it and squeezing with all their strength until her windpipe was crushed.

He looked at the report. Ingrid Tollefsen. Thirty-one years old, originally from Kolbotn, now residing in Majorstua. Employed at the Oslo office of the American pharmaceutical company Forum Healthcare. Educated at the Norwegian University of Science and Technology, NTNU, in Trondheim.

Sørensen cleared his throat and rocked back and forth in the chair.

"Norwegian girl killed in Rome this week," he said.

"I see that. What was she doing there?"

"Attending some conference or other. Something in pharmaceuticals."

"What happened?" asked Milo while he skimmed the rest of the report. It did not provide many answers.

"We don't know that much yet. We've had some . . . linguistic challenges, you might say."

"So now you want me to step in and translate?"

"Well, not just that, Milo. But hold on a little. I have to explain. This is damned touchy."

"Yes, you said that."

Sørensen spit the snuff pouches into a coffee cup and rolled over to the window. He opened it, fired up a cigarette, and blew the smoke in the direction of Grønland. But the wind blew it back, and Milo smelled the odor of tobacco as it seeped into the room.

"Ingrid Tollefsen was killed on Monday evening. Sometime between eight and midnight. There is no sign of a break-in. There is a lot that suggests she knew the killer."

"Or that she had just gotten acquainted with him?"

"You're thinking about a one-night stand?"

Milo nodded while he looked at the pictures.

"Nice-looking woman. I bet she couldn't walk a block in Rome without getting looks and comments."

"I'm sure that's right. But, based on the e-mails we've received from the Italian police, the killer has not left behind a single trace. No sign of sexual intercourse either. There is nothing whatsoever that indicates panic, rape or robbery. On the contrary, there's something calculated about the whole thing," said Sørensen.

Milo glanced at the pictures again.

"You'll assess that better than me. I'm still just a lousy Financial Crimes investigator, and I don't really know—"

"Does her surname ring any bells? Tollefsen?" Sørensen interrupted him.

"No. Should it?"

"Probably not. It's not exactly an unusual name."

The chief inspector plucked the cigarette butt in an arc out the window before rolling back into position behind his desk. He put his elbows on the desktop and fixed his eyes on Milo.

"But you do remember the Ingieråsen case?"

Milo nodded.

"Obviously. There isn't anyone in all of Norway who doesn't," he answered.

3

It was right before summer vacation two years earlier that the two homicides—or executions, as the press put it—at Ingieråsen Middle School in Oppegård municipality were carried out.

Even if what really happened was not a hundred-percent clear, technical findings and witness statements had drawn a picture of a gruesome incident: two killed, multiple perpetrators, but so far no one convicted.

Two murders that shocked an entire nation and which, for lack of a conviction, lay there like an infected abscess.

It was assumed that the young teacher was shot first. After that, the perpetrators killed the fifteen-year-old student. The boy had obviously gotten in over his head, and the police had no doubt that it was a group of Pakistani boys and young men who were behind it. Probably heavily involved in narcotics and other organized crime.

The boy had reportedly been an increasing source of worry at the school, without belonging to a gang, and in the past year had been a regular at a gym. It was not ruled out that he had started taking steroids, and that the killing could be connected to that environment. Either as a reprisal or simply a manifestation of blind, uncontrolled violence. A manifestation of an aggressiveness and hatred that was oiled on the steroid-laden bodies of the young second-generation immigrants who found no sense of belonging other than in the gang.

The teacher had been working late, and must have arrived just as the situation came to a head. At risk to his own life, he tried to intervene. Tried to convince. Tried to plead. The result was that he was shot in the head. Executed on the school grounds where he worked and tried to create a safe, problem-free school day for those who found themselves in the transitional stage between childhood and youth.

The student had turned around and started running, but was struck by three shots in the back.

Witnesses who heard the shots and approached the school described a gang of seven to ten individuals who calmly walked toward their cars and then disappeared. One witness did, in fact, tell that one of them stayed behind a few minutes and coldly and calmly took the time to assure himself that both were dead—he had leaned over the young boy—before leaving.

"I was the investigation leader on the case, and I haven't stopped thinking about it since," said Sørensen with his gaze directed at Milo.

The odor of tobacco was still hanging in the room, and something reminiscent of bitter insufficiency marked the voice of the experienced and controversial policeman.

"I remember the story about the teacher. He was popular. Hailed as a hero. Because he intervened, because he wasn't passive. Henriksen, wasn't that his name?" asked Milo.

Sørensen nodded, his fingers drumming on the snuffbox.

"Asgeir Henriksen. He became the very symbol of some-one who cared. Someone who put his own life ahead of others. Someone who was killed while trying to prevent violence. The whole thing was so meaningless."

Milo thought about the weeks and months of newspaper articles. All the letters to the editor and comments. Some bitter. Some confrontational. Some tentatively conciliatory.

There were those who maintained that immigration policy was to blame, with all the criminal gangs as a consequence. Others pointed to how young people on a downward path, es-pecially boys, must be taken care of. That this was a growing problem even in the established and prosperous suburbs. Many had called for child protection services.

"I remember the torchlight parades. What was the slogan again?"

"There were several. 'Turn your back on violence' and 'I care' kept coming back. Some even tried 'Crush violence.' It was a pretty aggressive atmosphere for a while, and it didn't get better when the suspects were not indicted and convicted, but walked away to their buddies and went on like before. We lacked tech-nical evidence and witnesses, but we know that several of them were in the vicinity of the scene of the crime," said Sørensen.

Neither of them said anything for a few moments, until Sørensen sighed heavily and opened his mouth again.

"The young boy who was killed . . . the one many thought was responsible for the teacher being killed, his name was Tollef-sen. Tormod Tollefsen."

"Tollefsen? As in Ingrid Tollefsen? The dead woman in Rome?"

Sørensen nodded and ran his hand over his shiny head.

"Shot in the back. And I wasn't able to get the one who did

it. I still remember Ingrid sitting here. In this office, in the chair you're sitting in, begging me to find the ones who killed her baby brother."

The experienced policeman swallowed a couple of times and stared out into space.

"That's what she called him. 'My baby brother.' Because of the age difference. She was thirteen years older than him. Just that . . . she was completely crushed. And the fact that they lost their mother so early . . ." he continued.

"Her mother is not alive?"

"She died right after Tormod was born. They were relatively old when they had him. She was in her forties, and there were complications. Blood clot. She never got to see her son."

Milo did not say anything. He did not know what he should say. Sørensen blew air out of his mouth. As if he was trying to get rid of his heavy thoughts. Without completely succeeding.

"It's really unbelievable how much bad luck some people can have. A family can lose both children. While, in another family, three can win the lottery the same year. Damn it, luck is not equally distributed in this life," said Sørensen.

"We're not talking about accidents or bad luck here. But can there be a connection between the killings of the two siblings? It seems more like a gruesome coincidence," said Milo.

"I don't know. He was shot in Kolbotn. She was strangled in Rome. I don't know if there's a connection, but it opens up a wound. And I need to find out."

"But where do I come into the picture?"

"The father of the two, Sigurd Tollefsen, called me from Rome. He's in the process of trying to bring home his second murdered child. He's calm so far—although in a brokenhearted way—but has run into Italian bureaucracy. It turns out that the hotel room is still closed off, and the Rome police refuse to release the body until the Norwegian police have sent a detective. This is really a job for the police liaison stationed at the embassy, but he's traveling and won't be back until next week." Sørensen looked at Milo and swallowed heavily.

"I can't let the guy sit there in limbo while I take a week to dig up an available man and an interpreter. Can you go down there?"

"To Rome? Yes, of course. When?"

"As soon as possible. Now. Will that work?"

"You saved my life once. Of course it works."

Milo stood up and took the case folder from the desk.

"Milo, I appreciate this. This is going to explode in the media, but I think we can manage to keep a lid on it a little longer. The only thing that has been in print so far is this item," said Sørensen.

He handed a newspaper to Milo. At the bottom in the corner there were six lines under the headline FOUND DEAD IN ROME. No name was mentioned.

"Journalists don't seem to realize that the real stories are hidden in these small news items," said Sørensen, taking out his pack of cigarettes again.

He rolled the chair over to the window and fired up a cigarette.

"You haven't thought about cutting down on the nicotine?" Milo asked.

The chief inspector gave him a disillusioned look.

"The point of tobacco, my friend, is to make time pass. It means I have something to do, while at the same time it shortens my life. That way time passes twice as fast."

4

The gold card let him check in at the business counter and then go through security on fast track. Only ten minutes after he parked the car, he entered the lounge to kill time before departure. The woman who scrutinized his card and ticket gave him one of the smiles she was paid to put on, and Milo nodded back.

He got himself a glass of beer and some snacks and settled down with his e-reader. On an Italian Web site he checked the latest news and weather report. October sun and seventy-five degrees Fahrenheit in Rome. Outside, the October wind was blowing the leaves from the trees and threatened overnight frost in Oslo.

For a moment he considered sending a text message to Theresa saying that he was on his way to Rome. She was only a two-hour train ride away—in Bologna—and a few days together in Rome was not to be looked down upon. They had a good time when they were together, and the bond between them had only grown stronger after they had spent the whole summer together. At the same time, the distance was still a problem. For that reason they had decided that they were together when they were together—but not necessarily when they weren't.

A kind of relationship, in other words.

But at the moment he was on his way to do a job, and he might risk making her sit around waiting. So he skipped the text message to her this time.

Not much of what his father had said to him while he was growing up had stuck, but one of his sayings had.

"It's not about finding the right one, Emil. The time also has to be right. The right person, at the right time. It's not easy, damn it. Most people end up with the wrong person at the right time. Others find the right person, but the time is never right," Endre Thorkildsen had told his son.

It surprised Milo to hear him say that. He hadn't known that his father was capable of talking about anything other than the stock market and the brokerage he ran, but gradually it occurred to Milo that there was something more there. It was just so well hidden behind the façade.

Where Theresa was concerned, Milo had no doubt that she was the right person. The girl, six years younger, whom he knew from all the summer vacations in Sardinia, had grown on him since their summer love affair a few years back. He felt it. He did not doubt the bond between them.

He was less sure about whether the time was right.

Milo set aside the e-reader and proceeded to browse in the sparse case folder while he thought through the conversation with Sørensen. Besides the dead body on the double bed, the pictures showed some clothing that had been draped over a suitcase, various toiletries and some medications on a bathroom shelf, and finally a passport, money and receipts in a small heap on the desk.

He browsed through the report again, signed by *Commissario* Benedetti, for whom he had already left a message on his answering machine. He let him know that he was en route, but had no illusions that the Italian policeman would answer him before Monday. It was doubtful he worked on Saturdays.

"*Nessun segno di effrazione o violenza sessuale*," it said in the letter that otherwise was characterized by bureaucratic Italian. No sign of break-in or rape, as Sørensen had said.

Ingrid Tollefsen had been dead between six and eight hours before she was found by the cleaning woman.

Milo made a mental note to speak with her before he returned to Norway. Sørensen would not have the opportunity to
arrange an interpreter over the phone, and something told him
that the woman would say as little as possible to authoritative
Italian police officers whom she feared might get her in trouble
with her employer or the tax authorities.

He got up for a refill of both beer and snacks, and let his gaze
sweep across the lounge. Normally it was full of men and women
traveling on business who basically sat alone, fondling their cell
phones and eating out of boredom. On Saturdays like this, on
the other hand, it was almost empty apart from four or five solitary men who'd had to upset the family weekend to take a long-
distance flight to some place in Asia or Latin America to be at a
meeting on Monday morning.

An American was sitting in a corner, trying to compensate
for the poor connection by almost shouting into the phone.

On his way back to his seat Milo heard his own phone ring,
and the display revealed his father's number.

"Hi."

"Emil! There you are."

The voice sounded gentle. A little too gentle, typical for
someone who was beating around the bush.

"I'm at the airport. On my way to Rome."

"Italy again? Has something happened?"

"No, just a short trip. Work," Milo explained.

"Okay, then I won't ask any more."

As director of one of the country's oldest brokerage firms,
there were limits to how much he could talk about work with
his son, the financial crimes investigator. And when the subject
wasn't work and stocks, the conversations had a tendency to bog
down. Milo knew that his father never called to chat, even if they

had gradually started seeing each other again after his mother's death two years earlier.

"What is it, Dad? Can you make it quick before I run to the gate?"

"No, no. Nothing in particular."

"Of course there was something," Milo answered impatiently.

His father hesitated.

"Well, I wanted to invite you to dinner tomorrow, but since you're traveling . . ."

"I'll send you a message when I'm on my way home. We can do it then."

"Yes, that would be fine."

Milo had rarely heard his father sound so uncertain on the phone.

"What is it, Dad?"

"Perhaps we could decide on a day now, so that . . . so that . . ."

"Are other people going to be at this dinner? Is that what you mean?"

"Well, yes. There is one more."

"Who is it, then?"

"Emil, this is a little touchy. A little hard to explain on the phone."

His father was the second person that day who'd had a "touchy" subject to talk about. He didn't know if he liked where this was heading.

"You don't want to say who it is?" he pressed his father.

"As I said, Emil, if we could say Friday, for example . . ."

But Milo was not in the mood to placate his father. It occurred to him what was coming. And if his father's future wife wasn't able to adjust her schedule and show up for dinner on a half-day's notice, it wasn't his problem. He knew that his father had had several relationships since his mother's hospitalization and suicide, but did not assume that the current one—no doubt with an attorney at Hilmersen Fuge—was entering such a serious phase that it was time to introduce her to his son. At the same time he noticed that he didn't care as much as he would have six months ago.

"I'll call you when I'm on my way home, then I'll come to dinner. It must be possible, damn it, for her to adjust her schedule if she's going to meet me—your only son—for the first time," Milo said while he took his luggage and headed for the gate.

"Uh, how did you know? . . ."

"I have to hang up, Dad. I'll be in touch."

"Yes, Emil. Good. Have a safe trip, then."

The flight had already started boarding when he got to the gate. He showed his boarding pass, and got yet another paid smile from an airline employee in return.

He found his seat, 5C and, as usual before a flight, he recited an "Ave Maria" to himself.

He had just made the sign of the cross from his forehead down to his chest and from shoulder to shoulder when his phone emitted a little *beep*. It was an e-mail from his cousin in Milan.

From: Cavalli, Corrado
Subject: FW: Regarding inheritance
To: Cavalli, Milo

Have you seen this message from New York?
I think that you or I have to go. But it's impossible for me in October or November. Can you go?

CC

Forwarded message:

From: Patmunster, Oscar

Subject: Regarding inheritance

To: Cavalli, Corrado

Dear Sir,

As agreed on the phone, here is some more information which you can share with your family.

On August 25 Ms. Brenda O'Quigly passed away at St. Joseph's Hospital. I am aware that neither you nor the rest of your family have ever heard of Ms. O'Quigly, however, she knew about you. She was connected to your grandfather, Antonio Cavalli.

I am the executor of Ms. O'Quigly's estate, hence my efforts to get in touch with the Cavalli family.

At this time, it will be necessary for a member of the Cavalli family to meet in person in New York for a signature and also for the handing over of some personal effects. The will is very specific on this point, and I am afraid it will be impossible to do this through an Italian attorney.

Unfortunately, I am unable to go into detail about the will at this stage, but let me convey my opinion that it will prove to be of financial and personal value to the family.

Please let me know at your convenience how we can proceed in this matter.

Yours sincerely,

Oscar Patmunster

Partner

Leary Patmunster Joyce

Milo read quickly through the e-mails once more. He had never heard about a Miss Brenda O'Quigly in New York.

It was obvious that Corrado did not have time in the next few months. Autumn in Milan was hectic for everyone in the fashion industry. Milo's cousin had made it big on the vanity market, and made good money on rich parents who wanted to prep their daughters for the catwalk.

This meant it would have to be Milo who made the trip to New York, and the thought did not bother him in the least. He liked autumn in New York, and it had been several years since he was there last.

The plane was taxiing on the runway when he responded to Corrado.

From: Cavalli, Milo

Subject: Re: FW: Regarding inheritance

To: Cavalli, Corrado

I can go.

Maybe next week.

Now I'm heading to Rome for work.

I'll call you!

M

As the plane took off, he thought about the strange e-mail from the American attorney.

Who was Brenda O'Quigly?

And how did she know his grandfather?

5

In the taxi from the Fiumicino airport en route to the center of Rome his thoughts returned to his childhood trips to Rome with his mother.

How she had loved that city!

He remembered how she'd quoted from one of her favorite films by her favorite director, Federico Fellini. The scene in *La Dolce Vita* where the gossip columnist Marcello Rubini, as portrayed by Marcello Mastroianni, and the rich, world-weary Maddalena have run away from the party and drive around the city in her Cadillac, before they go home with a prostitute and borrow her bedroom to make love. Maddalena is tired of the city, but Marcello can't get enough: "Personally, I love Rome. It's like a jungle. Damp and quiet. It's easy to hide here," he says.

Milo could not count how many times while he was growing up he had come padding down from his room and found his mother stuck in front of the screen. Either while she was watching *La Dolce Vita* or another of Fellini's films, *Il Bidone* or *I Vitelloni*. And he remembered how he dutifully sat down beside her and listened to his mother's commentary.

Personally, he could control his enthusiasm for *La Dolce Vita*.

He did not miss the film. But he missed the moments with his mother.

Every time they were in Rome, this quote came up.

"This city is like a jungle, Milo. Damp and quiet. It's easy to hide here," she always said. And every time with such great seriousness that he wondered what she was hiding from.

Now that she had hidden herself from the world forever, he regretted that he had never asked.

The afternoon sun was hanging over Rome, spreading a warm light over the city. Milo leaned his head against the window, watched the buildings flying past and tried to remember the last time he was there with her. One memory slipped into another, and it was hard to keep all the trips separate, where they had wandered around the city between museums, churches, restaurants and shops. And occasionally an out-of-the-way bookstore or antiques store. His mother never got enough of the city, and Milo loved experiencing it with her.

She often became thoughtful and could stand inside a church and whisper, "*Non capisco questa grandiosità*. I don't understand this magnificence," half to Milo, half to the sanctuary.

And he remembered the visits and dinners with Uncle Luigi, who was not his real uncle, but a close friend of the family. Luigi had been a professor at the university in Rome, with antiquity as his area of specialization, and lived in what Milo remembered as an enormous apartment with a view of Villa Borghese.

The rooms were filled with books, art and laughter. But mostly he remembered the smell of tobacco. Sweet, aromatic pipe tobacco. And Milo and his mother often stayed in the guest rooms and enjoyed Uncle Luigi's boundless hospitality.

But now they were gone.

Both of those who had taught him to love the "Eternal City" were dead, and he felt alone as the taxi cut between lanes into the city center.

Luigi had been diagnosed with lung cancer four years earlier and had died early one morning in September three and a half years ago. Milo remembered the funeral and the crowded church. And six months later his mother's problems took hold of her in earnest, and she had been hospitalized. It was still difficult for him to reconcile the fact that she had chosen to end her life by her own hand.

The taxi stopped in front of the hotel, Milo tipped generously and shortly after he was checking in at reception.

"Emil Cavalli?"

The young man behind the counter was not able to restrain himself.

"*Sei italiano*? Are you Italian?"

"My mother was Italian."

"Ah. I understand."

Milo took the key, found the elevator, and went to his room on the eighth floor. It struck him how seldom he stayed at a hotel in Italy. As a rule, he stayed at one of three places: the apartment in Milan, the family place in Tuscany or the summer house in Sardinia.

He looked down at the traffic and the many Vespa scooters moving around like wasps—as the name suggested—and called *Commissario* Benedetti. Once again he had to leave a voice mail. There was nothing that suggested that the Italian policeman had any intention of working on the weekend.

But Milo did not intend to wait until Monday to do what he had come for. He quickly gathered his money, credit cards and cell phone and left the hotel room.

On his way into the taxi the phone rang. He hoped it was Benedetti, but saw Theresa's name on the display.

"*Ciao, carina*! Hi, darling!"

"Hi. I was just talking with Corrado, and he said you were going to Rome."

"I'm here now. Landed an hour ago."

"Why didn't you say anything?"

Her tone was slightly reproachful.

"It just came up a few hours ago. An urgent assignment," Milo replied.

"But I want to see you. How long will you be there?"

"I don't really know. A couple of days, at most. A woman was killed here, and I'm going to help the family bring her body home."

"Oh. But I want to see you," she repeated.

"I want to see you too."

"There's a train to Rome arriving at quarter after nine. We could have a late dinner together."

"That sounds great."

"Will you meet me at the station?"

He looked automatically at his watch. That was only three hours from now, but in any event that was enough time for what he had planned the next few hours.

"Yeah, sure, I'll meet you at the station," he answered.

The courtyard was antique yellow with flower boxes in front of the windows. And between them were lines with clothes drying. As Milo went up to the entry and was about to ring the bell, the door opened and an old woman dressed in black toddled out.

"*Signora*," Milo greeted her politely and slipped through the door, relieved at not having to talk his way in by using the phone system.

The entry smelled like Saturday. A mixture of laundry softener and food cooking.

On his way up the stairs he could hear the sound of TVs turned on full blast, filling the apartments with noise from loud game- and talk shows. He came to the fifth floor and checked that the name on the doorbell matched. He adjusted his tie and rang.

Inside he heard the occupants calling to each other about who was busiest and therefore couldn't answer. Finally there was the sound of shuffling steps and the rattling of a chain being unhooked before the door was opened.

The man in the doorway was at least two heads shorter than Milo, and dressed in a white mesh undershirt and khaki pants that were fastened high above his navel. His hair, or the little that remained and which lay like a little wreath over his ears, was gray and matched what stuck out through the holes in the mesh undershirt. He stared uncomprehendingly at Milo.

"Signor Benedetti?" Milo asked.

"*Sono io. Chi é?*" That's me. Who are you?"

"I'm Milo Cavalli. From the Norwegian police."

Benedetti answered with a little "ah," before he hurried to explain that it was Saturday and he didn't work on weekends.

"We'll do this Monday morning, Cavalli," he said, while he tried to push him back and close the door.

Milo took a step forward, and right then Signora Benedetti came into view in the entry to see who her husband was talking with. Milo put on his best smile, and made a little bow.

"Signora, *che profumo!* What an aroma! What are you making for dinner?"

The woman lit up.

"*Tummala!*" she said proudly.

Milo turned his eyes skyward in recognition. He was familiar with the classic Sicilian gratin dish that contained everything from chicken, onions, tomatoes and celery to sausages, cheese and meatballs. It was one of his grandfather's favorite dishes from southern Italy, and he felt a sting of melancholy and fullness when he recalled how his grandmother made him finish several generous portions. Crammed full on the verge of unbearable. And then a little, ice-cold glass of *limoncello* after dinner was the only salvation.

"It smells heavenly! Tell me, do you make it with veal meatballs too, the way my grandmother always did?"

"Of course! But who are you?"

Milo briefly explained who he was and why he was there. Contact with the wife in the house was established, and her husband stood like an extra, almost clinging to the door.

"The problem, signora, is that my bosses require me to submit a report. They don't care if it's a weekend and that we poor foot soldiers only want to rest."

Kicking upwards never failed, and Signora Benedetti shook her head understandingly at how difficult bosses could be.

Milo continued.

"So I only wondered whether I could be so bold as to borrow your husband a short while, if I promise to have him back in time for dinner at nine o'clock?"

Even if *Commissario* Benedetti had said that they would soon be sitting down for dinner, Milo guessed that did not add up. Which his wife confirmed.

"Of course. No problem. Just take him along. Here he's just in the way," she said before returning to the kitchen and the saucepans.

Milo looked at the Italian policeman in the mesh undershirt and smiled slyly.

"Let's go."

"*Vengo.* I'm coming," Benedetti muttered.

6

They were followed by an overeager hotel manager, who glimpsed hope that the police could soon release the room and let him make money on it again. He inserted the key card into the door and invited them in with a bow.

The room was small and smelled musty.

Milo´s gaze drifted inexorably to the bed in the middle of the room, where Ingrid Tollefsen had been found dead a few days earlier. Now the bed was empty, and only a slight wrinkle on one side of the bedspread showed that someone had been lying there.

Milo held up the picture of the dead woman. Her hair spread out, one foot hanging limply off the edge of the bed. He moved around the bed and inspected the room. The other two observed him in silence.

"Where is her suitcase?"

"At the station. We have all her belongings," Benedetti answered, handing him a sheet of paper. "Here's the list of what she had."

Milo took a quick look at it.

"No laptop?"

"No."

"But she was traveling on business, wasn't she?"

"*Sì.*"

"Strange to go on a business trip without a laptop."

"*Sì.*"

Milo looked out the window. The street below was narrow, but people still managed to park on both sides of it. Granted that they made use of the sidewalk. A carabinieri car had squeezed in and blocked a pedestrian crossing. Right across from the hotel was an apartment building. Could anyone have seen something? He turned around.

"Commissario, has—"

"We've gone door-to-door in the building across the street. No one saw or heard anything. As you see from the pictures, the drapes were drawn," the Italian policeman interrupted him.

Milo looked at him. There was no hint of arrogance in his gaze, only a sincere desire to make the stay in the hotel room as brief as possible so that he could go home for dinner. Milo could not help liking him.

"Great. I'll just look at the rest of the room, then we'll go," he said.

It was a corner room, and the bathroom faced a small courtyard. Milo glanced into the bathroom, and at the same time looked at the pictures the Italian police had taken. The shampoo bottle on the edge of the bathtub, the tube of toothpaste on the shelf, the pillboxes by the mirror and the bottle of body lotion on the washstand had been removed. Now the bathroom was emptied, but still not cleaned. The faint odor of shampoo and perfume remained.

He stepped on the pedal of the waste container and could see that it too, was empty. Then he pulled the shower curtain completely to the side. All he saw were some soap remnants and a few strands of hair by the drain. On the wall there was a small window opening. It was closed. Alongside it a small air vent was cracked open. The courtyard air struck him.

"Was the window in here closed or open when you came? Did one of you close it?" he called out to the two who were waiting.

A couple seconds later Benedetti stuck his head in.

"It was closed."

"What about the air vent?"

Benedetti glanced at the wall.

"None of us have touched it. It's probably been open the whole time."

"What's outside there?"

"Just a courtyard with some trash cans, cardboard boxes and parked scooters."

"Hmmm."

"We've checked there," Benedetti answered.

Milo looked out, but the vent was too small to give him the overview he wanted of the courtyard.

He looked around. Pulled a little on the shower curtain, let his eyes move along the one wall up to the ceiling, where he could follow a little crack in the paint all the way over to the light fixture. He got out of the bathtub and stood in the middle of the room. Benedetti observed him, but did not seem to want to say anything.

Why were both the bathroom and the hotel room itself so orderly? Milo thought. Shouldn't there be traces that a life-and-death struggle had taken place here? The killer could not have broken in while Ingrid Tollefsen was asleep, because there was no sign that the door was forced open. But, at the same time, it was difficult to understand that she had given up without a struggle.

Milo tried to picture how she opened the door and stared at the killer. He saw only two possibilities: either a life-and-death struggle with howling, screaming and blows, or quickly taking refuge in the bathroom.

He took hold of the door handle and closed it. The bathroom

immediately felt smaller, and Benedetti took a step back toward the sink. As if the room was a bit too small for both of them.

The handle was round, the kind you twist around to open. The lock was a button you pushed in.

Milo tried to push it in, but as he let go, it sprang back again. It would not stay. He tried again. The same thing happened.

"It can't be locked," he said, looking over his shoulder at Benedetti.

The Italian policeman responded with a shrug.

Milo opened the door again and got down on his knees. He looked at the fitting on the door, and then at the fitting on the doorframe. The fitting was dull, but not everywhere. The hole in the doorframe, where the bolt of the lock slid in when the door was closed, was bent in a tiny bit, and there was a light scratch in the fitting facing into the bathroom.

He pointed at it, and turned toward Benedetti.

"This must have happened recently. This scratch is much lighter and doesn't have the same faded color as the rest of the fitting."

Benedetti came a few steps closer and looked at the spot Milo was pointing at.

"That might well be," he said.

"Someone used force to push open the door not too long ago."

Benedetti's face was expressionless.

"She locked herself in the bathroom. And then the killer forced the door," said Milo.

"That might well be. But then wouldn't the damage have been greater? There is no damage to the door itself," Benedetti replied.

Milo shook his head and stood up. He closed the door and pointed at the lock.

"The bolt doesn't go very far in. A person with a little muscle, or weight, could easily force open this door. That might also explain the damage to the lock."

He looked around the bathroom again. He was convinced that Ingrid Tollefsen had sought refuge in here. But why hadn't she screamed? he thought. And it struck him that perhaps she had. Without anyone hearing it other than the killer. Or else she was unable to. She could have been paralyzed with fright.

His gaze was drawn toward the bathtub again. Milo stepped into it for the second time, let one hand glide along the edge, leaned over, and with a paper napkin, removed the strands of hair in the drain and looked down into it. Then he straightened up and thoughtfully drew his hand along the wall tiles under the little air vent.

He caught sight of something in one joint. Between two tiles a short line had been scratched. He glanced at the other joints, but no similar marks were to be seen.

It looked like the line had been scratched on purpose. Was there an attempt to draw an arrow on the upper part of the line? In that case it pointed right up at the vent.

He moved his head even closer. Under the arrow he saw another two lines. He felt a tingling through his body when he recognized the initials I T.

Ingrid Tollefsen.

Milo turned toward the Italian.

"I'd like to take a quick look in the courtyard anyway," he said.

Benedetti shrugged his shoulders in resignation in an "as you wish" gesture. Milo smiled at him.

"*Commissario,* if it was you who had come to Oslo to investigate the killing of an Italian citizen, you would do the same," he said.

Benedetti looked at him. "*Certo.* Of course."

Six stories down, at ground level, the courtyard smelled even more like a rear courtyard. Even if it was too cramped and narrow for the sun to reach all the way down to the cobblestones, it warmed up enough that the garbage cans emitted an air of decay.

The hotel manager wisely stayed inside the door between the kitchen and the outside area, while Benedetti took a few steps into the courtyard for courtesy's sake. Milo tried to identify the relevant bathroom window.

"It's that window there, isn't it?" he said, pointing.

Benedetti looked up, then nodded in reply.

Milo did not know what he was looking for. He only knew that he had to make the rounds down here too. Sørensen would certainly have done it. And even if Milo's experience with homicide investigation was limited, he knew a lot about achieving results. About being the best.

"*Essere il migliore é una funzione di due cose: sforzo e persistenza.*" Being best is a function of two things: effort and persistence, his grandfather had always said.

Milo remembered especially well another of his grandfather's sayings, from a summer in Sardinia. There was a discussion at dinner that touched on the concept of talent. Corrado, his cousin, was talking about some talented individuals he knew in Milan. Probably a couple of young ladies whose actual talent was highly debatable. Then their grandfather, who was never one to dominate dinner discussions, proclaimed loudly and clearly, "I consider myself fortunate that I have never had any talent that I've let myself be fooled by."

The discussion died then and there.

Milo moved a few boxes and felt the sweat on his back. He longed for a shower before meeting Theresa. Behind him he heard Benedetti fire up yet another cigarette.

"A couple more minutes," he said, going carefully down on his knee to peek under a garbage can.

He glimpsed something white by one of the wheels. He stood up and started pulling on the garbage can, which stank of food scraps. Slowly it moved, and when he had pulled it all the way out, a small, round vial came into view. His pulse became stronger.

He picked up the vial. It was white and dirty and cracked. Probably from when the wheels on the garbage can had squeezed it down against the cobblestones. He rotated it in his hand and felt a flicker of satisfaction when he read the label taped to the vial.

"*Commissario*! Look!"

Benedetti came over to him. With his cigarette in the corner of his mouth, he took the vial and rolled it around in his hands while he read the label.

"*Che cazzo*! What the fuck!"

The label said "Antidiab" and under the Norwegian doctor's name was the patient's: Ingrid Tollefsen.

He opened it and looked up. It contained a few tablets, but also a small piece of paper. Benedetti stuck his fingers down and carefully pulled the paper up. It was wet, and almost in shreds after the dampness had penetrated through the crack in the plastic.

What had once been written with black color was now flowing over the paper, apart from a few letters.

"Verba . . ." Milo read out loud as they stood shoulder to shoulder in the courtyard pungent with garbage.

Five barely legible letters. The rest was a blurry, black scribble.

It was almost eight thirty when they left the hotel.

"I'll get a taxi and drop you off on the way back to my hotel," said Milo.

"I'm in no hurry. There's a bar right around the corner here," Benedetti replied, beginning to zigzag between the parked cars on the sidewalk.

"But I promised your wife—"

"Neither she nor dinner are going anywhere," the Italian policeman interrupted him.

The bar was a bar in the Italian sense. That is, a coffee bar during the day, but with the possibility to have a glass of wine standing at the counter in the afternoon and early evening. It was half-full, but the TV hanging up in one corner helped keep the noise level at maximum. They each brought a glass of prosecco out onto the sidewalk, and Benedetti took out his pack of cigarettes. He held it out to Milo, who thanked him and took one.

Benedetti provided a light for them both. Milo inhaled, and because he smoked so rarely, he immediately felt the sensation of dizziness that settled like a calming blanket over his thoughts.

"She may have known the killer," Benedetti began.

"Mmm."

"There was no sign of a break-in or that anyone has forced the door into the room. She simply opened for him."

"For him? Do we know it's a man?"

Benedetti looked at him with surprise.

"Of course it's a man who killed her."

"I think so too, but can we rule out that it's a woman?"

"Yes. Signorina Tollefsen was in good shape, relatively tall, but she was strangled without a trace of a struggle. The one who killed her was bigger and stronger. A man."

Milo did not contradict him.

"The fact that the bathroom door was broken open also suggests a man. She knew him, let him in, but then she realized what was about to happen. She must have locked herself in the bathroom, and then he broke open the door," he said.

Benedetti nodded thoughtfully while he took a substantial drag on the cigarette.

"But this was not a man who was after her body. It was not a man who was numbed by alcohol and fired up by desire, and who killed her in passion. There is no sign of sexual violence. The motive must have been something completely different."

"There's something cold and planned about the whole thing. The killer has obviously taken his time to remove his traces. No laptop, no papers, no flash drive," said Milo.

Benedetti nodded before he took a couple sips from the wineglass. They sat quietly a little while as Vespas and Fiats rushed past.

"Do you know anything else about what kind of conference she was at?" Milo asked.

"A pharmaceutical conference under the auspices of one of those international corporations. I have the papers at the office. You can get them tomorrow after we've been to the medical examiner."

Milo smiled in thanks. It was obvious that Benedetti had seriously abandoned any hope of a work-free weekend.

"Can I see the vial of pills again?" Benedetti asked.

Milo handed it to him, and Benedetti opened it. The slip of paper was still there, but it was impossible to decipher any more letters. "Verba" was the only thing that could be read. The rest of the word and any other words remained illegible.

"I'll get the lab to look at this. Analyze the tablets that are left and look at the paper," said Benedetti.

"Yes, it's worth a try. She must be the one who threw it," said Milo, as he let his eyes meet the gaze of a dark-haired woman in her thirties who was passing with a girlfriend.

"I agree. It wasn't the killer who did it. And she didn't lose it. It's just a shame that what she tried to write is illegible."

Milo took out his phone.

"What are the tablets called?" he asked.

"Antidiab."

Milo googled it quickly on the phone.

"A kind of antidiabetic agent, it says here," he said.

"Which means?"

"A diabetes medicine that contributes to lowering blood sugar."

"So she had diabetes?" asked Benedetti.

Milo shrugged.

"I'll get her whole medical history checked when I'm back in Oslo."

"*Va bene.*" That's good, said Benedetti, finishing the wine. He looked at Milo.

"Would you like to eat with us?"

"Thanks, but I already have a date."

"Okay, then. Another time, perhaps."

Milo nodded in reply. He thought about the aroma that had seeped out from the kitchen in their apartment. The traditional Sicilian dish meant that the Benedetti had family ties to the south. The way he also swallowed his words at times suggested that he was not born and raised in Rome.

"Where are you from, originally? You're not from Rome, are you?" Milo asked.

Benedetti looked at him attentively.

"What makes you say that?"

Milo commented on the food that awaited him at home with his wife, and the hint of a southern Italian dialect.

"That's right. I'm originally from the south. Naples . . ." he began.

But then it was as if he stopped himself and didn't want to complete the sentence.

"How did you end up in Rome?"

Benedetti let his gaze wander over the sidewalk and street, where more and more cars and people flowed past on their way home, or out, to dinner.

"It's a long story. Another time, perhaps," he answered.

7

She was easy to spot in the crowd of people on the platform.

Not because she was particularly tall. Or particularly short. Or because she was particularly stylishly dressed or particularly casual in terms of clothing. But because with her warm smile and eyes that were not hidden behind big sunglasses, she stood out from the other Italian women walking past. She had a smile that signaled a secure presence, happy to be there, happy to have her eyes on him, housing a warmth he did not often see in other Italian women of her age.

But her gaze held something else too, he noticed. Determination. As if she was there for a particular reason.

She pressed herself to him, reached up on tiptoe and kissed him softly on the lips.

"*Ciao, caro.*" Hi, honey, she said and hugged him.

"*Ciao*, Theresa," he answered, kissing her a long time and almost lifting her up from the platform.

She smelled faintly of perfume and tasted the way he remembered. She had on a nice pair of jeans that sat snugly around her slender thighs and rear, a light-blue blouse and an elegant cashmere sweater under her open trench coat. Her hair was shorter than the last time he'd seen her—it gave her a tougher look—but it was just as black as it had always been.

They found a taxi and drove toward the hotel. She held his hand firmly, while with the other she stroked the back of it.

"Do you want to take a shower and change before we eat?" he asked.

"No, afterward," she answered.

She waited in the taxi while he ran up with her bag, and fifteen minutes later they were sitting in a small restaurant. At the other tables most were finishing their main course and waiting for dessert.

The thought of the dead Ingrid Tollefsen was slowly giving way.

They got water and wine on the table and toasted cautiously.

"It's good to see you again, Emilio."

"It's good to see you too."

The appetizers came to the table. A tomato and mozzarella salad for Theresa and local sausages and cheese for Milo.

"*Buon appetito*," he said.

"*Grazie, altrettanto.*"

The waiter refilled their wineglasses, and they updated each other on studies and work. Theresa was studying art history in Bologna, but planned to start her studies in industrial design in Milan in the fall.

"Are you glad I came?" she asked.

The inquiry was simple and innocent enough, but something in her tone made it sound like a trick question.

"Yes, of course. I can't imagine anything better than sitting in a little restaurant in Rome with you."

"No?"

With calm movements she cut off a piece of mozzarella, speared a piece of tomato and brought it to her mouth.

"No, not really," he answered.

She chewed slowly and met his gaze.

There was something unexpressed between them, and both remained sitting in silence a little longer. The ball was in her court.

"So why didn't you call and say you were coming?" she asked finally.

And he understood what had been smoldering beneath the surface.

"I told you. I only found out about the trip this morning. It was something that came up suddenly. A Norwegian woman was murdered, and Sørensen—you remember he's the one I told you about—asked me for a favor."

"But you could have called."

He sighed and took a gulp of wine. It was only twenty-four hours since he had fought with Reeza Hamid, and his body still ached. It was less than twelve hours since he had been dragged into a homicide investigation. And it was barely an hour since he had inspected the scene of the murder of Ingrid Tollefsen.

The last thing he needed was more problems.

"Yeah, I could have called, but I didn't. Because I was at work, and because it's just a short visit. But since you're here, I'm very happy about that," he said sincerely.

"Sometimes I wonder what kind of relationship you really want."

"Haven't we talked about that? I think we do very well when we're together," he replied.

She rolled her eyes. "When we see each other, yes. The problem is that we almost never see each other."

"We were together almost every day this summer. That was really nice."

She looked at him, and her gaze suddenly turned glassy.

"That's just it. It was really nice. But then you just disappear again," she said.

"I don't disappear. You know where I am, and I come back."

"But it's off-and-on-and-off-and-on the whole time!" she exclaimed, drying the corners of her eyes with her napkin.

"I'm sorry, but right now—"

"Maybe those superindependent, mountain-climbing, downhill-skiing, athletic Nordic girls you're used to think it's just fine to turn a relationship off and on like that, but I don't," she interrupted.

He looked at her, but she lowered her eyes. Part of him wanted to get up and embrace her. Another part of him had no patience for this and simply wanted to end the meal and go to bed.

"There isn't anyone else," he said.

"How should I know that?"

"Because I say so."

"The thing is, Emilio, I love you. And miss you. And . . . I don't know how long I can bear having it like this. Either we're together, or we aren't."

They remained sitting silently a few moments. Theresa had said what she wanted to have said. The ball was in Milo's court.

"This is starting to sound like an ultimatum," he said.

He could never stand letting himself be controlled by others.

Milo was antiauthoritarian on the verge of extreme. Something everyone from teachers, coaches, employers and colleagues got to experience. Even the head of Financial Crimes noticed it when at the six-month interview Milo opened by saying that he "hadn't started in Financial Crimes to chase small-fry," and that he would quit if he didn't get to work on the big cases.

When faced with an ultimatum his gut instinct was to counter or to attack, but with Theresa it was different. There was no doubt that he was in love with her, and in the back of his mind a dawning sense that she had the right to demand more of him was gnawing.

"This is not an ultimatum, Emilio. But I can't hide what I feel. I just want to know what you think about this. I need to know what direction we're going in. Or, more precisely, what direction *you're* going in."

"I'm going in your direction," he answered, taking another gulp of wine. "But I don't know if I'm going at your pace."

She smiled and it reached almost up to her eyes.

"I'm not saying that you have to propose . . . yet . . ."

He smiled back.

"And I understand that you don't want me to move to Norway. But is it completely inconceivable, for example, for you to live in Italy?"

He squirmed a little in his chair, and the pain in his back made him moan. A sound Theresa immediately misunderstood as a response to her question.

"Is the thought really that unbearable to you?" she asked with a shadow in her eyes.

"Not at all, I was just moaning because my back hurts."

"Okay . . ."

"I have a job in Oslo—"

"—that you don't really need."

He sighed.

"That's perhaps where you're mistaken. Even though I don't need the money, I feel for the first time I can remember that I'm actually doing something important. It's correct that I don't need to work. I actually don't need to lift a finger the rest of my life, I can just live on money from the family fortune. But I would fall apart."

"You're not the type who falls apart, Emilio. Just because your mother—"

"We don't need to talk about her now. The point is that right now this is important to me. And in any event it will be for some time. But I have never felt about anyone what I feel for you."

"Okay."

"But I don't know if that's enough for you now."

She shrugged slightly.

"Me neither," she answered.

After the appetizers came the first course. Milo went for his favorite, *spaghetti alla vongole*—spaghetti with clams. The pasta was as firm—al dente—as it should be, and the cook had spiced up the dish with some *peperoncino*. Theresa had *penne al pesto*.

The food was good, but the atmosphere was not.

While they waited for the second course, they tried to make small talk, but both were aware of how much effort the other was making.

The veal they both ordered was served, and the waiter poured the rest of the wine into their glasses. Theresa, as always, sipped the wine carefully, but it was still enough to put a glazed layer over her eyes. Slowly her smile got warmer.

"Listen here, Theresa. Believe it or not, I'm happy that you're saying how you feel. The next few weeks will be very tough for me, but it would be great if we can talk this out properly after that."

"Of course. Finish up what you have to do. Now you know what I'm thinking, anyway," she answered.

They declined both dessert and coffee, and hailed a taxi to take them back to the hotel.

While Theresa took clothes and toiletries from her suitcase, Milo started to calmly undress. He hung up the suit jacket, and unbuttoned his shirt. As he was taking it off, he felt a shooting pain through the small of his back, and let out another moan. Theresa looked at him.

"You've really hurt yourself," she said, helping him take off his shirt.

Then she caught sight of the purple marks on his back and the scraped elbow, and exclaimed, "*Poverino*! You poor thing!"

Gently she stroked his back while she kissed his shoulder and on up his neck until she ended up at his mouth. Slowly they started to remove each other's clothing. She squeezed out of her jeans, and her blouse fell on the floor. Then she loosened his belt and helped ease his trousers down to his ankles.

While he kissed her, he led her toward the bed. She let herself fall backward, and he followed. They rolled around, and she set herself on top of him. Her golden-brown skin was warm and smooth. Slowly he undid her bra, and they rolled back again. He took hold of her black panties, and as he pulled them gently off her, she raised her rear to help out. She was lying completely naked under him and pulled him to her.

Afterward they showered together and there she did things—and let him do things with her—that no unmarried Catholic woman should really do.

SUNDAY

8

She was asleep when he left.

It was only eight thirty, and he had a lot to get done before lunch.

After a quick coffee and *cornetto* he hailed a taxi and went to the police station, where *Commissario* Benedetti was already waiting.

"I'm just filling out the documents you need to get the body released and sent home again," he said while he signed some papers and took out an envelope.

Milo had never experienced this sort of efficient, accommodating Italian bureaucracy, and something told him that it would probably be just this one time. What had gotten Benedetti to change from reluctant to accommodating he did not know, but he had no intention of asking about it either.

"*Grazie,*" he said, taking the envelope.

"*Niente.*" It was nothing. "Let's go."

• • •

The building was classically beautiful and could just as well be a museum. Milo commented on it, and Benedetti showed a set of brown teeth.

"I know what you mean. But this building doesn't house any old, dead objects. Just dead people," he said.

Inside they were met by a tall, slender man in brown corduroy pants, a checked shirt, a tie and a V-neck lamb's wool sweater. His narrow face was encircled by a thin beard and a high hairline. It was impossible to estimate his age, but Milo suspected that he had looked equally elegant and sovereign the past twenty years.

"*Dottore*," said Benedetti, extending his hand.

"*Commissario*. You are here because of the Norwegian woman, right?" the other man answered in a bass voice.

"Yes. Thanks for meeting us on a Sunday."

The other man waved him away and turned to Milo.

"*Dottore* Brizi. I'm the medical examiner. A pleasure."

Milo answered the handshake.

"Cavalli. *Polizia Norvegese*. A pleasure."

They took the stairs down to the basement, where the temperature was several degrees lower. In a little closet they put on green pouches over their shoes, hairnets and white coats.

A few minutes later they were standing around the corpse of Ingrid Tollefsen.

The light hair was no longer flowing around her head, but instead was in a ponytail under her left shoulder. The skin, which was pale to begin with, appeared chalk-white under the strong fluorescent lights, which made the dark flecks on each side of her throat stand out even more clearly. Like specks of blood in snow.

"Suffocation?" Milo asked.

"*Sì*," Brizi answered in a low voice, as if he did not want to disturb her sleep.

She was lying on a metal bench in the middle of the room. Along one wall were two large, white washbasins. Above the basins were dispensers with sterilizing fluid and brushes for scrubbing hands. Along the other wall were the medical examiners' tools. The razor-sharp scalpels. Scissors of all sizes. Knives. And at the far end was the bone saw, with the ergonomically designed handle. Everything in shining steel.

Milo moved around the body of Ingrid. Her breasts lay flat over her ribcage, and almost flowed a little past it. Her stomach was flat, but marred by thirty or so stitches that extended from under the navel and almost up to the breastbone where the pathologist had opened her to examine the internal organs.

She had been beautiful. And in good shape. She could have been one of his fellow students a few years ago, apart from the fact that she had studied science and technology, while he had taken economics. But she reminded him of a fellow student, or a young colleague.

This was a lady with guts, thought Milo.

At the same time, this was also a lady with baggage. The big sister who was only in her early teens when her life changed. She'd lost a mother and gained a brother. A baby brother. Who, fifteen years later, had been shot and killed in a quiet Oslo suburb. And now, two years later, she herself had met death. In a hotel room in Rome.

Milo had seen dead people before, but still reacted to their immobility. People who had lived, suffered, cried, run, loved and hated, and suddenly a line was drawn over all their exertions. Before him was a corpse. But it was also a daughter. And a star student who, in addition to her studies in Trondheim, had worked on fundraising campaigns for everything from orphanages in Rumania to famines.

But above all she had been a big sister.

What thoughts had raced through her head in the moment of death? Did she have time to feel panic? Was she paralyzed by fear?

"There's one thing I don't quite understand," said Milo, looking over at Brizi.

"What's that?" the medical examiner replied.

"Someone suffocated her, but the body bears no signs of struggle. Not so much as a scratch."

"It's because of this," Brizi answered, going over to her head.

He moved it slightly to the side so that the throat and parts of the neck were exposed, and pointed at a little red mark on the left side of the throat.

"What's that?" asked Milo.

"Anesthetic. Someone drove a syringe of propofol into her neck. After a few minutes she passed out, and then the person in question suffocated her. Without her being able to put up resistance."

Benedetti parked outside a little three-star hotel in the vicinity of Termini, the central train station, and let Milo enter first. They had agreed to meet in the lounge next to reception, and Milo immediately caught sight of him.

The man was sitting, bent over and passive. His gaze was fixed on a point on the floor, and his torso rocked slightly forward. A mentally ill man, many probably thought when they saw him, but Milo understood: Sigurd Tollefsen was grief-stricken.

Milo recognized the apathy. The soothing rocking of the

upper body because the loss of a dear one had settled in the stomach region and threatened to slice him into filets from inside. And when Tollefsen looked up at him, Milo saw a face drained of tears.

"Milo Cavalli. From the Norwegian police," he said, extending his hand.

Sigurd Tollefsen raised up a little from the bench and responded to the handshake.

"My condolences," said Milo.

"Thanks. It's—"

But the sentence stopped there. His gaze sought the floor again. He took a deep breath.

"Are you connected with the embassy?" he asked.

Milo shook his head.

"I got here yesterday. I'm working with Chief Inspector Sørensen, whom you spoke with on Friday."

Tollefsen nodded heavily.

"And what happens now? I understood that there is a long paper mill to go through."

"It's arranged. A flight leaves this afternoon with your daughter's casket on board. I've taken the liberty of reserving a seat for you too," Milo replied.

"But . . . my understanding was that it wouldn't happen until tomorrow."

"I got here yesterday."

"And you arranged it in one day? On a Saturday?"

Milo shrugged.

"I don't like to wait for things," he answered.

Tollefsen stood up heavily and firmly shook Milo's hand. His eyes were shiny and his lower lip was trembling. He cleared his throat weakly.

"Thank you. Now I understand what Sørensen meant when he said he had someone he thought could get the case moving."

Milo smiled.

"The only thing you have to do now is sign a few papers that my Italian colleague has here. Then we can talk again back in Oslo."

"When? . . ." Sigurd Tollefsen had to take a breath. "When do I get to see her?"

"Soon," Milo replied.

Benedetti took a step forward with a little plastic folder under his arm. He briefly greeted Tollefsen and expressed his condolences. A few minutes later the papers were signed, and Tollefsen was on his way up to his room to pack.

"Poor bastard," Benedetti mumbled while he gathered up the papers.

"I know. Thanks for arranging all this so quickly."

"No problem. I'm sorry I was so difficult in the beginning. The thought of yet another case with unpaid overtime is not tempting. I have a tendency to get stuck with the cases that have the least resources available."

"Why is that?"

Benedetti shrugged his shoulders, as if he didn't know the answer. But Milo saw through him.

"Are you unpopular with the bosses?" he asked.

The Italian detective snorted.

"I guess I'm not exactly known for my tactical qualities where scratching the right person on the back is concerned, no."

"Does that mean this homicide is not a priority case for the Rome police?"

Benedetti sighed heavily and cast a glance up at Milo. He searched for words.

"I'll do all I can. Within the limits I have," he said.

Milo knew that was true, but understood at the same time that the Rome police were not standing ready with the cavalry in this case.

"Thanks. But what was it really that got you to drop your free weekend and arrange this so quickly?"

"When we were in her hotel room, some memories came up," said Benedetti.

"What memories?"

"We've all lost someone, Cavalli. Personally, I lost my big brother over thirty years ago. It almost broke my mother and father and, when I saw your commitment, I was reminded of why I once became a policeman. To be able to help those like my mother and father. I was too young to do anything when we lost Giovanni, and I felt so helpless."

"I understand what you mean."

"You've also lost someone close to you?"

"My mother."

Benedetti nodded thoughtfully.

"Then we understand each other," he said.

They went out to the car and got in.

"What actually happened with your brother?" Milo asked.

"He died in a boat accident. A military cruiser that went down between Tunisia and Sicily in 1977. It was his last tour. He was going to start engineering studies after that."

"Why did it sink?"

Benedetti shrugged his shoulders while he turned out of the parking space.

"I tried to look into that . . . but got nowhere. The ship simply exploded. No one knows why. And the only one who survived didn't remember anything that could explain the incident."

9

He met Theresa outside the small, out-of-the-way restaurant. They kissed. Warmer than when they'd kissed at the train station the evening before. But cooler than when they had returned to the hotel room last night.

"Sleep well?" he asked.

"Very. Didn't get up until eleven," she answered.

"So you haven't eaten yet?"

She shook her head.

"I'm famished!" she said before they ducked in through the low doorway of the restaurant.

The room was small, and the ceiling low. Only six small tables were spread around, and only one of them was vacant. The unpadded chairs, the paper tablecloths on the table, the bare walls and small wineglasses signaled simplicity, but Milo knew that the food served at a place like this was anything but simple in taste and that this kitchen had taken more than a hundred years and three generations to be what it was: an out-of-the-way gem for the initiated.

The waitress came over to them, and they ordered water and wine. When she was back again, she rattled off the menu, which consisted of a couple of appetizers, three pasta dishes, two meat entrées and a fish entrée.

"What do you recommend?" asked Milo.

The answer came readily.

"Cheese and sausages as appetizer. Pasta from Sicily with vegetables. The fish."

Milo looked at Theresa.

"*Va bene per me.*" That's fine with me, she answered, taking a small sip of wine.

"Then we'll rely on you," Milo said, turning to the waitress.

It was never wrong to follow the kitchen's recommendation at a place like this. The waitress took the compliment from Milo as a matter of course, turned on her heels and called the order into the kitchen.

Milo tasted the Sicilian red wine while he looked around the place. The other guests appeared to be four couples and three friends at a table in the corner. Or there were at least three couples. The fourth pair he was unsure about. It could just as well be that the young man wanted to signal to the whole world that the small, dark curlyhead with the narrow mouth was his girlfriend.

Opposite Milo sat a man in his midthirties with sad eyes, the kind like dogs' eyes, that seem to pull down and get women to say, "Oh, how cute!"

Milo suspected that the eyes were more tired than sad, a distinction women were seldom attentive to.

The room was lit up by four wall lamps that occasionally dimmed and then brightened again.

"What are you thinking of?" asked Theresa.

"That the energy source for the lights in here is probably a guy on a stationary bicycle in the back room. The youngest son. And occasionally he has to lower his pace to refill his water or wine, and then the lights dim."

She laughed out loud, and took hold of his hand.

"I like it when you make me laugh," she said.

"And I like that you make me want to make you laugh," he answered.

The appetizers came to the table. Simple in appearance. Complex in taste. And perfect with the wine.

They ate and chatted. She asked about what he had done that

morning, and he answered evasively. A description of the session at the morgue was hardly a good prelude to a meal.

The conversation flowed better than the evening before, but not without a certain sense of exertion, as if they both tried not to mention the elephant in the room.

"When are you leaving?" she asked.

"This evening."

"And in a few weeks we'll see each other again?"

He nodded.

"Yes. I'm going to think about what you said," he answered.

"Fine. But you don't need to look so serious. It's actually a compliment. I like being with you. And I don't like *not* being with you," she said.

He looked at her.

"I understand that. I don't like it either when we're away from each other."

"But it's not so bad that you want to do something about it?"

"We'll have that discussion next time," said Milo, asking for the bill.

As he got off the plane at Gardermoen, he sent three text messages. One to Theresa to say that he had arrived and that he'd had a nice time with her, one to his father to say that he could make it for dinner the following day, and the last to Sørensen to set up a debriefing.

He had not even passed customs before his phone beeped again.

I MISS YOU. T.

Then his father answered and asked him to come at six o'clock the next day. The thought of meeting his father's lady friend, and probable future wife, was not at all tempting, but he knew that it was something he had to get through.

He had just gotten in the car when Sørensen texted his order: 9 TOMORROW. THAT COFFEE PLACE OF YOURS.

MONDAY

10

Dolce Vita on Prinsens Gate eased the transition from Rome to Oslo. Alessio behind the counter nodded in recognition, and Antonello Venditti was streaming from the speakers.

They found a table in the far corner. Milo with a cappuccino and cannoli, Sørensen with an *Americano* and snuff.

"Tell me!" he ordered.

"Fine. There are a couple of things that bother me."

Milo told Sørensen about the investigations at the hotel, the conversation with the medical examiner Brizi and the cooperation with *Commissario* Benedetti. Sørensen listened, sipped his coffee and sucked on the snuff.

When Milo was finished, he leaned back with his arms crossed.

"So someone was able to drug her. Probably someone she knew, since she must have let that person in. At the same time, someone, probably her, threw a pill bottle down into the back courtyard. With an illegible note in it."

"We could make out the letters v-e-r-b-a. Verba."

"Verba? What's that supposed to mean? The beginning of a name? Is there an Italian name that starts with those letters?"

Milo shook his head.

"Not as far as I know."

"So we have an almost illegible note with some incomprehensible letters. We have no witnesses, no biological traces in the hotel room and no laptop or anything from her," he summarized.

"That's right," Milo replied.

Sørensen sighed heavily, spitting the snuff pouch into the empty coffee cup.

"That's not too damned much," he observed.

"I know," said Milo.

"We'll have to start by finding out what she was doing at that conference," said Sørensen, getting up.

He put on his topcoat and wrapped a scarf around his neck as if he were going out into a storm.

"I have an appointment with the head of Forum Healthcare in Lilleaker, where she worked. Do you have time to come with me?"

"*Certo!*"

"Huh?"

"Of course."

Sørensen shook his head.

"Milo, you're in Norway now. Knock off the Mafia talk."

Milo put on an innocent expression while he raised his shoulders and held both palms up in front of him at shoulder height in an apologetic gesture.

"*Scusa!* Sorry!"

"Nitwit! We'll take your car," Sørensen said, waddling toward the exit.

• • •

Their arrival was announced, and CEO Thomas Veivåg appeared with the legal director and public relations director too, both of whom introduced themselves with names Milo immediately forgot.

As a Financial Crimes detective Milo was accustomed to companies showing up in force, but Sørensen did not like being in the minority.

"Sheesh, the whole bucket brigade," he muttered to Milo.

They were shown into a vacant conference room that was featureless and functional. The conference table had room for ten to twelve persons, a projector was hanging from the ceiling and the view toward the Lysaker River was covered up by exterior blinds.

Milo and Sørensen sat down at one end of the table, the three others on the opposite side.

"Well, I don't know how this sort of thing is done," Veivåg began while he poured coffee for the two police officers.

"The way it works is that we ask questions and you answer," Sørensen said drily.

He set his notebook on the table along with his snuffbox, and searched for his pen. Milo took out his Mont Blanc pen and gave it to him.

"But, first of all, of course we must also express our condolences to you for the loss of a capable colleague," said the chief inspector.

The three on the other side nodded back as if on command.

"Thank you. It's quite incomprehensible," Veivåg replied. "Ingrid was . . . a great girl. Professionally accomplished, accessible, extremely well liked."

The two others nodded in affirmation.

"Tell us a little about the company first, and then about what she worked on," said Sørensen.

"Okay."

Just then the legal director leaned over the table while he smoothed out his tie in an almost caressing motion.

"Just something very brief to start with. If that's okay, Thomas?"

Veivåg nodded curtly, and the other man directed his attention across the table.

"Just so we are clear on this. What kind of meeting is this, actually? In formal terms. Are we talking about an interrogation? Or is this just a background conversation?"

Sørensen inserted two pouches of snuff and dropped the box onto the table.

"This is an investigation," he answered.

"I understand that, but purely legally—"

"Purely legally, we are trying to find out who killed Ingrid Tollefsen, arrest the person in question and get that person convicted."

The legal director looked uncertainly from Sørensen and Milo to his boss.

"This is not an interrogation," said Sørensen.

"Okay, fine, thanks," he answered, leaning back in his chair again.

Thomas Veivåg cleared his throat.

"Then I'll begin by telling a little about the company and about . . . Ingrid and what she worked on here."

"Fine," Sørensen answered, emptying his coffee cup.

Veivåg gave them a condensed version of the company's history, which he had obviously done countless times before. Forum Healthcare Norway was part of the international pharmaceutical giant Forum Healthcare Inc. Listed on the New York Stock Exchange and one of the world's three largest pharmaceutical groups. The Norwegian part, formerly called NorMed had been acquired eight years earlier. NorMed was originally a sister company to NewMed, but the two companies developed in different directions. While NewMed merged with a British pharma giant, which was later swallowed up by EG Health, NorMed continued for a few more years as an independent company. Until the definitive breakthrough with the company's own glucocorticoid tablets.

"What did you call that?" asked Sørensen.

"Glucocorticoid. Better known as cortisone," Veivåg explained.

"I've heard of cortisone."

"It's used for a lot of things, but especially for prevention of bone brittleness, or what's called osteoporosis," the head of Forum continued. "NorMed got its breakthrough with cortisone products in both capsule and liquid form, and in a few years got a reputation as one of the world's leading research environments in just osteoporosis. And not long afterward the Americans were knocking on the door."

"Why did the owners decide to sell the company?"

Sørensen resembled a journalist as he sat taking notes on his pad and interjecting questions. He had the same impatience. The same antipathy for authority.

"Because, in the pharmaceutical industry, the laws of big numbers rule. The bigger you are, the more you have for research, development, sales and distribution. In practice we were sitting on a gold mine, but lacked the infrastructure to make the gold known and transported out into society," Veivåg answered.

"What was the company worth when you sold it?" asked Milo.

"About eight billion kroner," the director answered.

The coffee carafe made its way around the table while Veivåg continued talking.

"It's really quite incredible, but from 1890 to 1905 a number of pharmaceutical companies popped up in Kristiania, and a few down in Vestfold. And in the course of a century several of them became global leaders and spearheads in some of the world's biggest companies."

"Spearhead? Aren't you just a subsidiary that has to make what the Americans tell you to?"

The way Sørensen pronounced "the Americans" made it apparent that these were not his favorite people, and that this was connected to a political stance he had adopted sometime in the 1970s. And which he had maintained since.

Thomas Veivåg shook his head slightly.

"Forum Healthcare has actually invested large amounts to develop the Norwegian entity. We have an R-and-D department that—"

"R and D?"

The chief inspector looked inquisitively at him.

"Research and development," Veivåg explained.

"Okay."

"We have a research and development department with thirty employees, and our research director is head of departments for several European countries besides. So then, our owners have control, but we don't feel like a subsidiary," said Veivåg.

"And what did Ingrid Tollefsen do here?" Sørensen asked.

"She worked in the R-and-D department."

Tollefsen had been a student at NTNU in Trondheim at the biotechnology institute, as well as an exchange student at Università degli Studi di Roma and their Pharmaceutical Biotechnology Center.

"She studied in Rome? When was this?" Milo interrupted, glancing at Sørensen.

If she had lived in Rome, she had a social circle there, which meant that the investigation must be expanded. *Commissario* Benedetti would be notified as soon as the meeting with Forum was over.

"She spent her last year as a student down there. And then she had an internship in the World Health Organization too, when they still had a Rome office. Then she started with us, about three years ago now. So it must be almost four or five years since she lived there," said Veivåg.

"What kind of conference was she attending in Rome last week?" Sørensen asked.

"You should really talk with her immediate supervisor, Anders Wilhelmsen, about that. I thought I would show you around afterward, show you her workplace and introduce you to him. But from what I know, it was a conference on molecular research," Veivåg answered.

Milo thought about the white slip of paper in the pillbox they had found.

"Does 'verba' mean anything to you?"

They looked at each other and then at Milo.

"No. Should it?" answered Veivåg.

"I don't know. I'm just wondering. Verba something-or-other."

Veivåg shook his head.

"No, it doesn't ring any bells."

They continued talking a few more minutes before they packed up for a short guided tour. While their cups were placed on the little wheeled cart by the wall, the public relations director ventured a question.

"What do we say if the media calls us?"

"Nothing. Nada," Sørensen answered.

"But 'no comment' never sounds good," he protested.

"Say that you are cooperating with the police and contributing the information we need," said Milo.

The public relations director nodded seriously.

Sørensen allowed himself a smile.

"That's nice. Cooperation with the police is never wrong," he said and spit the two snuff pouches out into a wastebasket.

The Research and Development department was separate from the rest of the company, with its marketing people, accountants, secretaries and directors. From reception they went down a stairway and were shown into a cloakroom. For the second time in two days Milo had to put on a white coat, foot protectors and a hairnet. But this time it was to enter a place where they worked to save lives. Not like last time, in Rome, where it was to look at a corpse.

"This is Anders Wilhelmsen," said Thomas Veivåg once they were inside and were met by the head of R & D.

Wilhelmsen filled out the white coat amply. He was the same height as Milo, but twice as wide. His hair was pulled far back, and revealed a high—not to say missing—hairline.

"Welcome. I'm just sorry it's under such circumstances." His handshake was firm and his voice deep.

"I'm sorry about the loss of a capable employee," said Sørensen.

"She was one of the best," said Wilhelmsen.

"We understand that. Can you show us around a little and explain what she was working on?"

The head of R & D nodded and turned around. He started talking, and guided them to the middle of the premises. Around them employees were sitting, bent over microscopes and computer keyboards.

"I don't know how much Thomas has told you, but Ingrid worked on various projects directly connected to the development of new products for Forum. We do everything from pure basic research to clinical testing of new products," Wilhelmsen explained.

"What was she doing in Rome?" asked Sørensen.

"Research conference. She wanted to go down there to get updated, and I'm positive about that type of professional replenishment."

"How did she fit into the environment here?"

"Very well. She was highly respected and well liked."

"But did anyone notice any changes in her behavior recently?" asked Sørensen.

Wilhelmsen thought about it.

"No, not really."

"Not really? What do you mean?"

The head of research made a slight pause and moved his weight over to one leg.

"When she had been working for us for a year, that thing with her brother happened. Yes, I'm sure you're familiar with the story. He'd gotten on the wrong track, and . . . well, it's just unbelievable that they're both dead now. Poor family."

"How did she take what happened to her brother? Did her behavior change?" Sørensen wanted to know.

"In the beginning, naturally enough, she was crushed. Who wouldn't be?" Wilhelmsen replied.

He forced her to take sick leave the first couple of weeks, but then she came and asked for a leave of absence.

"Leave of absence?"

"Yes, she was a very conscientious person. Felt guilty about being on sick leave. So she asked for two months' unpaid leave."

"To do what?"

"Grieve, I assume. Pull herself together. I don't really know. I just said okay, and took her off the projects," said Wilhelmsen. "Two months later she was back, and after that she wasn't absent a single day."

"Where was she for those two months?" asked Milo.

Wilhelmsen shrugged his shoulders.

"I don't know. You'll have to ask the family. We had no contact during her leave, and when she was back, we didn't talk about it either."

Both Milo and Sørensen noted key words. The leave of absence was a black hole in Ingrid Tollefsen's timeline, and they had to know what she had been doing. Two months was a long time. At the same time Milo knew what it was like to grieve. He himself had sought refuge in Italy after his mother's death, before he came home again, resigned from his stock-analyst job in Bremer Securities and started as a special investigator in Financial Crimes.

"Okay, what we need now is a complete list of the projects she worked on since she started," said Sørensen.

Wilhelmsen looked over at Thomas Veivåg uncertainly. This was obviously a signal for the boss himself to say something, but it was the legal director who cleared his throat and came to the head of R & D's rescue.

"Now, the sort of things that go on in this department are subject to strict confidentiality clauses. We are, as I said, listed on the stock exchange, and all information must be handled—" he began, but was interrupted by Sørensen.

"We know what confidentiality is. But we need to get a complete picture of what she was working on, who she was in contact with, e-mails in and out, reports and so on."

"But this is not information we can automatically give out," the attorney protested.

"You can't?"

"No, unfortunately. I have clear instructions from our attorneys in the U.S. that this must go through them."

"Through the U.S.?!"

Sørensen snorted and tried to make eye contact with Veivåg instead, but the managing director kept his gaze firmly fixed on the attorney who was speaking.

"Yes. This is also connected with the fact that we are subject to American financial legislation," the legal director explained.

Milo took a step toward Sørensen and gave him a look that said, "I'll fix this." Turning to the Forum directors he said, "I understand that. I can initiate a case with Financial Crimes, and make contact with your head office and the Securities and Exchange Commission."

"What the hell is that?" asked Sørensen.

"SEC. The American financial regulatory agency," Milo replied.

"Initiate a case? Make contact with the SEC? Is that necessary?" Thomas Veivåg asked uncertainly.

"You want to make this formally correct, and of course we understand that. This is pure routine," said Milo.

Veivåg looked at his legal director, who cleared his throat worriedly.

"I'll inform our New York office. We will obviously do what we can within the legal framework over there to help you. Perhaps it is not necessary in formal terms to set up a separate case," he said.

"Fine. Because if not, we'll have to say that we don't perceive that you are cooperating if the media were to call us. And it is going to sound a damned lot worse than if you say 'no comment,'" said Sørensen, turning and walking toward the exit.

11

Milo let himself into the apartment, went upstairs and changed to workout shorts and a T-shirt. He had time for a round with the boxing bag before going out to his father's for dinner.

He warmed up with some light punches on the bag while he shook himself loose. The soreness was still there after the struggle with Reeza Hamid a few days earlier but, fortunately, he seemed to have escaped serious injury.

After a minute or two he switched to direct hits against the bag. Let the force come from his hips while his fists rang against the sack. The chains it was hanging on rattled with every blow that hit, and Milo felt how the force from the blow of his fists against the sack was transmitted up into the aching shoulder. He clenched his teeth and continued, and gradually the warmth spread in his body and the pain in his shoulder was reduced to a murmur.

He took a little break and shook loose, before picking up the pace. Simply by standing and hitting intensely against the sack for ten or fifteen minutes he worked out most of the muscle groups in his body.

He finished with a minute of rapid, continuous blows against the sack, and was gasping for air when he was done.

He still felt his pulse pounding when the phone suddenly rang. It said "Unknown Caller" on the display, and Milo thought immediately of Benedetti.

"*Pronto!*" he answered loudly and clearly while he dried the sweat from his forehead with a towel.

But it was not the Italian detective.

"Uh, I would like to speak with Emil Cavalli."

The voice was a woman's.

"That's me. Who is this?"

"Hi. My name is Ada Hauge and I'm calling from *Klassekampen.*"

"I see, but I'm not interested. I'll stick with the Saturday subscription, I don't have time to read the paper during the week," Milo replied.

"I'm not trying to sell you a subscription. I'm a journalist."

Milo did not reply, but went into the office and sat down heavily in a chair.

"Hello? Are you still there?" she asked uncertainly.

"I'm here. What's this about?"

"It's about Ingrid Tollefsen. I understand that you were down in Rome to investigate the case."

Milo cursed to himself. He mostly wanted to hang up. Just say to hell with it, but he was too well brought up. At the same time he knew the tactic from other journalists he had been in contact with. When they wanted to confirm information they weren't sure about, they often asked a question to make it sound like they already knew. He had experienced that when he worked as a stock analyst. Journalists who didn't ask "Is it true that you are the one working on the acquisition of . . ." but instead opened with "I hear you're working with the acquisition of . . . and have a few questions in that regard." If you answered that type of question, you were already trapped. Answering with "How do you know that?" only confirmed the information, and often that was what the journalists were after. They simply took a chance.

What did Ada Hauge know about the murder of Ingrid Tollefsen?

"I never give statements to the press," Milo answered.

With that he neither confirmed nor denied anything.

"I'm not looking for statements. I'm looking for information."

"I'm not the right person."

"Listen here, I know that you were in Rome over the weekend."

"I didn't know that *Klassekampen* had its own crime reporters," said Milo.

He tried to change the subject by avoiding confirming anything at all.

"We don't. I work on domestic news. The fact is that I had an internship at *VG* when her brother was killed. Among other things, I covered the court case afterwards."

"I see."

"And then I became acquainted with Ingrid. We are . . . were the same age . . . and yes, we got well acquainted at that time."

Milo did not say anything, but let her talk.

"We stayed in contact. Met for coffee occasionally, and I was going to see her last Friday. She didn't come. I tried to call her. Over the weekend too, and today. And then I called her father earlier today. He was the one who told me."

Milo realized that it was no use denying it.

"I understand. But, as I said, I don't want to be interviewed."

"And, as *I* said, I don't want quotes. I'm looking for information."

"It's Sørensen you have to talk with, he's the chief inspector."

"And I will. When we've finished this conversation."

Milo stood up and took out the headset for the phone. While he talked, he texted Sørensen.

"Listen here. There's nothing I can say about the case. You obviously know that I was in Rome, but I would prefer that you keep my name out of it."

"That's fine, but you have to help me."

She was tough, but not unpleasant. Milo felt like he was in negotiations. Give-and-take.

"What do you want to know?"

"If there is a connection between the killings."

"It's too soon to say anything about that."

"But what do you believe?"

"We don't believe anything. We investigate. And this is something that we have to find out."

"So you're not ruling out that there may be a connection?"

"We're not ruling anything out," Milo replied.

He heard her fingers running over the keyboard while they talked, and felt an intense need to finish the call.

"You'll have to talk with Sørensen, but I doubt that you'll get anything out of him," he said.

"I doubt that too. But I'm going to write something regardless."

"That's too bad."

"Why is that? Because it may damage the investigation?"

Milo did not have time to answer before she continued.

"It's only a question of time before it leaks out in the press. The Oslo police are like a sieve. And wouldn't a sober article from us be better for you than *VG* disclosing this and rolling out the cannons?"

"Could be."

"And I understand that you don't want to be bothered by us journalists, but look at it from the bright side."

"Which is?"

"It shouldn't be difficult to get enough resources for the investigation anyway as long as the media is following the case."

She had a point. And he didn't like it.

"Can I ask you a question?" he asked.

"Yes, sure. Fire away."

"Why were you going to meet her on Friday?"

"We got together occasionally. I don't know . . . there was a kind of bond between us back then."

"How often did you meet?"

"Well . . . the last time must have been last spring. So it wasn't like we were knocking down each other's doors exactly."

"I understand. Was it you or her who took the initiative to meet this time?"

Ada Hauge remained silent on the other end. And when she spoke again, some of the professional certainty was gone. She hesitated to answer.

"It was Ingrid. She sent me a text message."

"Did she say anything about what she wanted to talk about?"

"Nothing specific."

"But?"

"She said that she wanted to discuss something with me."

"What was that?"

"She didn't say."

He could picture the dead Ingrid Tollefsen on the cold metal bench in the basement of the morgue in Rome. Did what she wanted to discuss with Ada Hauge have a connection with the killing?

"Can you think of anything she wanted to talk about? Had she hinted at anything earlier when you talked?"

He could hear her clearing her throat on the other end.

"That's an awful lot of questions you're asking. I'm actually the one who should be asking the questions. I'm a journalist, after all," she said.

"Yes, but you were also her friend. And this may actually be important to the case. Can you recall whether she talked about anything? Relationship trouble? Work problems?"

"I remember she said once that she missed the university."

"Was she unhappy at work? Did she say anything about that?"

"No. Not directly. Just that she missed the academic world. But she probably wouldn't have said that if she was a hundred-percent satisfied with her job."

Milo noted *Dissatisfied with work?* on a sheet of paper.

"No, perhaps not. What was she like, really? As a person, I mean?" Milo asked.

"A very fine woman. Smart. Tough. Nice."

"Did she talk much about her brother?"

"At first she didn't talk about anything else. She reproached herself. You know perhaps that their mother died when he was born?"

"Yes, I heard that."

"Ingrid was about thirteen or fourteen then. I got the impression that she took on a kind of maternal role. Feeding, diaper changes, going to day care. You get the picture."

"Yes. But she couldn't take care of him all the time. So why did she reproach herself for what happened to him?"

"I think she had a kind of counterreaction as she got older. Went away to study. Get a little distance. And that meant she wasn't there when he started having problems. I think that deep down she thought he wouldn't have gotten into trouble if she'd been around."

Milo made further notes on the paper while he listened to what she had to say. He was starting to feel cold after the workout and longed for a warm shower. He looked at the clock and realized that he would be late to dinner with his father.

"I understand that it must have been tough for her," he said.

"Yes, but it wasn't true that she buried herself in sorrow. She grieved, yes, but she got back up. That's what I mean when I say that she was tough. Do you understand?"

"Absolutely. But I'm a little late for an appointment now."

"That's fine. I have what I need," Ada Hauge answered.

"No quotes, right?"

"No quotes. You're going to see that I'll handle this case carefully."

"Good," said Milo.

"But can I expect to be able to call you again later?"

There it was again. The negotiation. I do something for you and then you can do something for me later.

"Just call, but don't assume that I can give you anything."

"I understand that. But the day you actually can say something, I'll be at the top of your list. Fine?"

"Fine."

They ended the call.

Twenty minutes later he was done showering and dressed, ready to be introduced to the new woman in his father's life.

12

It was his father who answered the door, dressed in charcoal-gray suit pants, light-blue shirt and a checkered apron.

"Nice apron, Dad."

"Emil, come in, come in."

The nasal, posh voice did not go well with the checkered apron.

They hugged awkwardly, and his father took Milo's topcoat and hung it up.

"So, where is she?"

"She's in the living room, but before you go in, there's something I would really like to say."

"I see, and what is that?"

His father came toward him.

"I've thought about telling you this many times, but it's been damned touchy, you understand. So I thought it was just a matter of pulling the bandage off quickly, instead of dragging it out."

Milo sighed.

"I know it's been tense. I understand that you're not going to be alone for the rest of your life, that you'll find someone new."

"Well, it's not that simple—"

"Can I just go and say hello to her? Let's take it from there" said Milo.

Without waiting for an answer he set a course toward the living room with his father limping after.

"Hold on a second, Emil—"

But it was too late.

What the hell! thought Milo.

She was sitting on the couch with her legs crossed, reading

a magazine, and was about twenty years younger than he had imagined. Besides that, her attire and appearance were completely unexpected. The dark jeans with a hole on one thigh, the short, stringy hair. And not least the little diamond in one nostril.

"Hi, Milo," she said, getting up.

She could not be much more than twenty. Slender as a child.

Milo turned toward his father.

"What the hell is going on here? Have you lost your mind?"

"I tried to explain. Emil, this is Sunniva."

"Hi, Sunniva," Milo said curtly.

"She's my daughter. Your half sister," said his father.

"Oh, shit!" answered Milo.

Endre Thorkildsen told the story while he stood and tried to make eye contact with his son.

Sunniva was twenty-one years old, and her mother had been his colleague. She was an accountant in the brokerage firm he had been part of founding, and "one thing led to another," as he explained.

Sunniva came into the world, and there was never any question that her father would not support her. Contact was sporadic as she was growing up, but the past few years they'd had more contact than before. She was studying industrial design, and planned to stay in either Berlin or London at an art school starting in the fall.

"Why didn't you say anything before?" asked Milo.

His father looked at them both.

"I couldn't. At first I thought you were too young to understand, and that it was simplest to keep things separate. And later it was hard to talk about it, after Maria . . . your mother . . . got so bad," he answered.

"Did she know about this?"

His father nodded silently.

"And what did she say?"

"That stays between me and her," he answered firmly.

Milo stood up, pulling his hands through his hair and folding them behind his neck.

"Sorry, Sunniva, I'm sure you're a nice girl, but this was a bit much. I had prepared myself to meet Dad's new fiancée."

She let out a little snort of laughter.

"Do you think this is funny?"

"A little, yes."

She smiled self-confidently, and Milo could only smile back.

"Yes, maybe it is, but—"

"I have a roast in the oven that I have to take out," his father interrupted.

"I'm not that hungry," Milo replied.

"But I am," said Sunniva.

"For crying out loud, Emil! You're not leaving now! Can't we just sit down over a meal? Get acquainted a little. Can that be so bad?"

"I don't know."

"Emil, she's your sister, damn it!"

"Half sister!" Sunniva and Milo responded in chorus.

He stayed. And they had a kind of family dinner. The conversation flowed slow like cement, and at times seemed as if it was an interview. Sunniva and Milo answered each other's questions, and their father interjected information he found suitable, but that only made the situation even more uneasy. "Is that so? Emil has always liked swimming a lot too. There you have something in common!"

After a couple of hours they left, and Milo offered her a ride. A short time later he was accelerating onto the E18 in the direction of downtown Oslo.

"Did you think it was awkward?"

"I was just surprised. I'm an only child. I'm used to it just being me. Now I suddenly have a half sister. I just have to digest that."

"Are you mad at Dad because he never said anything?"

For a moment he was taken aback that she called his father Dad. That he was also someone else's father.

"I'm upset at him because of a lot of things," he answered.

"Yeah, so I've heard."

She looked up at him.

"I went to see you once."

He glanced at her.

"What?! When?"

"A couple of years ago. I stood outside your apartment in Briskeby. I wanted to ring the doorbell, but I knew I couldn't."

She remained quiet a moment, and Milo did not know what to say.

"I saw you coming out with a girl. Probably your girlfriend. You were holding hands."

"What did she look like?"

"Shorter than you. Of course. Dark, medium-length curly hair. Almost a little Spanish."

"Kristin."

"Are you still together?"

"No. That ended a long time ago."

"Do you have a girlfriend now?"

"I have a girl in Italy. Theresa."

"Pretty name. Is it serious?"

"I'm seriously fond of her, yes. But we'll have to see. What about you? Do you have a boyfriend?"

"Well . . ."

"What's his name?"

"Her name is Elisabeth."

"Okay. I didn't know that—"

"It's okay. Before her I was with someone named Howard."

"Really."

There was less than ten years between them, but Milo suddenly felt that there was a whole generation's distance.

"I'm not so preoccupied by gender. I fall in love with people," she said, drawing figures on the windowpane.

He changed the subject.

"Where do you live?"

"Majorstua. Neuberggata."

"Okay. Then we'll drive there."

They sat silently, and Milo concentrated on driving. He liked to drive fast and, as always, his thoughts flowed freely. He thought about what Ada Hauge from *Klassekampen* had said. That Ingrid Tollefsen wanted to talk to her about something. What was it she had been doing recently in Rome that had led to such a tragic end to her life?

And what had actually happened in that hotel room? How was someone able to drug her without her having screamed or fought back? Could there have been several people in her room? One who held her still and one who drugged her? Or was there just one person who held her down while he stuck the syringe in? It must have been done by a person with experience in using syringes.

His thoughts went to Forum Healthcare. Ingrid Tollefsen's

employer. He did not count on any of the suit-wearing bean
counters he had met there being able to handle a syringe. But
there were certainly others in the company who could.

He parked outside her apartment and turned off the engine.

"You wanna come in for a while?" she asked.

He thought about it a moment. His irritation with his father
was still there. But at the same time she was family. And family
came first, regardless of how inconvenient it was.

He nodded and followed her up. The hall was overflowing
with shoes, boots, jackets and coats. They could hear loud talking somewhere in the apartment, and by the doorway to the
kitchen was a garbage bag someone had neglected to take down
to the courtyard.

"I share with three others. Sorry about the mess," she said,
going ahead of him into her room.

It was big and messy, with a bed, writing desk, wardrobe,
and an easel in the corner.

"You paint?" he asked.

"A little. Not much. Trying out some techniques," she said
while she took out a photo album she wanted to show him.

There was a knock on the door, and an attractive woman in
her early twenties stuck her head in.

"Oh, I didn't know you had a visitor," she said, blushing
when she saw Milo.

"Hi, Rannveig. It's not a problem. This is my brother. Milo."

He went over to her and shook her hand.

"Milo. A pleasure," he said.

"Rannveig."

She had short hair and was tall like a model, and her handshake was both warm and soft.

"Well, I won't disturb you. Nice to meet you, Milo," she said and withdrew.

He turned around and looked right at a smiling Sunniva.

"My God, you're quite the charmer!" she exclaimed.

He smiled, and looked for a place to sit down. He ended half reclining on the bed, with a pile of pillows as support.

They remained sitting and browsed through her collection of photo albums for half an hour and chatted about what they had been up to all these years. Cautious questions while they moved in circles around what they really wondered about.

"When did you find out that Dad was your father?" Milo asked at last.

She thought about it.

"I saw him occasionally when I was little. He was my dad who came for a visit now and then. But it was probably not until I was nine or ten that I started asking questions. About why he didn't live with us. For a long time I thought Mom and Dad were divorced, but gradually I understood more."

"So he came to visit you?"

"Yeah. We celebrated my birthdays. Just the three of us. And sometimes he was there when I came home from school. They might be sitting at the kitchen table with a cup of tea, talking."

And she told about the feeling she got of not wanting to disturb. Just sneak in, make herself unnoticed, and sit in the living room and hear the sound of their voices.

"I didn't want those moments to stop," she said.

She smiled absently as she said that. As if now, as an adult, she was feeling like the little girl she had been.

Milo looked down at the pictures from a birthday. Sunniva with a crown on her head, smiling from ear to ear. His father sitting in a chair. Suit and tie. He must have come directly from work. And after the presents and cake he had stood up, said thank you, got in his car and drove home to Milo and his mother.

"Did your friends know who he was?"

"They knew I had a father I saw now and then."

"So you talked about it? You weren't told not to talk about him with others?"

"That wasn't a problem."

"But he wasn't afraid that others would find out, and that then I would find out too?"

"Milo, I grew up in Furuset. You grew up in Nesøya. They are worlds apart."

"I'm sure you're right. But it must have been frustrating for you."

"My early teens were the worst," Sunniva answered.

For a while she had asked and pried about how her mother and father got together. Why they hadn't moved in together. How her father could have two families.

"And what did she say, your mother?"

"She didn't like to talk about that in particular. 'The situation is what it is, Sunniva.' I understand now that it must have been frustrating for her too. She really liked him. But she was always so bloody . . . understanding."

"Understanding?"

"Yes. She always said that it wasn't easy for Dad. I remember I yelled at her, 'Why did he have me then?' "

"And what did she say?"

Sunniva shrugged her shoulders.

"She started talking about coincidences. About how she was supposed to start working somewhere else, but quite by accident got an internship with Dad. 'Life is a series of coincidences,' she always said. 'If I hadn't started working there, if I hadn't moved from Trondheim, if I hadn't started night school, if Endre hadn't started that brokerage firm, then you wouldn't have been born,' she said."

"Must have been tough to have thrown in your face."

"Well, yes, but I think she babbled a lot. I was only concerned about why I didn't see him more often. She got a little vague when she talked about that. 'Even that shipwreck in Italy was a coincidence that finally meant that you were born,' I remember she said. She took her line of reasoning pretty far afield."

"Shipwreck in Italy? What did that have to do with it?"

"No idea. Some military ship that went down."

Milo frowned and stared at her. What in the world did a shipwreck in Italy have to do with Sunniva?

"What kind of ship was it? And when?"

She thought a moment.

"Well, let's see. I was fifteen or sixteen when she mentioned it. She never talked about it again. But I got the impression that it must have been long before I was born. In the 1970s. I guess I really just thought it was a way for her to obscure what I wanted to talk about. Why do you ask?"

Milo thought about Benedetti. He had also mentioned a military vessel that went down with his brother on board. More than thirty years ago, he had said. In other words, sometime in the 1970s.

How many Italian military vessels could actually have sunk at that time?

"I don't really know. But you're the second person in a few days who has mentioned a military vessel that sank in Italy," he answered.

TUESDAY

13

"Bless me, Father, for I have sinned. It's been four months since my last confession."

"God have mercy on you so you can repent your sins and believe in His mercy."

"I don't know if you remember me?"

"Yes, sure. And now you're back."

"Now I'm back, yes."

"What do you want to talk about, my son?"

"I've acquired a sister."

"I see. But isn't your mother—"

"Dead?"

"Yes. Dead."

"Well, yes. She's gone. But it turns out that I have a half sister."

"My word!"

(Pause.)

"I've had a half sister for over twenty years without knowing it. Then, suddenly, out of the blue, she's sitting there at home with my father."

"It must have been somewhat of a surprise?"

"You bet."

"How does it feel?"

"As if I've been betrayed. As if Mama was betrayed."

"And she was, too."

"Yes. He says she knew about it, but it must have been a great sorrow for her. He brought her here to Norway . . . and I always think that she must have felt so isolated. Even if we've been able to talk about her suicide, I can't get rid of the feeling that he betrayed her."

"I understand. But you know that things are often more complicated than they appear. And the fact that he is now telling you . . . that you get to meet your sister . . . could that perhaps be an outstretched hand from him?"

"Maybe so. I know in any event what Mama would have said."

"What would she have said?"

"*Devi essere pieno di amore*. She always said that to me."

"Full of love, right?"

"Yes. 'You must be full of love.' "

"That's beautifully stated."

"She truly believed in love. For everyone, really. She is the most generous person I've ever known."

"It sounds like she was a lovely person, my son."

(Pause.)

"And if she knew about your father's daughter and stayed anyway, isn't there a kind of forgiveness in that?"

"Well, yes. Certainly. But it wasn't like she could just leave. Your type doesn't exactly advocate divorce."

"We are probably more advocates of forgiveness."

"Yeah, I guess you are."

(Pause.)

"Do you still think a lot about your mother?"

"Almost every day. Not as strongly every time, but I can't free myself from the thought that it was very difficult for her at the end. And it's in the back of my mind that she was sick. That she had a mental illness. And diseases can be hereditary."

"But you aren't your mother. You are a separate individual, with your own characteristics and circumstances."

"I know that."

"I understand if this is difficult to talk about for you, my son, but sickness has always been a trial for us humans. You feel your own limitations. Your impotence. And, inevitably, you are forced to think about your finitude."

"Finitude?"

"Your mortality. That our lives too have an end."

"Thanks for the encouragement, Father."

"But sickness also has another side, my son."

"Yes?"

"It can also bring with it a new form of . . . shall I say . . . maturity."

"In what way?"

"It can get people to see things more clearly, peel away what is unimportant. It can get you to distinguish between what is essential in your life—and what is unessential."

"Maybe so."

"And it can get the person to come closer to God. By turning to Him."

"I guess it's just as common that it leads to the opposite, that you turn *away* from God."

"That can happen too. You're right about that. There are probably many who need someone to blame. But you are still sitting here. That means you haven't turned away. There is a possibility of seeking refuge in Him—and His word."

"What you said about distinguishing between what is essential and not . . . I understand what you mean."

(Pause.)

"I have a girlfriend in Italy. We've been together for a while."

"I seem to remember you mentioned her, yes."

"She's impatient."

"In what way?"

"We live in separate cities, in separate countries. She doesn't think we see each other often enough."

"And what do you think?"

"Until now I think it's been fine."

"Until now?"

"Yes. It's been good for us. And free."

"Ah, freedom, yes. Which you young people prize so highly."

"Well, Father, you yourself have chosen a life without a partner. There is a form of freedom in that."

"Maybe so. Or else you might say that God is my life partner. What I have devoted my life to—"

"Don't say you didn't choose the solution that suited you best, and you alone."

"This is not about me, my son. Obviously, in the end, one should choose the solution that is best for oneself—"

"Exactly."

"But one also has a responsibility for those around us. Does she love you?"

"Yes."

"Do you love her?"

"Perhaps."

"Well, regardless of what you decide, you must take the feelings of both into consideration."

"I know. It's just that I've always thought that I have plenty of time, but now she's beginning to demand answers. And it's not just the thing with Mama that reminds me of . . . my finitude, to use your words. In my job I am constantly reminded of . . . last weekend I was in Rome to bring home a Norwegian girl. She was killed . . . and when I saw her lying lifeless on the metal bench at the medical examiner . . ."

"I understand."

"She was my age."

"So you are investigating her murder?"

"Yes, I'm part of the team."

"So you are investigating a murder while you still are not through processing your mother's death. At the same time you have just found out that you have a half sister, and you must decide what to do with regard to your sweetheart?"

"It sounds like a soap opera when you put it that way."

"Life is like a soap opera. You wouldn't believe all the stories I've heard sitting here. But I understand that it can be tough for you."

"I'll handle it."

"I don't doubt that."

(Pause.)

"Shall we pray together, my son?"

"Do you think I need that?"

"I think we both need that."

14

"I called Benedetti in Rome. He's checking Ingrid Tollefsen's circle of acquaintances down there. I'll call him again later today."

Milo talked while Sørensen studied a pouch of snuff before putting it under his lip. On the table a copy of *Klassekampen* was open to the article by Ada Hauge. She was right when she said she would write a sober article, but nonetheless it had triggered an avalanche of phone calls from other journalists. Sørensen had finally reacted by turning off the phone.

"Can't bear those monkeys right now," he said.

Alongside the newspaper was the printout of the telephone log for Ingrid Tollefsen.

"I also sent a copy of her work hard drive to the computer team at Financial Crimes, and I've sent off an inquiry to the attorneys at the Forum head office in New York. I'll follow up in the course of the day," said Milo.

Sørensen got up and paced around the room.

"It's the motive we're struggling with. Just like with the little brother. Why the hell shoot a fifteen-year-old boy in the back and head? And who strolls into Ingrid Tollefsen's hotel room, drugs her, strangles her and removes all traces?"

Milo shrugged his shoulders.

"I don't know. Should we view the cases under one or as two separate investigations?" he asked.

"Officially, there's only the one. The case with the brother was closed. We weren't able to get good enough evidence that time. But, unofficially, we have to see whether there's a connection," answered Sørensen.

"What do you think? Is there a connection?"

"I feel it in my bones that there's some link or other. That's not to say that she was killed because her brother was killed. But I don't believe in coincidences. I believe in a series of events," Sørensen said.

He was interrupted by the door opening. Assistant Chief of Police Agathe Rodin came in followed by a young man Milo had not seen before.

"We're forced to hold a short press briefing, Sørensen," said Rodin.

She was in uniform and wore her three stars with a straight back and a proud expression.

"We can't prioritize that now. We have a pile of—"

"It will only take fifteen minutes," she interrupted, snatching a folder out of the hands of the young man following on her heels.

"Magnus is from the public relations department, and he's written a short press release."

The young man cleared his throat quietly, and took a step forward.

"It's very short and sweet, actually. We confirm the identity, say that the investigation is in full swing and avoid making speculations," he said.

Sørensen looked down his nose at it.

"Can't you just send it out? So we don't have to waste time?" he said.

Magnus smiled indulgently.

"For the newspapers that's fine, but the broadcast media don't like to read from press releases. They need to have people on the TV screen talking right into the microphone."

"What a fucking circus!"

Agathe Rodin straightened up another notch.

"Yes, I know, but that's how it is now. By the way, has it been awhile since you had media training?"

Sørensen looked at her with annoyance.

"I don't think so. There must have been a meeting last year—"

"—that you didn't show up for. Magnus will run a quick round with you now. We have less than an hour."

She waved her hand in the direction of the public relations adviser, who ran out into the corridor and came back with a small video camera.

Sørensen sighed audibly and scratched his head. Milo wisely kept quiet.

"I've made a Q and A that you can look at while I set up," said Magnus, holding out a sheet of paper.

"Q and A?"

"Questions and answers. The questions we think you might get, and how you should answer."

"You don't need to tell me how to answer," said Sørensen without taking the paper.

"Oh well. Then let's go, okay?" asked Magnus.

Sørensen grunted something in response and placed himself in front of the camera. First with his arms hanging down, then folded in front of his stomach and, finally, behind his back. Like a little general.

The public relations adviser started the camera and began the questioning.

"What can you say about the investigation?"

"We are investigating this case broadly and cooperating with the Italian police," Sørensen answered.

"What do you know about the cause of death?"

"We don't wish to release details about that."

"Does this mean that you know the cause of death, or not?"

Sørensen rocked a little back and forth on the soles of his feet.

"I don't want to comment on that."

"But what theories are you working from?"

"We are working in several directions and investigating broadly."

"Can there be a connection between the murder of Ingrid Tollefsen and the murder of her brother, Tormod Tollefsen, a few years ago?"

"It's much too early to say anything about that."

"But you're not ruling it out?"

"We are not ruling anything out."

Agathe Rodin took a step forward.

"That will do," she said.

She looked at Sørensen, and then at Magnus.

"That answer only invites speculation, wouldn't you say, Magnus?"

The public relations adviser nodded.

"The lead-in will be that the police are not ruling out a connection, and thereby you trigger an avalanche of speculations."

"But it's true. Should I lie, then?" said Sørensen.

"Of course you shouldn't lie. But you don't need to say everything that's true," Rodin replied.

"But damn it, it says in the paper today that we aren't ruling out a connection," said Sørensen, pointing at *Klassekampen*.

"But what they write is their own responsibility. We mustn't confirm it. You should simply repeat that this is not something you want to speculate about, and that the investigation will have to show what happened," said Magnus.

"One more time," said Rodin, stepping back.

"A few things, Sørensen. You have a tendency to look into the camera instead of looking at the interviewer, and you're also a little restless and rocking on the balls of your feet. Both things make you seem uncertain. The way TV is, no one remembers what you say, only how you say it. If you look comfortable and secure. Or nervous. It's quite merciless, seen that way," said Magnus.

"This is a lot of nonsense. That's what it is."

"If you just lean your weight over on one leg, your upper body will automatically stay still. Then you won't wobble. And then keep your line of sight toward the interviewer."

"Hmpf."

"What?"

"Fine!"

They ran through the same questions, and came back to the question about the connection between the murders.

"So, in any event, you're not ruling out a connection?" Magnus asked in his best journalistic voice.

"We don't wish to speculate about that. The investigation will have to take its course and show what actually happened," Sørensen answered dutifully.

Rodin nodded contentedly, but Magnus was not done.

"But are you the right person to lead this investigation, considering that you didn't succeed in the investigation of the murder of the brother?"

An irritated frown appeared on Sørensen's forehead.

"What kind of idiotic question is that?"

"It may come up, and then it's a good idea to practice for it. We can't control the questions from the journalists, and they aren't especially concerned about being polite," said Magnus.

Sørensen looked at Rodin, who smiled back. A smile from a boss to an underling that said, *Be damned sure to do as you're asked*.

"Just answer the question," she said.

The question was repeated, and Magnus shoved the microphone uncomfortably close to Sørensen, who answered by casting an irritated glance down at it before saying, "In my book, we solved that case. We found the perpetrators, but didn't get them convicted," he bellowed.

"Under no circumstances will you say that. Then we'll have a lawsuit against us at once, and then you won't have any time for the investigation," the assistant chief of police exclaimed.

"So what the hell should I say?"

Magnus cleared his throat cautiously.

"I've put a suggestion in the Q and A," he said, holding out the paper.

"Let's see, then!" said Sørensen, snatching it.

He skimmed it quickly and mumbled something incomprehensible before he said, "Fine. Let's take it one more time."

"But are you really the right man to lead this investigation, since you failed in the investigation of the murder of the brother?" Magnus asked.

Once again he shoved the microphone dangerously close to the chief inspector. But this time Sørensen did not turn away. He held his gaze, and answered in a calm voice.

"I'm doing the job I was assigned to do, so that's a question you will have to ask my superiors. The important thing now is that we put our available resources into the investigation so that we can clear up this homicide."

Rodin clapped her hands.

"Good! That will do it." She looked at the clock. "The briefing begins in forty minutes. Come down fifteen minutes ahead, then we'll talk through this one more time," she said and marched out of the room.

Magnus quickly packed up the camera, nodded to both of them and disappeared after the assistant chief of police.

Sørensen went straight to his desk and took out the snuff-box. He shoved in two pouches before turning toward Milo.

"And what are you sitting and smiling about?"

Milo shook his head.

"Nothing. That was very . . . educational," he answered.

"Certainly," Sørensen said drily. He sat down heavily. "I've been promised more resources, but I still need your help."

"Not a problem."

"I know you have plenty to do over at Financial Crimes, but I hope you don´t mind."

"It's pretty quiet now," Milo replied.

"Good. Then you'll continue checking several of the things we've talked about."

He made a theatrical pause.

"And then I´ll get to join the circus downstairs."

15

Milo parked in the Sentrum parking garage, and two minutes later he was walking through the passageway into the offices of Financial Crimes.

Astrid was enthroned in reception, and he tossed out a *"Ciao, bella"* to her on his way to his office among the others on the money-laundering team.

He turned on the computer and checked his e-mail. Then he took out the printout of the telephone log to Ingrid Tollefsen. He browsed to the last page. The last call to her was from an Italian number. He made a note to e-mail it to *Commissario*

Benedetti. There were no other incoming calls that day, but she had made two other calls the day she died. In the morning she called two Norwegian numbers in succession. He browsed through the papers. She called both numbers at regular intervals, one more often than the other.

He got up, taking the papers with him. On his way he picked up two cups of coffee before he knocked on Temoor's door.

"Just a moment."

Temoor was sitting with his back to him. The slender fingers were pounding on the keyboard.

Milo took a step into the room and encountered the aroma of overtime. In this case, a mixture of sweat and Red Bull.

Temoor Torgersen was Financial Crimes' constantly working and consistently communist computer expert. He turned toward Milo and automatically extended his hand for one of the coffee cups.

"I really hope you're not coming to harp about the hard disk already? Even *you* aren't that impatient, Milo."

He rolled back to his place and continued keyboarding.

"No, I thought we could do something together for a few minutes," said Milo to his back.

"So you have more work with you?"

"I thought we could spend a little quality time together," Milo replied.

"Nitwit!" Temoor finished typing and turned around. "What do you have?"

"Two phone numbers I have to check."

"You can do that yourself, damn it."

"Yes, maybe, but then I'm going to need help finding out more about the numbers, so we might just as well do that together. You'll do it in two minutes, I would take thirty."

Temoor held out his hand and Milo handed him the papers.

"I put a star by the two Norwegian numbers," he said.

"I figured that out!"

He rolled over to another machine, and let his fingers do the work. Two minutes later he had the answer.

"Sigurd Tollefsen at the one number. Ingrid Tollefsen at the other."

Milo looked over his shoulder.

"Ingrid Tollefsen? But wasn't the call made from her phone?"

"And to her phone too."

"Certain?"

Temoor continued typing.

"Look here. Two numbers registered to Ingrid Tollefsen. The one she called from, and the one she called to."

"Why did she call herself?"

"No idea. I don't know that sort of thing. I only work with *what*—not *why*."

"Can you do me another favor?"

"Here it comes, okay. Didn't I know it," said Temoor laconically.

"Just look at the number she called to, her own, that is. Is it still active?"

Temoor clicked and pressed, and brought a list up on the screen.

"It's active, yes."

"When was the number last in use?"

"Yesterday. One call in, one call out."

Milo finished his coffee and stared out into space.

"Why did she call her own phone the day she was murdered? And why is the phone still in use more than a week after she died?" he mumbled.

"That's probably just what you have to find out," Temoor replied.

He tied his blue belt around his waist, adjusted his outfit and stepped onto the mat. He was still tender in a few places after the fight with Reeza Hamid and yesterday's workout, but he needed to clear his head.

Some were doing individual warm-ups, while others chatted and waited for the instructor. Milo looked around the training center and noted that the ancient instinct was still thriving when he saw the female green belt flirting with the only black belt.

A dojo—a training center for martial arts practitioners—is a perfectly organized hierarchy, where the color of the belt decides the placement on the rank scale. And where the women exclusively flirted upward, while the men happily flirted downward.

So far Milo had never experienced a female practitioner, for example, flirting or getting involved with a man with a lower belt. It was as if their instincts forbade it and instead drove them to search closer to the top of the rank, the black belts. As if they were the tribe's strongest warriors, and in the best position to protect.

He had seen the same in the financial industry when he was part of that carousel. How the men fought for the women's favor, and where the size of the wallet was decisive. You might smile at it, distance yourself, intellectualize it, this endless cattle show of status symbols. But the fact was that it worked. Milo knew that the big watches, expensive suits, rumbling cars and gold-colored credit cards were in reality nothing other than the black belts of the financial industry.

They lined up in a row in front of the trainer, got on their knees in greeting by placing their palms on the orange mat and bowing their upper bodies forward.

Then there was a light warm-up and sparring with someone with the same belt.

He had often experienced that the solution to a problem came easier if he let his subconscious work in peace. If he tried to push for an answer, it got stuck. Sometimes it was important to think about other things.

And he didn't know of anything as effective as focusing on getting an opponent made of ninety kilograms of muscle down on the mat and under control as quickly as possible.

He had called Benedetti on his way to the workout, and informed him about the Italian phone number. Benedetti informed him at the same time about the charting of Ingrid Tollefsen's acquaintances in Rome.

Before he left work, Milo had also arranged to have Tollefsen's other phone traced. If it was still in use, he had to find out who had it, and where the person in question was.

But all this was shoved to the back of his mind as the six-foot-four training partner came toward him and dished out kicks and blows. Milo made a side move to the right as he quickly marked a kick in the stomach of the other, who bowed forward. Then Milo took a step right toward him, marking a blow against his kidneys before setting his hip against him and throwing him to the mat. The exercise concluded with control holds.

Then it was Milo's turn. He threw out a kick and followed up with a blow, but his partner moved sideways as he was supposed to. Milo felt the other man's foot in a controlled kick against his stomach followed by a blow before he was picked up and thrown onto the mat with a thud.

The only thought in his mind as his body rotated in the air was to land in a controlled way.

He was on his way back to the apartment when Temoor called.

"I'm not done with the hard drive, but I thought you'd want to know that there's been activity on the phone you asked me to monitor. Brief, to be sure, but enough to find a base station."

"Brilliant, Temoor! Tell me!"

"It's a base station at Kolbotn."

"Kolbotn?"

"Yes. Outside Oslo. That is, southeast of Oslo, but you probably don't know—"

"I know where Kolbotn is," Milo interrupted.

"I can't give you the exact address where the phone is, but the base station is on Liaveien."

"Thanks a lot. We'll talk tomorrow."

But Temoor had already hung up.

Milo looked at his watch. Almost ten o'clock. The training had made him alert, and he knew that at home it would be several hours before he got into bed. He entered Liaveien on the GPS and turned the car around.

Less than twenty-five minutes later he turned off the E18 at Mastemyr and followed the signs and GPS toward Kolbotn. He passed Stabburet and then a big industrial building. The voice on the GPS told him to go to the right in a traffic circle, and then he drove into a small parking lot in front of the post office in Kolbotn. He stopped with the engine running. The place was dead. On the other side of the street was an imposing pyramid-like concrete building, which Milo assumed was the town hall. A little farther away was the Kolbotn shopping center, which must have been developed recently along with the low, modern blocks a little farther away. He remembered that he had played soccer against a team from Kolbotn when he was young, but none of this seemed familiar.

He started to stroll ahead when he caught sight of the sign.

"Ingieråsen School," it said, and it pointed ahead and to the right.

His heart noticeably skipped a few beats, and he automatically sped up. A small path led him up onto a narrow gravel track. And on the rise was the school.

It was dark and deserted.

He looked around. By one of the entrances, illuminated by an outdoor light, stood a group of boys. He could see the glow of a cigarette being passed around. Suddenly he became aware of a movement along the fence. A girl in dark clothing was walking and kicking pebbles. The only color she was wearing was a pair of bright red Converse sneakers.

Suburban idyll. Smoking teenage boys and solitary teenage girls, thought Milo.

How different it must have been two years earlier. There, on the same gravel track below the Ingieråsen School, Tormod Tollefsen and Asgeir Henriksen had been methodically executed.

And not a single person who lived in the buildings a few dozen meters away had come to their rescue.

A confused teenager with bad friends. And a teacher who tried to make a difference.

Milo walked once around the school before returning to his car and calling Sørensen. Briefly he told about the tracing of the phone to the close proximity of Ingieråsen School.

"So a cell phone in Ingrid Tollefsen's name is still in use

more than a week after her death. And right in the vicinity of the school where her brother was executed two years ago?" the chief inspector summarized.

"That's right," Milo replied.

He heard the sound of a lighter and Sørensen inhaling.

"I don't like it. I don't like it one damned bit."

WEDNESDAY

16

He borrowed one of the interview rooms at Financial Crimes to hold the videoconference.

It looked like an ordinary office, but was sparsely furnished, almost bare, so that there would be no distractions during questioning.

He could not count how many interviews he had conducted since he started in Financial Crimes. The first few times he was an observer, but after training in interview techniques was over, he was responsible for a number of interrogations himself.

He liked it. Liked the game, liked reading the person on the other side of the table. Whether it was the accused or a witness, as a rule the person in question had an agenda. Plus hope and fear. And if he found out what the person hoped for and feared, there was almost no limit to what he could get out of them.

He sat behind the empty desk and turned on the apparatus in front of him. It looked like a TV, but was used for video recordings and videoconferences with the various police districts. But this time it was Rome on the screen. That is, the sound was there, but the picture was missing. He could hear Benedetti fiddling and cursing.

"Porca putana!"

Then there were several voices, and suddenly the back of the Italian detective's head appeared.

"There. I see you," said Milo.

Benedetti turned around with a confused look on his face.

"There, yes."

He sat down at the table and sorted papers while he lit a cigarette.

"Everything okay, Milo?"

"Yes, thanks. And you?"

"Sì sì sì."

"Okay, what have you got?" Milo asked, taking out his notebook.

"A couple of things that are quite interesting. Maybe not a breakthrough, but there are a few things that must be followed up."

"Like what?"

"Well, for one thing, we assumed that she came here to Rome from Oslo, but when we double-checked, we found out she came from New York. Did you know that?"

Milo shook his head. New York? No one at Forum Healthcare had mentioned that she was in New York before she went to Rome. What was she doing there?

"The other thing we're doing now is charting the academic environment she was in, her circle of acquaintances and her work at WHO. I've got the name of her adviser for her final thesis. A certain *Professore* Salvatore. Furthermore, we know that she had a boyfriend here three years ago. Whose name is"—Benedetti browsed in his papers—"Giampiero Donatello."

Milo made a note: New York. Prof. Salvatore. Giampiero Donatello.

"What about the Italian number she was called from?"

"Phone booth in Trastevere."

"One that can't be traced, in other words."

"*Esatto.* Exactly."

At the other end of the video link Benedetti put out his cigarette.

It was Milo's turn to talk. He went through the past twenty-four hours, and told about the tracing of her cell phone, which showed it was still active.

"You have to find out who is using her phone," said Benedetti.

"I know. We're tracking it, and I'll be notified when it becomes active and moves."

They were about to conclude the brief update sequence, but Milo had saved one question for last.

"Benedetti, you mentioned something to me that I've been wondering about. It has nothing to do with this case, but . . ."

"What is it, then?"

"You mentioned a shipwreck. That your brother died. When was this?"

"In 1977."

"And it was a military vessel?"

"*Sì.* It went down between Tunisia and Sicily."

"But were there other military vessels that were shipwrecked in the 1970s?"

Benedetti shook his head and lit another cigarette. He blew the smoke toward the screen, and for a few seconds it settled like a veil over the image.

"No. Just the one. It was a national disaster. Over a hundred dead. Why are you asking?"

"Because someone else mentioned that same shipwreck recently."

"In what connection?" the Italian policeman asked.

"Family matters, I guess you could say."

"I see."

"But what really happened? Why did the ship sink?" asked Milo.

"Don't know."

"But aren't you curious?"

Benedetti took a deep drag on the cigarette and blew it out into the room. Then he looked around, as if to assure himself that he was alone.

"For a few years I tried to find out. I worked in Naples at first as a policeman and, among other things, I went to Sicily to talk with the families of several of the victims."

He had used his free time on his own little investigation, but encountered silence wherever he turned. Which had reinforced the suspicion that it was not an accident, but a criminal act.

"And it's not difficult to guess who you might suspect, if someone actually blew up the boat," he added.

"*La mafia*," Milo replied.

"*Esatto.*"

"Do you really think the Mafia was behind it?"

Benedetti shrugged his shoulders.

"I never found out anything. But there were many who

didn't like me asking questions, and finally I was offered a position in Rome. And let me be clear that I judged that more as a
warning than as a reward."

"So you let it go," Milo observed.

He did not mean it as criticism, but obviously hit a sore spot.

"What the hell should I do? I had nothing to go on. Should
I risk my parents losing their other son too?"

"No, I understand."

Benedetti scratched himself on the chest, while he stared
absently out the window of the little meeting room in Rome.

"Of course I wondered what happened. I still find myself
thinking about it. But I'm getting older. And I've learned and rec-
onciled myself that certain things in life you never find out. You
just have to let it go."

He moved his gaze from the window and toward the camera and Milo.

"And that shipwreck definitely belongs to the category of
things you ought to let go."

Temoor's office was empty. Of people anyway. The computers
and stack of empty Red Bulls was still there, but the skinny computer nerd's chair was unoccupied.

Milo could not recall the last time he had seen that, and went
over to Astrid in reception.

"I can't find Temoor. Do you know where he is?"

"Surprise, surprise. He's sick today."

"Sick?"

She smiled at him.

"It does happen," she said.

"Do you have his address?"

"Shouldn't he be allowed to be absent?"

"Of course. But not when I'm working on a case," said Milo, adding a smile to show that he was not a hundred-percent serious. Only ninety percent.

She wrote Temoor´s address on a piece of paper, and a few minutes later he was driving out of the garage in the direction of Trosterud. Fifteen minutes later he parked outside an apartment building that was as foreign to him as the mosque on the other side of the highway.

He found his way to the right entrance, noted T. Torgersen as the only Norwegian name on the series of doorbells. Now, to be sure, Torgersen was not his birth name. Temoor was born in the slums of Bangladesh, but came to the Torgersen family as a malnourished three-year-old. Without having talked about it—Temoor never discussed personal matters at work, and it was not Milo's strong suit to share private details—he understood that growing up in Vestfold had not been rosy. Among spoiled rich kids, somewhat less spoiled upstarts, dropouts and everyday racists, Temoor Torgersen had his ups and downs.

And once he had his degree in hand, he got on the first train to Oslo.

In the capital he had embraced the radical Blitz community, and Blitz embraced him. For several years his days consisted of demonstrations and studies in informatics with the occasional arrest and building occupation. Before he miraculously got a job with a small computer investigation company and was then picked up by Financial Crimes. To be sure, after thorough investigation by the Police Security Service due to his "youthful rebellion," as the head of Financial Crimes so diplomatically called it.

The lock on the entry door was broken, and the elevator out of order. Milo tackled the stairs. The entry was cold and sterile, and he wondered for a moment if he ought to be worried about

Temoor. A door slammed one floor above him, and a young immigrant of indeterminate origin came shuffling down the stairs. The aroma of strongly spiced food struck Milo.

They looked at each other without saying anything.

He continued up to the sixth floor, and found a handwritten paper with the name "Torgersen" taped to one door. He put his ear to it, but did not hear a sound.

He wondered what was awaiting him. Was it true that Temoor was still a practicing anarchist? But only in his own apartment? As a kind of refuge for old Blitzers, where they smoked pot and dreamily discussed the coming revolution?

He rang the doorbell, but heard no sounds from inside. The doorbell obviously did not work. If only he didn't have to break down the door to find out if there was life inside.

With a clenched fist he pounded three times on the door. Shortly after, a chain rattled and the door was opened by a woman in her late twenties or early thirties.

"Yes?" she said, friendly but inquisitive.

"Hi. I was actually looking for Temoor. Torgersen. But—"

"He's sick. Is it important?"

"Yes. Well. I work with him. . . ."

"Are you Milo?" she asked.

"That's me."

"I almost guessed that," she said, letting her eyes glide from his head down across the open topcoat, tie and shoes. "So come on in!"

She opened the door and invited him in.

He remained standing in the foyer and waited until she had locked the door.

She was short and round, and dressed in comfortable—but

not very elegant—running pants. She had on a white T-shirt, and creeping up her arms to her shoulders were tattoos in various styles. One ear was pierced with a little spike, and her hair was cut short and blue on one side.

"I just put some rolls in the oven," she said, both sounding and looking like the housewife from hell.

Milo was still not sure if he had come to the right place.

"I'm Grete, by the way," she said, extending her hand.

He took it and reeled off "A pleasure."

"I live with Temoor," she explained.

"Oh yes, I didn't know—"

"That he was living with someone, no." She laughed so that her breasts and belly shook. "No, I can imagine that. But I know who you are," she said.

"Is that good or bad?"

She measured him with her eyes again.

"To put it that way, you're the only one of his colleagues I've heard about. And met. Take it as a compliment," she said, brushing past him and into the kitchen.

He followed, and continued into the living room.

He had half expected to find it full of computer equipment and cables, but instead it was a motley mixture of ugly and old. An inherited couch, a coffee table from a flea market.

But the rolls smelled divine.

Out of the one door came Temoor, also in a T-shirt and running pants.

"Milo, what the hell—"

Then Grete came padding in with a plate of rolls.

"Is that any way to greet a guest, Temoor?"

"What are you doing here?" he asked.

Once again it was Grete who spoke up.

"He's here to see how you're doing. Isn't that nice?"

Temoor snorted.

"Milo is here because he needs something, and it can't wait until tomorrow. You can bet your ass on that. Isn't that right, Milo?"

"No, I just wanted to visit my favorite coworker," he replied.

"Sure."

"Temoor! Give up! Now let's have some rolls and tea," she said.

They sat down, and Milo got their story. How they met at Blitz. Love at first protest march.

"Didn't think you had time for a girlfriend. You're always at work," said Milo.

"Nonsense. You're the one who's never there. You're always out somewhere. But since I'm always there when you come back, you think I'm always there," Temoor answered reproachfully.

"But you do work quite a bit even so," said Grete.

She turned toward Milo.

"I'm a nurse's aide and work a lot of nights. Then I sleep during the day and I'm gone at night. So he can actually work as much as he wants," she explained.

They sat and chatted a little more before she left them in peace to talk about work.

"I just wondered whether you've found anything on the hard drive you were going to look at? And if you could check it against a couple of names I have here?"

Milo gave him a paper with the name of the Italian ex-boyfriend and the professor Ingrid Tollefsen had as an adviser in Rome.

Temoor got up.

"Come with me," he said, and went into a little guest room filled to the brim with computer equipment, cables, game consoles and a guest bed covered with cardboard boxes.

He sat down at one of the machines while he looked at Milo's paper. A short time later the printer started working. He got up and retrieved the printouts.

"I didn't find anything right away on the ex-boyfriend, but here's an e-mail exchange with the professor," he said, giving him the papers.

"Thanks a lot," said Milo.

They had nothing else to talk about, so Milo stuck his head into the kitchen.

"I'm leaving now. Thanks for the rolls and tea. It was nice to meet you, Grete."

She smiled warmly back.

"It was nice to finally meet you, Milo."

At the front door he turned toward Temoor.

"Get well soon! And thanks again for the help."

Temoor nodded curtly.

"And Grete seems really nice. Can't get over that you haven't said anything."

The look from Temoor said, *This stays between us*, but his voice said, "Thanks for stopping by."

He drove straight to the police station where Sørensen was writing a report and refining his arguments for more resources.

"Sit yourself down, Milo," he said as he finished the sentence.

"How did the press briefing go yesterday?" asked Milo.

"Good enough. I did as they said. Stood stiff as a post, stared the journalist in the eyes and answered as briefly as I could."

He came around the desk and served coffee from the worn-out coffee percolator into the even more worn coffee mug that read O LD'S EST D D.

"By the way, I had a talk with Sigurd Tollefsen a little while ago. He knew nothing about his daughter going on leave for two months," he said.

"Didn't know? Are you sure he's telling the truth?" Milo asked skeptically.

Sørensen waved the objection away with an unlit cigarette.

"He's not lying. He's not the type," he said, taking out his lighter. He fired up a cigarette and went over to the window to blow out the smoke. "Families have secrets. That's just the way it is. Yours no doubt has secrets too."

Milo shrugged his shoulders and took out the printout he had just received from Temoor.

"What do you think about this e-mail exchange?"

Sørensen took it and read the brief text.

From: Salvatore, Chiara
Subject: Re: Re: Arrival?
To: Tollefsen, Ingrid

Oops, of course.
Regardless, looking forward to seeing you again.
    Have a safe trip,

    Chiara.

———

From: Tollefsen, Ingrid
Subject: Re: Arrival?
To: Salvatore, Chiara

Hi Chiara,
I would prefer that you use my personal e-mail (ingtoll@me.com).

Ingrid

P.S. I arrive in the morning. I'll call you from the hotel.

———

From: Salvatore, Chiara
Subject: Arrival?
To: Tollefsen, Ingrid

So nice to talk with you again, Ingrid.
And of course I have time to see you. By the way, Lucca asked about you too. Let's have dinner together one of those evenings!

When are you arriving? Just so I manage to clear a space in my calendar and take time off (here in New York people almost never take time off!)

Hugs from
Chiara

Sørensen frowned.

"Chiara Salvatore was Ingrid Tollefsen's adviser when she studied in Rome," Milo explained.

"But she's in New York?"

"Looks that way. I'll have to tell Benedetti in Rome. He's trying to get an appointment with her. But what about the e-mail?"

Sørensen read it again.

"I react to three things. First: Ingrid Tollefsen asks her not to use her work e-mail. Second: She called and asked to speak with her. I don't know what else she was going to do in New York, but if that was the only reason she went there, we have to talk with this Chiara Salvatore pretty damn soon."

"And the third?" asked Milo.

"Who the hell is Lucca?"

Milo took back the printout.

"I don't know. But we'll find out. Right now there is suddenly a lot that points toward the U.S. We have the attorneys at Forum besides, waving legal clauses."

"You'll have to ask that Benedetti when he can get a flight over the pond," said Sørensen.

Milo thought about what the Italian policeman had said in Rome. About how he had cases thrown at him, but not resources. The question was whether he would get a green light from his superiors for a New York trip. Milo knew in any case that he wouldn't have the patience to wait very long for the Italian police to prioritize it. If it dragged out, Milo was going to step in. He had no such resource problems.

He thought about the e-mail from his cousin Corrado and the American attorney. He had no desire to mention it to Sørensen. But that and the leads in the case that pointed in the direction of New York were bouncing around in the back of his head. The Italian professor in New York. Ingrid Tollefsen, who had flown from Oslo to New York to meet her, and then to Rome. Where she was killed.

"I'll ask him. This Professor Salvatore may be one of the last persons who talked with her before she was killed in Rome."

Sørensen nodded thoughtfully.

"But we still have leads to follow up on here in Oslo."

"I know. I can't let go of what that journalist said about Ingrid being dissatisfied with her job. Maybe she was thinking about quitting. The question is why?" said Milo.

As if on signal, his cell phone rang. He looked at the display, which showed TEMOOR MOBILE and answered.

"Milo."

"Temoor here. It's in use."

"What is?"

"Her cell phone."

"Where?"

"Blindern. Five minutes ago. But I'm guessing it's in motion. I'll call you when I get anything else," he said and hung up.

Milo looked at Sørensen.

"Ready to move out?"

17

They spun out of the parking space, made their way through Gamlebyen and out onto Mosseveien in the bus lane past all the traffic. Sørensen drummed his fingertips on his thigh, now and then leaning over and looking at the speedometer.

"So you couldn't find a smaller car than this," he said while demonstratively trying to stretch his legs in the little Fiat.

Milo responded by pressing harder on the gas pedal. The 160 horsepower moved the small car with a powerful lurch, and the chief inspector's head hit the neck support.

"What the he—"

"I can pass anyone in this thing."

"Yes, I realize that," said Sørensen and fell silent.

Milo's phone rang again, and he took it on speakerphone.

"Temoor here. New signal from Oslo S, and now most recently a little southeast. Do you want me to—"

"We're already on our way," Milo interrupted.

"But you don't know where these people are going!"

"A thousand kroner that he's sitting on the Ski train now and getting off at Kolbotn station," said Sørensen.

"Okay, fine. I'll report if there's more activity," said Temoor.

They passed Sjursøya and had to slow down when the bus lane disappeared at Ulvøya. South of Nordstrand the traffic thinned out again, and when there were two lanes at Fiskevollbukta, Milo pushed the car for all it was worth.

Before the exit at Mastemyr the car was up to 170 km an hour, and Sørensen did not say a word.

Milo followed the signs to Kolbotn just like last evening, but drove all the way to the shopping center this time. They stopped and jumped out of the car just in time to see the Ski train leave the platform.

"Damn it, we're too late," said Sørensen.

"No, look, people are trickling out of the station area now," Milo said, pointing.

From the station there were basically two ways to go. Either away from Milo and Sørensen toward the old shopping center and Skiveien, or toward the new one. The same direction as Ingieråsen School.

"He's going this way. For sure," said Milo.

The train commuters came steadily closer and there seemed to be more of them all the time. Men on their way home from their bank jobs. Teenagers going to school in Oslo. Students.

"But who are we looking for?" Sørensen asked, irritated.

Milo scanned the crowd. At first he had only been focused on arriving before the train did. Now he felt the possibility gradually slipping away as the people came closer and started to disperse in various directions.

Suddenly he had an idea.

He fished out his cell phone and entered the number to Ingrid Tollefsen's cell phone as he spied out over the crowd. The closest ones, the most eager to get home for dinner, were now only a few meters away. The slowest were about fifty meters back.

Toward the back he saw a young man in dark clothing stop. Milo did not see his face because of the hood that covered it, but could see him take a cell phone out of his pocket and stop to look at it.

Milo felt his heart pounding and let it ring. No voice mail took the call. He could see the young boy stand and look down at his cell phone. Slowly he raised it to his ear.

Milo heard the ring tone stop and a faint "hello."

Bingo! he thought contentedly and began to walk toward the boy.

"Hi, I'm trying to get hold of Ingrid Tollefsen," he said into the phone.

But the other did not answer.

"Hello! Do you hear me?" Milo said louder.

Then the boy raised the hood and looked around. It took him a moment to catch sight of the two men in topcoats coming toward him. One with a phone at his ear.

Milo saw the boy turn and run back toward the train underpass.

"Damn it! Come on, Sørensen, that's him!"

Milo ran after, unbuttoning his topcoat to get free arm movement. He sprinted into the tunnel and came out on the other side, where he was met by a steep stairway. The boy was nowhere to be seen. Milo powered up the steps, already feeling his pulse beating too hard from such an explosive transition from stationary to full use of his leg muscles.

At the top of the stairs he saw the boy disappear up toward the old shopping center, and he set out after him. Sørensen hadn't yet reached the bottom of the stairs.

Milo hurried as fast as he could, and the distance narrowed. But the boy was fast. At the shopping center he disappeared down the stairs behind the building.

Milo could see him looking around in confusion, uncertain which direction to take. He was on his way across the parking lot, and Milo was in the middle of the stairs, which he descended in long leaps. The distance was barely thirty meters when a car suddenly started up in reverse. The boy saw it too late and tried to jump out of the way, but the car struck him and knocked him down.

He screamed, before getting to his feet. An older man got out of the car, but the boy limped off. Milo quickly followed.

The boy limped off in the direction of the train tracks and threw the sack over the fence. While he howled in pain after the collision and the blow he had taken, he started to climb and threw himself over the fence just as Milo arrived.

"Stop!" he shouted, but the boy didn't listen and hobbled off toward the rails.

Milo climbed over the fence, but he was heavier than the boy, and it swayed severely. As he leaned over, his topcoat got stuck. He quickly freed himself, but that gave the boy a new head start as he limped across the tracks.

Milo ran toward him, but stopped abruptly in front of the tracks at the sound of a loud signal. He looked to the side and saw a freight train come thundering toward him. It roared past, and Milo felt the draft tear at his clothes and hair.

"Fuck!" he shouted while he saw the boy disappear down toward the road. He could see that he was starting up the mesh fence out toward the road.

Milo sprinted across the tracks, jumped down the slope and threw himself against the fence with all his strength. The boy was almost at the top, but had to stop when it started to sway.

"You can just forget about getting away from me!" Milo shouted, throwing himself against the fence again.

The forceful movement made it impossible for the boy to climb further, and instead he clung to the fence as best he could. Then his one leg lost footing, and he fell to the ground with a shriek.

Milo was over him immediately, tore off the hood, and stared down at a girl who could be anywhere from fifteen to twenty-five years old.

18

The queue at the emergency room was longer than Milo could bear, so he took her to the Volvat private clinic for an examination, where they determined that nothing was broken. She was only badly bruised.

After that it was down to the police station and a very impatient chief inspector.

"Who are you? Why do you have Ingrid Tollefsen's phone? When did you last see her? Did you know her brother? And why the hell do you run away when the police want to talk with you?!"

Sørensen spit out the stream of questions while he paced back and forth in the room.

"I didn't know you were policemen," the girl said quietly, looking down at the floor.

She spoke good Norwegian, but not without an accent that revealed she was not a native speaker.

"What did you say?! Take off that fuckin' hood so we can hear you," said Sørensen, pulling it back.

She shrank even more. As if the hood protected her.

"I said that I didn't know you were policemen."

"Who the hell did you think we were? Jehovah's Witnesses?"

She did not reply, and Milo sat down right across from her. He tried to make eye contact, but her gaze wandered. She was skinny, dressed in worn jeans with a checked shirt under the hooded sweatshirt. Her clothing was youthful, but there was nothing about it that suggested fashion awareness. On the contrary, there was something thrifty about her, as if the clothes were inherited. Or given to her. The pants were a few sizes too big, and the sweatshirt was dirty and faded.

"Let's take one question at a time," Milo said calmly. "What's your name?"

She cast a quick glance at him, but did not answer.

Sørensen took his snuffbox from the jacket that was tossed over a chair. He inserted two pouches before turning toward them.

"Okay, here's the situation: You have the cell phone of someone who was killed. I hope for your sake you have a good explanation for that."

This time she kept her eyes on Milo.

"Is Ingrid dead?" she asked.

"Yes, she is."

"How—"

"Murdered. In Rome last Monday. Didn't you know that? It's been in the newspapers and on the Internet."

She shook her head, and he could see the tears running down her cheeks.

"I almost never read Norwegian newspapers. And I haven't had time to be on the Internet lately."

By the window he heard Sørensen take a breath as if he was about to say something, but Milo waved him away.

"I was afraid that something had happened. But she told me not to call her. She was going to call me when she got back. How . . . was she killed?"

"She was strangled."

The girl leaned over the table, put her head on her arms and her entire slender body was shaking. Milo set some paper napkins beside her.

"We're investigating the killing. And as you understand, we got on your trail by way of Ingrid's cell phone. We know she called you last Monday. You are probably one of the last people she talked with before she was killed," Milo explained.

The girl was still crying.

"So you must realize that we have a lot of questions, and we think you have a lot of answers. Will you help us find out who killed Ingrid?"

The girl sat up again, dried her tears and blew her nose on the napkins.

"Can I get a little water?"

Milo went out and came back with a glass, which she emptied in one gulp.

"Thanks," she said.

Then she told her story.

Her name was Oriana; she was from Chechnya and was studying chemistry at the university in Oslo. She lived in a small rented room in Kolbotn, near Ingieråsen School, and had met Ingrid on the same gravel track where her little brother had been killed. She had seen Ingrid there several times after the killing, and when she realized she was the sister of one of the victims, she told Ingrid what she had experienced on the evening of the shooting.

She had fallen asleep on the couch that evening, but was wakened by the sound of a car engine revving up. When she went over to the window, she saw several persons on the gravel track. She thought no more about it, assumed it was some boys who lived in the area, and sat down with her books again.

But then she heard the shots.

"You didn't see anyone shooting? Just heard? How did you know they were shots and not a car backfiring or some other sharp sound?" Sørensen interrupted.

"Because I know what a shot sounds like. It's not the first time," she answered.

Quiet, but convincing.

The sound of the shots made her leave her room, and when she went over to the track, she found Asgeir Henriksen, the dead teacher, and Tormod Tollefsen. The boy was barely moving, and she had leaned over him.

Milo recalled the witnesses who said that one of the killers had stayed behind and leaned down to assure himself that the two were dead. Most likely it was Oriana they had seen.

"He died in my arms," she said.

"I don't remember you from when we worked on the case. Were you questioned?" asked Sørensen.

She ignored him and continued telling what she had also told Ingrid Tollefsen. Right before Tormod died he looked at her and whispered, "The Unitor building."

"The Unitor building?"

Milo made a note.

"Yes, the Unitor building," she repeated.

He had also been holding something in his hand. An ampoule labeled *Crescitan*, which he'd slipped into Oriana's hand.

"He talked to you and gave you an ampoule?"

Sørensen slammed his palms on the table so that her water glass turned over and she jumped back in her chair.

"None of the witnesses said this when we investigated the case! Why the hell didn't you make a report?" he shouted at her.

"Because . . . you arrested them!"

"What happened then? Did you leave? Did you take the ampoule with you?" Milo asked.

He caught her gaze, tried to calm down the situation.

"I ran inside to call the police, but when I came into the room I heard sirens. Someone else had already done it."

For that reason she stayed away.

"Did you take the ampoule?" Sørensen was plainly irritated. "This is obstructing the work of the police," he continued while he rubbed his bald head.

"I was going to turn it in, I thought, but . . . but then I met Ingrid."

"And so you gave it to her?" Milo suggested.

Oriana nodded, biting her lip.

"She said she would take care of it."

"But you still should have gone to the police," Milo said calmly.

They looked at each other. She did not say anything, but he understood. And she realized that he understood.

"But why didn't you come to us?" asked Sørensen.

Not angry this time. More resigned.

But it was Milo who answered.

"Because she doesn't have a residence permit."

"Oh, shit!" the chief inspector replied.

"And your parents? Where are they?" asked Milo.

"My father's in Chechnya. My mother is dead. They were deported. Mama died six months later. She was sick . . . and she didn't get any treatment. I don't know exactly where Papa is now. I heard from others that he'd been arrested again."

"That sounds awful. But what made you stay behind?" Milo asked as gently as he could.

"I was allowed to finish high school. I had only a few months left, and they would send me home when I turned eighteen."

She didn't say anything else.

"But now you're done with high school and studying at the university. What happened?" asked Milo.

"I went underground," she said quietly.

Right after her last exam at high school she went into hiding with a family, and then moved on to new hiding places. Until she finally got help with false papers and found the rented room in Kolbotn.

"Who got you those papers?" asked Milo.

She shrugged her skinny shoulders, but Milo held her gaze.

"I don't really know. I wasn't the one who arranged it," she answered at last.

"Okay. We can take that detail later. But what else happened? After you became acquainted with Ingrid?"

"She helped me. She took care of me," said Oriana.

"In what way?" asked Milo.

"She helped me with money for the rent when I didn't get paid what I should for cleaning jobs. Got me textbooks. Pressured my lawyer not to give up the process with the residence permit. Gave me her old phone, and paid for minutes and gave me access to her user account to download apps and music on it. She helped me with everything. Big and small."

"Why did she help you, do you think?" Milo wanted to know.

Oriana drew patterns with her index finger on the tabletop.

"She had a very bad conscience, I think. She was not doing well. She and her brother had a close relationship, but the past few years she had been studying and working. I don't know, but maybe helping me was a way to try to make up for that. As a kind of penance. She even took leave from her job for a while."

Milo thought about what the research director at Forum Healthcare had told them about the unpaid two-month leave. So she had helped a young asylum seeker, who was the last person to see her brother alive. But what else had she used that time for?

"I wish you had made a report when we were investigating the case," Sørensen said.

Oriana looked at him dejectedly.

"Don't you understand? I have no rights here in Norway. You would have used me and thrown me in the trash when you were finished. I can't risk—"

She bit off her own sentence.

"What is it you can't risk?" asked Milo.

No reply.

"Is there someone you fear if you had come forward as a witness?" he continued.

"My life is constantly made up of choices. Just like yours. But where your choices don't have major consequences one way or another, I'm almost always at a crossroads. Perhaps I made the wrong choice that time, but . . ."

Once again these incomplete sentences. Milo was convinced

that she was not telling all she knew, but he did not want to pressure her.

"You're studying chemistry, you say?"

"Mmm."

"This ampoule. Crescitan. What is it?"

"You can just look it up."

"I know that, but I'm guessing you already have."

"It's an anabolic steroid. A derivative of testosterone," she answered.

Sørensen's eyes opened wide.

"So that's what he got himself involved in. At the gym where he started hanging out. Poor kid," he said.

"Tormod Tollefsen got mixed up with bad company, and started using steroids. And for one reason or other he was shot. But why?" Milo asked, turning toward Sørensen, who was sitting behind the desk turning on his computer.

"I don't know. Money? Talked back? No idea."

Milo turned toward Oriana, who was staring silently down at the tabletop.

"How did Ingrid Tollefsen react to the fact that her brother was using steroids?"

"She took the whole thing very hard. As I said, I think she blamed herself that she hadn't been there more for him," Oriana answered.

Her finger drew a figure-eight pattern on the table while she sniffled.

"What did you talk about when she called on Monday?"

"She said she was in Rome. That she would be there a few more days, and then she wondered how things were going for me. She said she wanted to see me soon."

"She wanted to see you? Did she say why? Was there anything special she wanted to talk with you about?"

"No."

Oriana hesitated a little with the answer.

"But did you get the impression that she wanted to see you soon? Or was it more the case that it had been a long time since you'd seen each other and that it was time to get together?"

"She didn't say anything in particular. Just that we must meet."

"Must? She used that word? 'We must meet.'"

Oriana nodded barely visibly, and Milo thought about Ada Hauge, who'd said that Ingrid had something she wanted to talk about with her. So Ingrid Tollefsen had been sitting in Rome, and thought that when she came back she had to meet both Ada and Oriana.

"Do you know anything else about what she was doing in Rome?"

"No, but I think it had something to do with work. A seminar, or something like that."

"Did she say anything about who she was with?"

"No. But she seemed a little . . . I don't know the right word . . . fired up, maybe."

"Fired up?"

"Yes, it seemed like she was in a good mood. Said something about it being exciting."

The word remained hanging in the air. Exciting could mean any number of things. An interesting conference with capable, inspiring people. Or else it wasn't about the conference at all. But a meeting with a person. Who had been more exciting than she could have foreseen.

Milo stood up and gathered his notebook and pen.

"Come, I'll drive you home."

Sørensen looked up from the keyboard.

"And don't you run off! Stay in the vicinity and answer if we call!" he ordered her.

She nodded seriously and put on her sweatshirt.

While she was doing that and pulling the hood protectively over her head, Milo took out his phone and googled Crescitan.

The answer came quickly, and he got a feeling of having taken a small step in the right direction.

He held out the cell phone for Sørensen.

"Look who manufactures Crescitan," he said.

Sørensen squinted at the screen.

"Forum Healthcare," he read.

19

Milo drove Oriana home, letting her sit in silence during the drive. Between shifting gears his thoughts wandered. It was obvious that he had to follow the steroid track. He had to talk with Forum again and find out more about Crescitan and why the hell they produced steroids.

And then we have to visit the gym where Tormod Tollefsen hung out, thought Milo.

He was willing to bet that Ingrid Tollefsen had started playing detective on her own. The fact that she had not gone to the police with the information about the ampoule of steroids supported that theory.

He stopped the car outside the house where Oriana rented a room.

"Are you okay?" he asked.

She nodded silently, but he saw the tears just below the surface, ready to pour out as soon as he had left.

"Do you have anyone to talk to?"

A curt shake of the head in response.

"You have my number on your phone. Put it in the contact list and call me if there's anything."

"Pretty soon I won't have any minutes left on the calling card," she answered.

"Do you have a job?"

"That's not so easy when you're here without a permit. I have cleaning jobs, but they don't pay very well. And sometimes nothing. They still owe me for two months."

"What about your rent? Is that paid?"

"I'll think of something."

He looked at her and decided.

"Don't go anywhere. I'll be back in ten minutes."

She looked inquisitively at him.

He drove down to the shopping center and got there right before it closed. Ten minutes later he was knocking on the door to the rented room. She let him into a small entry porch. Inside he glimpsed a simply furnished room and a small sleeping alcove. On the made bed were two teddy bears, a big dark brown one and a smaller light brown one.

She's just a child, it struck him.

"Here. Take this," he said, handing her four receipts.

"What's this?"

"Refill cards for your cell phone. You just enter the code that's on the receipt."

"I know how to do that, but—"

"And then take this," he interrupted her, giving her a bundle of bills.

She looked at him, and then at the bills. Slowly she counted the ten thousand kroner.

"But I can't take this," she said.

But Milo had already turned his back and was on his way out the door. This was not something he would tell Sørensen, who would certainly react to him giving money to a person who had withheld information. And who perhaps was still holding something back. But, in any event, that was a chance Milo himself was willing to take.

"I don't want to hear that," he said.

Outside he turned around.

"We'll call you later."

He saw her struggling to hold the tears back, and heard a quiet "thanks" before he went toward the car.

It was almost nine thirty, and it was too late to think about exercise. But he had to eat something. If he was lucky he had some mozzarella and tomatoes at home, so that he could fix himself a *caprese*.

He was driving in the direction of E18 Mosseveien when he happened to think of what Oriana had said about Tormod Tollefsen's last words.

"The Unitor building."

He stayed at sixty kilometers an hour while he googled Unitor on his phone. He found a Web site connected to a large shipping company, with an address in Lysaker. On the other side of the Oslo Fjord. Unitor appeared to have been a company that manufactured ship parts, but had changed owners and moved long ago.

He passed the Mastemyr area and got a sudden impulse. Quickly he googled "Unitor+Mastemyr." The first result that came up was an article in *Østlandets Blad*. It was several years old, but nevertheless was just what he needed. The headline was

BREAK-IN IN UNITOR BUILDING, and the case described problems in "the large storage building at Mastemyr by Kolbotn."

He was already on the expressway toward central Oslo, and accelerated to the exit to Holmlia. Over the bridge, and out on Mosseveien again, back toward Kolbotn and Mastemyr.

He had to check that building.

Four minutes later he turned toward Mastemyr and slowed down to thirty kilometers an hour. He came to a crossroads. The road to the left appeared to lead toward a residential area, while the road to the right led toward a hotel. He continued straight ahead, and after a few hundred meters he saw the building. He recognized it from the picture in the newspaper article.

He glanced to the side. The building was big and brown, and looked like it was designed by an architect who had studied in the former East Berlin. Brown metal plates, dark windows, gray concrete.

He let the car roll along the edge of the road and turned right to follow the building's façade. A large row of signs with company names showed that the once stately headquarters for a company listed on the stock exchange now housed a motley collection of small companies. It was impossible to tell from the company names what they actually did, except for two: The Gym spoke for itself, and Milo could glimpse the illuminated entry and rows of machines. The sign for Quick Storage was also self-explanatory. He continued past the entry to the gym, and came to a freight door with entry to Quick Storage.

It was closed, and Milo could see the panel where you entered a code to get in.

He passed and stopped by the side of the road a little farther ahead while he kept an eye on the door in the side mirror. After a few minutes a car with a trailer stopped outside. A man who looked to be in his sixties got out, entered the code and got back in the car again. Milo could glimpse a young woman in the passenger seat. As soon as they disappeared through the entry, Milo left the car and walked quickly after them before it closed.

Inside the door he came into a large indoor parking area. In the past there would have been freight trucks loading ship parts. Now a few cars were parked there, and by the wall a row of blue-and-red four-wheel trailers.

The older man with the trailer turned the car while the young woman directed him. It appeared to be father and daughter. A little farther away was a dark blue Audi A4 sedan, with tinted windows and the frame lowered a little.

Pathetic, thought Milo.

What had formerly been one big storage hall now consisted of hundreds of small storage spaces divided on two levels. Small cubes arranged in different sizes and available to rent so that people could store the things they didn't really need, yet couldn't bear to part with.

The older man cast a glance at Milo as he approached, as if for a second he wondered if he was responsible for checking this person who had followed him without entering the access code, but saw that Milo looked respectable enough. For that reason he concentrated on his daughter's furniture and boxes on the trailer. A floor lamp, a couple of bookcases and an office chair. She might be in her late twenties, and Milo guessed that the load of furniture was the result of a break-up. She had sad eyes, and she and her father did not say much to each other. He silently helped her set the boxes on a cart, which he then pushed ahead of him toward the corridors with rows of small storage compartments a short distance away.

Milo took out a key ring in an attempt to look like someone

who was going to retrieve something in his storage unit, and went the opposite way. He did not know what he was looking for, but was driven by a gut instinct. The last words of a dead little troublemaker a couple of years earlier had been the name of this very building.

The corridor he was in was barely a meter and a half wide with compartments on either side. Orange doors with bronze-colored padlocks. The corridor was like a path in a labyrinth. After a few meters he could choose to go left, right or straight ahead. Ahead of him he could see a freight elevator and a stair-way. He went that way, and took the stairs one flight up. There were more corridors in another labyrinth pattern. More com-partments in a row.

From various directions he heard the sounds of compart-ment doors being opened, and furniture and cartons being moved. An iron pipe hit the concrete and clanked before it rolled into the corrugated iron wall. A man cursed.

Then an iron door slammed, and the freight elevator was put into motion. Milo walked toward it, and through the grate he saw the father and daughter slowly sinking down to the main floor. From the railing in front of him he had an overview of the parking area and entry. He saw the man put the cart back and the daughter get into the passenger seat. The man went up to the door, entered the code, and while the large freight door slowly opened, he jogged back to the car. He started the engine, and the car rolled quietly out of the building.

A minute passed before the door slowly glided down into place, and as it struck the concrete with a deep thud, Milo felt a sensation of claustrophobia. He did not have the code to open the door, and it was almost eleven o'clock. His hope was that someone in the parked Audi would also soon be going out.

He was on his way toward the stairs when the door opened again. A van came rolling in and stopped right inside the door so that it partly blocked the exit. The engine rumbled deeply before it was turned off, and three men got out. Their upper bodies revealed that they had carried a lot of heavy objects; not boxes and furniture, however, but iron and metal. And probably helped by the intake of simple chemical substances. All three had gorilla arms that hung slightly bowed out from their bodies and with the knuckles pointing straight ahead instead of to the side.

Three specimens of the missing link, thought Milo, waiting to go down the stairs. The way they parked and the way they now stood leaning against the car aroused his suspicions. As if they were waiting for someone.

Could he be the one they were waiting for? In that case, how did they get on his trail, and what did they want from him?

He went back to the place by the railing with a view of the cars, but stayed two steps from the edge so that he was not readily visible. In the corridor right below him he heard the sound of a cart and two men talking excitedly together. The language was not Norwegian.

He cast a glance at the three men, who evidently also heard the sound from the corridor. Two of them moved calmly away from the vehicle, while the third made rotating movements with his head and neck to loosen up the muscles. He resembled a wrestler ready for combat.

Not good at all, thought Milo, looking at his watch again. He did not have time to think further before the voices below were raised.

"What the hell are you doing here?" he heard one of them say.

He looked quickly over the railing and saw two Pakistani

men who had stopped between the parking area and the corridor they had come out of. Both were broad-shouldered like the three others by the van, but at least a head shorter.

On a cart they had six large boxes.

"What are we doing here?!" shouted one of the oversize men.

Milo was unable to hear the rest of what was said, but made out words like "our area" and "Pakis."

He cast a glance over the railing again, in time to see one of the Pakistanis take out his cell phone. That was like a signal to the other three.

Suddenly it was like there was an explosion on the level below, and Milo watched as several hundred kilos of muscle attacked the two who were standing by the cart. But in contrast to fight scenes you see in movies, which could almost be beautiful as the opponents danced around each other thrusting and parrying, this scene was only raw, brutal, and brief.

The two Pakistanis tried to fight back as best they could, but the Norwegians went right at them. Milo could see how the one who, two minutes earlier, had loosened up his neck and prepared for battle, fended off the blow of one Pakistani before head-butting him. Blood spurted from his nose, and the man screamed while he tried to bring his knee up into the Norwegian and get out of his iron grip. But the other fired off another head-butt, and the Pakistani fell to the ground with a moan.

The other Pakistani was also down for the count on the concrete, and the three Norwegians pounded the two prostrate men with blows and kicks.

Milo could literally hear the blows breaking bones in their bodies every time they struck.

He pulled back and took out his cell phone to summon help, but determined that there was no coverage where he was standing.

Going downstairs would be pure suicide, so instead he tried to move the phone calmly around to see if he could capture a signal. He had to go all the way over to the railing again, and crouched down to text Sørensen.

"R in Unitor building. Gang clash. No coverage. Call local police!" he wrote, and hoped the chief inspector had his cell phone nearby.

He was about to crawl back and out of view when he heard one of the Norwegians say loudly, "I think I saw someone moving up there."

The answer was lower, but audible.

"Their car is the only one here. No one else is here."

Milo lay completely still and hoped the railing and weak lighting camouflaged him. Through the mesh on the railing he saw the three shaved heads and tattooed bull necks.

"Someone's up there. Let's check!"

Two of them set off at the same time. Milo got to his feet and started moving as quickly and quietly as he could down the corridor as the two set a course toward the stairs. The third guarded the two battered Pakistanis. One of them was still moaning while the other was motionless.

Milo felt his pulse pounding. He turned left down another corridor, then right, then left again. Farther and farther away from the stairs and the freight elevator.

There must be an emergency exit, he thought.

He could hear tramping somewhere behind him, as if a couple of elephants came thundering.

The corridor abruptly ended in a wall, and he turned around sharply. Took a new route at the first crossing and continued all the way until that corridor ended too. The light was dimmer, and there was not a single emergency exit sign in sight.

He began going back again while he tried to get control of his breathing. The voices and steps came closer. The two had divided up and were now obviously searching corridor by corridor.

Milo was literally backed into a corner.

The only way out was the way he had come in. And that might just as well have been walled up with concrete.

"He must be around here," he heard one of them call and was startled at how close the voice sounded.

"There's no one here!" came the answer a few corridors farther away.

Milo looked desperately around again, glanced up and made a decision. He ran over to the compartment door with the strongest padlock, put one foot on the lock and shoved himself up while his fingertips took hold around an edge. The compartments did not go all the way up to the ceiling, and with an exertion of strength he halfway pulled himself, halfway shoved himself up. With his foot on the padlock and his palms on the roof of the compartment, he raised his body farther up and rolled onto the compartment roof, away from the corridor.

The roof was made of netting, the type used for garden fences, and swayed slightly under his weight. He spread his arms and legs to distribute his weight so that the net roof would not pull on any of the attachments, and peered down through the netting. The compartment below was three-fourths full of cardboard boxes, a sofa on edge, car tires and a bicycle.

He heard the voices approaching, and concentrated on lying as quietly as he could. He realized that his phone was not set on mute, and he prayed a silent "Ave Maria." He hoped there was no coverage in here either. One little peep on the phone and he was finished. Hopefully Sørensen and the local police would not call him first, but instead storm through the door.

What is it with me and storage buildings? he thought.

He remembered a warehouse in Milan and the hunt for a Norwegian arms dealer. That time he had bluffed his way out of it. But these were not the type you bluffed. These were not the type who stopped and listened to what you had to say. These were the type who hit first and asked afterward. Or who just hit.

"Not here either," he heard a voice say, less than two meters away.

Then he heard them both.

"He can't just fucking disappear."

"I didn't see a thing, and we haven't heard anything either. Come on. Let's go!"

It was quiet, but he heard no steps. They were standing below him, listening.

"Be quiet," the one said.

Milo breathed calmly through the net roof and tried to ignore that his thigh itched, and that a loose steel wire on the netting roof scraped against one cheek.

He heard his own heart pounding and only waited for one of them to climb up and discover him.

Suddenly the compartment door below him thundered.

"Damn!"

The force of the blow was transmitted all the way up to Milo, and his body swayed gently in the uncomfortable net roof. The steel wires scraped more skin off his cheek, making it sting painfully.

"Got nerves, huh?" he heard the one ask.

"Shut up!"

Slowly they started moving again, and he heard their steps die away down the corridor.

After five minutes he took the chance to roll over on his back.

He heard the rumbling sound of the van starting up, but waited another five minutes before he stuck his head over the edge.

Finally he rolled back to the edge of the roof, got a foothold on the padlock on the compartment door, and let himself quietly down on the concrete. He rubbed his cheek, which responded by stinging even more.

Calmly he went through the dark corridor in the direction of the parking area, but stopped when he heard the sound of the door opening again and a car that stopped with screeching brakes. He crept cautiously to the end of the corridor and looked carefully around the corner, and saw three Pakistani men come jogging toward the two on the floor. One limped over to the car while leaning on his friend, while the other had to be carried away.

Two minutes later the car turned quickly and left the building.

Milo started to run toward the door as it was closing. He just had time to lie down and roll out before the door hit the concrete with a thud.

He got up and ran over to his car while he looked around for the car with the Pakistanis or the van of Norwegians who had beaten the living shit out of them.

But no one was visible.

As he started the Fiat, there was a beep on his cell phone. The text message was from Sørensen.

DAMN. FELL ASLEEP ON THE COUCH. KEEP CALM! I'LL CONTACT THE LOCAL POLICE.

THURSDAY

20

There are fitness centers. With a receptionist, exercise rooms, pastel colors, bowls of fruit, flat screens, modern apparatus and posters with promises of more vitality.

And then there are gyms. With no schedules or spin classes, just free weights, a worn couch and posters with promises of muscles.

This was definitely a gym. The reception area was an unstaffed desk, and the ventilation system was not adequate to take away the odor of muscle building.

Sørensen and Milo passed a couple of rowing machines from the last century and tackled a spiral staircase that went down to the basement, where the ventilation system was even less functional, and the muscle building was even more intense.

Tormod Tollefsen had spent his time here a few years ago. Along with several members of the Downtown Gang. The same people that Sørensen suspected of the killing at that time, but whom they had been unable to convict in court.

The question both Sørensen and Milo now asked was whether this was where Ingrid had gone after Oriana told her about the steroid ampoule.

The room they came down to was ten by fifteen meters in size, and one wall was covered with mirrors from floor to ceiling. In front of the mirrors and along the entire wall there was a rack of dumbbells. Along the short wall was the bench press and incline bench. A Pakistani was exhaling in short bursts and concentrating while he worked to find the optimal grip around the weight bar. His friend stood behind, ready to help.

Milo looked at the weights and noted that there were fifty kilos on either side of the bar.

At the incline bench alongside, a third man set the barbell back with a thud and jumped up. He immediately met his own gaze in the mirrored wall and took a gulp from his water bottle.

In front of the mirror a Norwegian was lying on a small bench, doing chest exercises with heavy dumbbells, while two Pakistani men alternated doing deadlifts in the corner.

Sørensen sauntered over to the bench press, where the lifting was now in progress. Milo stayed in the background.

The Pakistani on the bench tensed his legs on the floor, and his back was like an arc as he lifted what had to be more than his own body weight. Behind him stood his buddy, encouraging him.

"Come on! One more. You can do it."

Sørensen inserted a pinch of snuff while he waited. When the man on the bench was done and sitting up again, Milo recognized him from when they had done surveillance on the Downtown Gang. He went by the nickname Banno, but his real name was Omar Boqhat.

"Hi, Sørensen. Gonna work out?" Banno smiled broadly,

looking past Sørensen and over at Milo before looking back at Sørensen.

"Sheesh, who's the kid in the suit?"

Milo stared hard at him, but did not say anything. He let Sørensen do the talking.

"Don't you recognize Milo? He was the one who neutralized Reeza and brought him in," Sørensen answered.

Banno stared at Milo and measured him from head to toe. His gaze was marked more by surprise than respect, as if he thought Sørensen was making fun of him. At last he sent a nod in the direction of Milo before turning to Sørensen again.

"And what can I do for you today?"

"Tollefsen," Sørensen replied.

Banno sighed audibly and took a gulp of water.

"Aren't you done with that case yet? It's over. We were released."

"The case isn't over, and you know as well as I do that it won't go away on its own," answered Sørensen.

Banno shrugged his shoulders.

"I'm working out. Can this wait?"

"No. But it will be quick," answered Sørensen.

"Okay, what do you want? I didn't know the kid. He died. I—"

"He was killed. Executed."

Another shrug.

"But this is about his sister," Sørensen continued.

Banno's face showed no reaction.

"Okay, and so?"

"I just want to know if she ever came here and asked questions about her brother."

"Not that I remember."

The answer came quickly and without hesitation.

Sørensen took a photograph out of his pocket and held it in front of Banno, who looked at it.

"Sheesh, is she dead too?"

"Killed. She was killed too, yes."

"Well, then I understand why you're so edgy. Two killed. No one arrested."

Sørensen held his gaze and Milo could see the vein on his neck pounding.

"A simple question, Banno. Did she come here and ask questions about her brother? You know I'll find out, but I want to hear it from you."

"I've never seen her."

Neither of them said anything else.

Neither of them blinked.

Both kept staring.

Around them everyone was sitting or standing calmly, with their eyes aimed at Sørensen, Banno and Milo. No one moved so much as a dumbbell. Only the defective ventilation system was heard. Banno seemed calm. His self-confidence threatened to burst his undershirt.

Suddenly the door to the changing room opened, and everyone's eyes automatically moved toward the sound. A cleaning cart was pushed out, and behind it stood Oriana.

Milo's eyes opened wide, but her gaze—which at first showed surprise—shone with fear and begged them not to talk to her. Sørensen must have seen the same thing, because he also managed to resist the temptation to say something.

She stood as if frozen, staring at the men in front of her. The bald chief inspector in the slightly oversize suit, the challenging posture of Banno, the misplaced, well-dressed Milo a few steps away, and the passive bodybuilders who followed Banno and Sørensen with their eyes.

Banno was still looking at her. Could he also see Oriana's fear? Could he see Sørensen exert himself not to show that he knew her?

"Don'tcha have work to do, or what?" the burly Pakistani shouted at her.

She hurried and put the cleaning cart in a closet, and went quickly up the stairs.

"Was there anything else you wanted, Sørensen?"

"No. Not this time. The rest we can take up at the police station later," Sørensen answered, turning around.

He passed Milo on his way toward the stairs.

"Bring it up with my lawyer!" Banno shouted at him.

"You'll hear from me!" Sørensen shouted over his shoulder.

Banno moved his gaze over to Milo, and took a few steps toward him.

"I'm sure we'll meet another time, boss."

"I hope so," Milo answered and left.

Oriana was nowhere in sight when they came up to reception again. He would have to call her later. It could not be a coincidence that she had not appeared as a witness when she worked at the gym frequented by several of the suspects in the murder of Tormod Tollefsen. She was the link between the two homicide cases, because it was after Ingrid Tollefsen talked with Oriana that she most likely started her own private investigation into the killing of her little brother.

An investigation that had cost her her life.

They got in the car and drove toward Mosseveien. They

were heading in the direction of the city center, but they would continue to the other side of the city. To Lysaker.

"What the hell was she doing there? Did you see her eyes?" said Sørensen.

"Yes."

"I thought she was going to pee her pants," said the chief inspector.

"Yes, she was scared. I wonder what they have on her? That must be the reason she didn't report herself that time. She could have risked reprisals. If they could kill a young Norwegian boy on a light summer evening, they would have no problem getting rid of a solitary asylum seeker," Milo replied.

Sørensen grunted and drummed his fingers on his thigh.

"Did you find out what you wanted otherwise?" asked Milo.

"Yes. I got it confirmed that Ingrid Tollefsen really had been there, asking questions about the killing of her brother."

"But he denied it."

"He's lying."

"How do you know that?"

"I know when people are lying."

Sørensen stared out the window at the traffic on its way toward Oslo, while Milo maintained good speed.

"It would have taken us three weeks to bring him in for questioning along with his attorney. Now I know."

Milo glanced at him.

"And what do you know, in concrete terms?"

"I know that Tormod Tollefsen got on the wrong track and had an ampoule of steroids in his hand when he died, and that his teacher was killed. I know that Ingrid Tollefsen found this out and started nosing around in the killing of her brother. And I am reasonably certain that she confronted Banno and the gang."

Milo turned off the E18 and found the road to the office and industrial park by the Lysaker River.

"And I know that Forum Healthcare, Ingrid Tollefsen's employer, is the company that produced the ampoule Tormod Tollefsen was holding in his hand when he died."

"Both steroids and growth hormones are completely legal products," Thomas Veivåg explained.

Alongside the CEO of Forum Healthcare sat the legal director with the forgettable name, nodding supportively.

"I thought steroids were prohibited," Sørensen answered skeptically, as he leafed forward to a blank page in his notepad.

Veivåg straightened up in his chair.

"Anabolic steroids in themselves are not prohibited. Along with growth hormones, they are used to treat a number of different diseases, and—"

"Which ones?" Sørensen interrupted.

"Well, persons who need to build muscle tissue. And muscle mass. For example, after an accident. Or to correct youth who are behind on the growth curve."

"Youth? Do you mean that doctors *push* steroids on young people to get them to grow?"

Veivåg shook his head.

"No, no, no one is *pushing* these products."

"Then you haven't been to a gym," Milo interjected.

Veivåg stopped in midsentence, and moved his eyes from Sørensen to Milo. He sighed barely audibly.

"Once again. We make completely legal products that every single day give patients all over the world a better life. These are medicines given to patients after careful medical assessment by doctors. Sometimes the body needs help."

"But what about the illegal sale of steroids at gyms and other places? I don't expect that all the juicers in Oslo get this by prescription from their doctors?" asked Milo.

"No, of course not. But we don't sell to them either," answered the head of Forum.

"But they are the same products, aren't they? What builds muscle mass in an accident victim can build muscle mass in a bodybuilder too, right?" asked Milo.

"In theory, yes."

Now it was Sørensen's turn to sigh.

"But damn it all, Veivåg! Do you deny that your products can end up in gyms and be sold illegally?"

It was as if the word "illegally" was the keyword the legal director needed. He leaned over the tabletop and started talking.

"Just to make this completely clear: Forum Healthcare does nothing illegal. As Veivåg has said, we make products for patients who need them. We are subject to both Norwegian law and the laws of all the other countries where we do business. And since we are a global company, we have adopted an international set of rules. Forum Healthcare is, among other things, part of the UN Global Compact and CSR is high on the agenda."

"CSR? Cut out the jargon!" said an irritated Sørensen.

"Corporate Social Responsibility," the legal director explained.

"Which means?"

"I don't know what the best—"

"Taking responsibility for a company's impact on society," answered Milo.

Sørensen looked with confusion from Milo to the two Forum directors.

"Do you sit here and brag that you are taking social

responsibility? And that you don't break the law? Is this racket really so bad that you have to spell it out that you are operating legally?"

Veivåg cleared his throat, but Sørensen continued.

"There's something a bit Nixonian about it, isn't there? 'I am not a crook.'"

Milo could not help smiling, while Sørensen continued the interrogation.

"I understand that you make legal products for patients, but at the same time it's obvious that these products also get diverted."

"We only have responsibility for production, and sell through lawful channels—"

Veivåg was interrupted by Sørensen's palm thundering on the tabletop.

"But the products end up on the black market anyway? How does that happen?"

Veivåg's expression now showed irritation.

"With all due respect, that is probably something you in the police ought to be able to answer."

"What a fucking cocksucker!"

Sørensen was drumming his fingers on his thigh while Milo maneuvered the Fiat between lanes.

"We'll get to the bottom of what their business is in that building. Are you after the American lawyers and authorities to get more access?"

"Yes, I'll call them again tomorrow. They've promised me an answer then."

"Good. We should turn that place upside down," said Sørensen.

"What about the storage facility where I saw the Pakistanis get the living shit beat out of them yesterday?"

"I spoke with the Follo police station this morning. They aren't aware of any problems there," Sørensen replied.

"But I was there, damn it! They almost killed them."

"And now they've headed to the hills."

Milo sighed. He thought about the cart the two Pakistanis had been pushing, with a number of cardboard boxes.

"It wasn't a load of furniture they were pulling. I can promise you that. What if that's just where they have their storage of steroids?"

"That may be, Milo, but we can't just turn every single compartment upside down and search through hundreds of people's personal belongings. It just won't work."

"I understand that. But what I can do in any event is to get hold of the names of everyone who has a lease there. Then we'll check the names against our registers," Milo answered.

"That sounds like a damned good idea," Sørensen replied.

Milo let him off at the police station. From the car he called Temoor and asked to him to get hold of the list of everyone who rented space from Quick Storage.

"Check all private persons against our registers, and if there are any companies that are listed as renter, then check as many as possible connected with them. I'll be back in a couple of hours," he said.

"A couple of hours? Loads of time, in other words," Temoor answered drily.

"Don't want to press you too hard, you know. Since you've been sick."

Temoor sniffled in response before he changed topic.

"That asylum-seeker woman you brought in . . ."

"Oriana?"

"Exactly. She was in the vicinity of the kid when he was killed. And she was a friend of his big sister, right?"

"Yes. That's right. What about her?"

"I don't know if it means anything, but I checked on her a little. Looked at her papers. By the way, I put the folder on your desk. But did you know she has a sister?"

Milo thought a moment.

"No. Where is she?"

"That's what's a little unusual. I don't know."

"What do you mean?"

"Well, they came here five years ago. Her mother and father. Oriana, who was fifteen then. And Olena, age eight."

Milo took out his notebook and jotted down some key words while Temoor talked. If Olena was eight when she came to Norway, she must be thirteen today.

"The mother and father were sent back, where the mother died a short time later. And Oriana has explained in the interviews that she got to stay and finish high school, and then she went underground."

"And what happened with the little sister?"

"She disappeared," Temoor replied.

21

Oriana was done with the lectures, and he met her outside the chemistry building at Blindern. They found a bench near the building, with a view toward both the university and NRK at Marienlyst.

Despite the autumn wind she wanted to sit outside.

"I sit inside a lot," she explained.

Young students sauntered past, either on their way to the

cafeteria, lectures or the reading room. Most were occupied with their own narrow world, but a few cast glances at the mismatched couple on the bench. The small woman who sat fumbling with the strap on her bag, and the well-dressed man who leaned back and met the eyes of those who looked in their direction.

"How long have you worked at the gym?" he asked her.

"A couple years," she answered.

"And why were you so scared when you saw us there?"

"I wasn't scared."

"You looked like a kid who'd been caught red-handed. And who feared being punished."

She did not answer.

"But who were you afraid of being punished by? Us or them?"

"Them? Who is them?"

"Do you know who we were talking with?" asked Milo.

"I think his name is Banno."

"Exactly. And do you know that he's part of the Downtown Gang?"

She shrugged her shoulders in response.

"And I'm sure you also know that he and several of his friends were indicted for the murder of Tormod Tollefsen? A murder that happened less than a hundred meters from where you live, and about which you neglected to contact the police to testify."

"You know why I couldn't do that. I don't have a residence permit, and—"

"And now it turns out that you work where they exercise, and get terrified when you see us talking with them. What do you know that you're not telling? What do they have on you?"

"I don't want any more problems," she answered, looking in a different direction.

"More problems?"

"I'm living underground. Studying under a false identity, and I have two cleaning jobs to make ends meet. If they realized that you knew me, I would have been without a job that day. I can't afford that."

She pulled her scarf tighter around her neck, and they let a noisy group of students pass before they continued.

"I don't think you're telling everything you know," said Milo.

"You can think what you want."

"I'm going to look at the papers in your residency application and the rejections from the authorities."

"Why is that?"

"To see what we can do about it, if we can get your situation straightened out."

He could have brought her in for more questioning, played hardball. But he chose another approach, even if it would take longer. There was something defiant in her slender body and her curt answers. Something told him that she had been exposed to far tougher things than a couple of policemen trying to get her to answer questions.

She looked at him with a mixture of surprise and contempt in her eyes.

" 'To see what we can do'?! There's nothing more to do."

"There's always something you can do."

"It must be nice to have your inflated self-confidence. Going around believing, no matter how idiotic it is, that you can fix every problem. But my attorney has tried everything. The rejection is final," she said.

"We'll see about that. I probably don't have any more self-confidence than you do. I just have a few more resources available," answered Milo.

She stood up and threw her pack on her back, getting ready to leave.

"Oh well. Speak up when you've hit the wall too!"

He looked up at her. The autumn sun blinded him, so he had to tilt his head a little to the side so that she was blocking it.

"I'll let you know when I have something to report, yes. But you're not leaving yet."

She looked at him impatiently, and then looked in the direction of the university.

"I have to do a little studying before I go to work again," she said.

But he did not intend to let her run off quite yet.

"First I have to find out what happened with Olena."

She stiffened and was not able to stop the question.

"How did you know—"

Then she bit off the sentence.

Milo inspected her face. Once again those frightened eyes.

"We've checked your papers. You must have known we would find out. But what really happened?"

"She disappeared right before Mama and Papa were forced to go back."

"Disappeared? How and why?"

But Oriana did not answer.

"You can't help me. That is, I'm very grateful for the money and the calling cards, but . . ."

She stopped, looking vacantly into space.

"Oriana, what happened to Olena? She was eight years old when you came to Norway, and must have been about ten or eleven when this happened."

"She had just turned eleven."

"But did she go underground, like you?"

Oriana shook her head.

"Not like me," she said in a low voice.

Milo studied her and saw that she was not lying. Not exactly. But she was holding something back. He had read stories about refugee children who disappeared. And you didn't need much imagination to begin to speculate about what might have happened.

A quick kidnapping of a little child at the Vestby refugee camp, a waiting truck, right out onto the E18. An hour later they could be in Sweden. Twenty-four hours later she might be in Germany, and put to "work." Was she one of these little girls you could see in the evening at rest stops along the Autobahn? Who got these older men with their twisted needs to stop, and where the money disappeared upward into the system to the men behind it?

"Where is she now?" Milo asked.

"I don't know."

He let her return to her books, while he remained sitting on the bench a little longer. As if the slightly damp air that seeped in through the opening of his topcoat could clear his thoughts.

He did not know what it meant that Oriana's little sister had disappeared. Or if it meant anything at all. But the sense that Oriana was holding something back had only gotten stronger.

The phone rang, and Milo considered a moment letting it go to voice mail. But when he saw Temoor's name he answered.

"Hi, Temoor."

"Hi. I've checked the storage things for you."

"That was quick."

"Well, you'll have to do the rest of the work."

"Okay, but what have you got for me?"

Temoor explained that the cross-checking of all the renters against the police register had produced few hits. He had found one drunk driver among the renters and a couple of tax evaders, but nothing of significance.

"But I have a list of three companies that you should look at more closely," he said.

"Okay. What are they?" asked Milo.

"I'll e-mail the list in a bit."

They finished, and Milo took the car back to the office. On the way he picked up a baguette for lunch, which he started eating while he turned on the computer. He had time to eat the whole thing in the time it took to bring the screen to life and enter all the passwords. The police computer system was not exactly up to date.

In his e-mail inbox were the names of the three companies Temoor thought he should check more closely: Suveren AS, Alfonso AS, and Baltic Services AS. He understood why Temoor had picked up on these three. The names were not exactly self-explanatory, and the fact that none of them even had a Web site of their own meant that it might be worth checking what kind of activity they were actually involved in.

He searched for Suveren AS in the Brønnøysund Register Centre, and saw that it was a company whose business was in "consulting." Which did not tell Milo anything at all. The owner was a fifty-four-year-old from Nordstrand, and when he googled his name, he got several hits. Apparently the company only had one employee, namely the owner himself, and a short article in *Management Weekly Journal* told about an employee in Tine who had taken a severance package to work as "coaching for managers in HR and communication." Milo looked at the accounting numbers for Suveren, and determined that the startup had not gone well at all, and that the company was not making any money. Failed, but hardly criminal, he thought.

He proceeded to look at Baltic Services. Eastern Europe always triggered curiosity, but a quick search confirmed that it was a small company that supplied tradesman services. And judging by a couple of comments on the Web, these were services of mediocre quality. But cheap. In other words, right on target for the Norwegian market.

Then he checked the third company, Alfonso AS.

The numbers he found in the Brønnøysund registries showed higher activity than for the other two companies, and it looked like the company owned an apartment building in central Oslo. It was wholly owned by Alias AS, which immediately struck Milo as a familiar name. Where had he run across it before?

He searched for it too in the Brønnøysund registries and immediately saw that he had hit the mark. One of the board members in the company was Omar Boqhat. Better known as Banno.

Through Alias AS, he and his friends controlled several companies that dealt with property and stock investments. Alias was, in turn, owned by other companies, and Milo remembered how income from fast-food stands, hairstylists and car washes was plowed into the companies. And in the midst of this cash flow also came the money from criminal activity. Dope, ladies and torpedo activities. Then the money trickled further into the system, and was converted into assets such as apartments, land, cars and so on. Laundered and clean.

Milo picked up the phone and called Sørensen to explain.

"So, one of the companies that Banno and the gang control rents storage in the building Tormod Tollefsen said the name of right before he died, where you saw two Pakistanis get beat up?"

"Right."

"I'll fix the papers. You talk with the landlord."

It was two o'clock when they arrived at the Unitor building where Quick Storage was located. A patrol from the Follo police station was already waiting, having a chat with a skinny guy in a leather jacket that was too large. He introduced himself as the general manager of Quick Storage.

"We're going to number 1051," he said as he entered the code to the big door.

Milo noted that it was four digits, and simple. He had entered 1-2-3-4. Not exactly Fort Knox.

The door glided up, and they entered the building.

The parking area was empty, and Milo automatically glanced in the direction of the place where the Pakistanis and bull-neck Norwegians had fought.

Some dark bloodstains on the concrete clearly showed that it had been intense. Milo could still hear the blows, the screams of pain, and the sound of bones breaking.

He thought about the cart of cardboard boxes, and was convinced that it must be dope of one kind or another. He would soon find out, when they got the lock to the compartment cut off.

They went toward the middle corridor, the same one Milo had seen the Pakistanis come out of, pushing the cart of boxes. His eyes swept up toward the ledge on the second floor, where he had stood in the darkness and looked down on the fight.

The man from Quick Storage led the way, and as they passed a light switch, he pounded on it and the light fixtures over the corridor came on. Behind him Sørensen and the two from the Follo police followed, one with a sturdy bolt cutter. Trailing them was Milo.

They passed the row of orange compartment doors in silence, and Milo thought about how the night before he had hidden while they searched for him. He wondered what awaited them now. Was it steroids for illegal sale to the bodybuilder community they were storing in the compartment? In that case it would explain what kind of company Tormod Tollefsen had gotten mixed up in. But what about Ingrid? Had she stumbled across this too, and in that way had to pay with her life?

Even if they were to confiscate a large shipment of steroids, it was not a given that they would be able to find the link to her murder. Which, after all, had taken place over two thousand kilometers away.

"Here it is," said the general manager, stopping in front of a compartment marked 1051.

The door looked like the others. The only difference was a much sturdier padlock.

One of the Follo policemen went up to the lock and cut it off with the bolt cutters.

"Be my guest," he said with a serious expression to Sørensen and Milo.

Sørensen went up and opened the compartment door. It let out a metallic screech, and Milo felt an expectant pressure in his chest.

"Damn it!" the chief inspector said when he opened the door wide, and the light from his flashlight swept through the space.

Milo took a step forward and saw that the compartment was empty, apart from two pallets in the middle of the floor. He went into the little room of about ten square meters, and let his eyes sweep across the floor and walls. Not so much as a scrap of paper was left behind.

"Porca putana!" he shouted, but only got his own echo in response.

Milo stayed in the car after the others had left. He felt like driving far and fast, and had to force himself to sit calmly.

Irritation that they had managed to empty the storage compartment made him eager for revenge. At the same time he felt like they were banging their heads against a wall. What did they really know about the connection between the murder of Ingrid Tollefsen in Rome, the killing of her little brother here at home, and the Downtown Gang? Tormod Tollefsen had evidently gotten mixed up in a gang of steroid users, most likely Banno and his friends. But they still lacked evidence that the Downtown Gang also pushed steroids.

At the same time he was waiting for answers from the lawyers in Forum Healthcare concerning what projects Ingrid Tollefsen had worked on. The only connection between Forum and the killing of the little brother was the ampoule with the Forum-produced steroids. But that proved nothing. He also knew that if Ingrid had fallen out with her bosses, she had made powerful enemies.

If you mess with the pharmaceutical industry—just like the oil, tobacco and arms industry—you had to be prepared to take one on the chin, he thought.

And in the middle of his stream of thought was Oriana. Milo had to get her to talk, but nothing more would come out until her situation was secured.

He had her folder with him in the car, and he took it out and skimmed through the letters from the lawyer. Milo was struck by how brief and weakly worded they were, as if Oriana was one of many clients, where he simply replaced name, country and dates, but basically used the same argumentation for residence as in all other cases. Arguments that the authorities didn't buy.

He needed someone to look at her case with fresh eyes. Put some effort into it.

A name suddenly came to mind, and he tried to push it away.

A name that made his blood pressure rise.

He tried to keep reading, but the name had bitten firmly into his brain.

Damn it all! he thought and started the engine.

Necessity makes the devil eat flies.

22

Twenty minutes later he parked at Aker Brygge.

On his way out of the parking garage and across the open plaza among others dressed in suits he happened to think of a comment from Sørensen.

"A hundred years ago this area was full of prostitutes," the chief inspector had said once when they were walking across Vika on their way to Aker Brygge, before he made a little stage pause and continued. "And it's still only lawyers and stockbrokers around here. There's something poetic about that."

The statement had been followed by hoarse laughter.

And now Milo was on his way to buy a service.

The reception area was worthy of a prominent law firm. Neutral but exclusive, with a well-dressed receptionist who smiled just as sweetly whether it was a corporate executive or an embezzler who arrived. Or a Financial Crimes investigator.

"Hello, how can I help you?"

The voice was as sweet as the smile.

"I'm here to see Philip Lehman," Milo replied.

"Do you have an appointment?"

"No, but he'll see me," he answered, giving her his card.

"One moment," she said, picking up the phone and dialing a number.

"There's a visitor for you . . . a Milo Cavalli . . . yes . . . from Financial Crimes, yes . . . no, just him . . . okay, fine."

She turned to Milo again.

"He'll be here in a few minutes. Would you like some coffee in the meantime?"

"No, thanks, but I wouldn't mind a little water from the dispenser over there," he answered.

"Go right ahead."

He drank a plastic cup of water while he thought about the times Lehman had grilled him in the courtroom. It had been absolutely unpleasant. The nasal know-it-all voice. The meticulous adjustment of the cuff links. The overbearing smiles to the judge at Milo's answers. The accusatory tone.

Philip Lehman was extremely well paid for defending wealthy individuals and corporations, and he almost always delivered the goods.

And after these encounters in the courtroom he and Milo had developed a mutual distrust. Which bordered on contempt. But which, nonetheless, was based on recognition of the other as a worthy opponent.

"Milo Cavalli! To what do we owe this pleasant surprise?" said Lehman with outstretched hand and pasted-on smile.

Milo knew that only moments earlier the attorney most likely had minutely scrutinized the list of clients and wondered who in the hell "that fucking dago" had come to talk about.

But Milo had decided to be honest, so he got right to the point.

"I need your help," he answered, taking the outstretched hand.

"Help? What?" Lehman answered with a facial expression that said, "Why the hell should I help you?"

"You'll have to come into my office," he said.

They each sat down on an elegant leather couch in the large office, Lehman leaned back with his legs crossed and Milo leaned forward with his elbows resting on his knees.

He began by telling him about Oriana and her situation. About her incompetent attorney, about the Immigration Appeals Board (UNE) and Norwegian Labor and Welfare Administration, about the family and how he wanted Lehman to take her case and put UNE in its place so that she got a residency permit.

But he avoided going into details about her role in the investigation of the murder of Ingrid Tollefsen.

"Why me?" asked Lehman.

"Because I can't think of anyone worse to be rear-ended by."

Lehman smiled broadly.

"Thanks. That was well put. And why this interest in this woman?"

"Because she doesn't have anyone else. The one she had is no longer around."

"I see."

Lehman was not someone who fell for emotional appeals.

"It's not important why *I* want this. What's important is why *you* will do it," said Milo.

The attorney let one hand adjust the already perfect knot of his tie.

"And why in the world should I take on such a case? You know very well this is not my area. I'm a business and defense attorney. I don't deal with social insurance law."

The words "social insurance law" were pronounced with such a large dose of contempt in his voice that you might think he was talking about something indecent.

"For three reasons. First, because it would make me extremely grateful. I would see it as a big favor."

Lehman snorted.

"Second, because it would involve extremely valuable publicity for you. Instead of an overpaid attorney with doubtful financial investments in the Cayman Islands and the tax authorities breathing down your neck, society would see an attorney who cares because he takes the time to help a poor, talented immigrant. Completely pro bono," Milo continued.

Lehman stood up and buttoned his suit coat.

"No, you know what, Cavalli, I don't deal with pro bono cases, and—"

"Third, because it will give you the opportunity to tap into my bank account," Milo interrupted.

The attorney raised one eyebrow.

Milo continued.

"You take this as a pro bono case outwardly. I pick up the tab. No one has to know anything. If it leaks out that I've paid you, I'll come after you with everything I have."

He leaned back and met the eyes of the attorney he disliked more than anyone, but whom he knew was the country's most exorbitant. Lehman went over to the desk and picked up the phone.

"Halvor, it's me. We have a new case. Can you come in?

Great! And bring along the phone number for the TV2 journalist we talked about in connection with the Grefsen case," he said and hung up.

Milo went back to the parking garage, and on his way looked up the number for Einar Gade-Broch. His father's golf buddy and best friend. Surgeon at University Hospital. There was a favor he needed.

Gade-Broch did not answer until after ten or twelve rings.

"Sheesh, Emil, hi! I just had to finish another call first. So, how are things with you?"

"Just fine."

"It's been a long time."

"Yes, I know. But Einar, I need a little help from you. Or a tip."

"Okay, what can I do for you, Emil?"

"Steroids and growth hormones. What do you know about them?" asked Milo.

"Well, not exactly my specialty. Why are you asking?"

"Work. I need to know more about both the legal and illegal uses."

"As I said, not exactly my field. But I think I know who you should talk with, an acquaintance of mine at the Norwegian School of Sport Sciences."

"What's his name?"

"Her. Anja Nyhagen."

23

He parked at Sognsvann and zigzagged between puddles in the direction of Toppidrettssenteret, the Elite Sports Center. He stood out in the tights-clad crowd on their way into the forest, and reminded himself that he should never do his runs up here. There was something jittery about the men with the big pulse counters and focused gazes rushing past.

They had agreed to meet by the main entrance, and he stood and checked his e-mail while he waited. A long-distance runner he recognized from sports broadcasts came rushing into the place, gasping for breath. He did a few stretches before he put his index finger against one nostril and sent a glob of snot to the pavement.

Charming, thought Milo, moving a few meters away.

A few minutes later a woman in her late thirties came out of the building. She walked toward him, smiling.

She had workout clothes on. Black tights that sat as if molded around her thighs and a black workout jacket. Her hair was oak-brown and shoulder-length, but gathered in a ponytail. Her face was narrow, with clear features. She had the cheekbones of a model, but at the same time a dozen freckles, typical of people who spend a lot of time in the open air and sunshine. She was one of the most beautiful women he could recall having met.

"Anja. A pleasure," she said.

The handshake was warm, and along with her ruddy cheeks this told him that she had just finished a workout.

"Milo."

"So you're Milo. I've heard about you," she said.

"I see. And what have you heard?"

"This and that."

There was something teasing about her smile.

"You shouldn't believe everything you hear," Milo replied.

She hummed in response and scrutinized him, and Milo immediately felt like he was being assessed.

"Thanks for being able to meet with me so soon," he said.

"No problem. Or rather, yes, there is a little problem. Since we talked on the phone, something has come up. I have to fill in for someone who's sick. Have to talk with some students about diet"—she looked at her watch—"in five minutes, actually."

"Okay. But can we talk afterwards?"

"That was just what I was going to suggest. I'll be happy to contribute information, but I'm going to meet a girlfriend afterwards for a bite to eat. My husband is out of town, and I can't bear any more meals of crackers. What if we met over a glass of wine after that?" she asked.

"Absolutely. Where?"

"I'll text you a little later. Now I have to run," she said.

He watched her leave with long, quick strides toward the main entrance while she loosened the ponytail and let her hair fall down over her shoulders.

There was not a man in the bar who did not follow her with his eyes as she came in the door.

She had the self-confidence her sisters ten years *older* lacked—and the experience her sisters ten years *younger* lacked. Something that gave her an attractive force she was well aware of.

He noticed how the conversations at the tables around almost stopped, and how the gazes of both men and women sought her out where she stood at the entrance, looking around.

Her gaze scanned the bar and tables and stopped at last at Milo, who was sitting at a table for two in a quiet corner.

She sent him a smile that struck home, and maneuvered

between the table with the six businessmen having a drink before dinner and the table of students covered with beer glasses.

He got up and took her hand, and responded to the cold squeeze she gave him.

"I took the liberty of ordering a glass of white wine for you," he said, pulling out the chair for her.

"That's nice," she said, sitting down while he pushed her chair in.

She had on a pair of jeans that fit tightly and elegantly over her thighs and behind, and a tailored jacket that meant she could waltz into any boardroom or nightclub whatsoever and only get approving looks.

"Cheers," she said.

"Cheers."

They went through the mandatory introductory questions about common acquaintances, and the kind of work they did. Anja Nyhagen was a trained physician, but specialized in sports and nutrition and now had the title of sports professor.

"It actually sounds like a contradiction, sports professor. But I am a kind of body expert, you might say," she said, sipping her wine carefully. "And now you want to talk about doping, right?"

Milo nodded.

"Steroids. Growth hormones. Anything you can tell me about their use, and possibly if you know how they end up in the gyms. If you know, that is," he said.

"Oh yes. I know. I know all about that. But I think you need to have a couple of things clear first. Steroids and growth hormones are not solely for the monkeys who hide in the gyms."

"What do you mean?"

"Today there are about a hundred thousand Norwegians

who use these types of preparations in one form or another. And not all of them are beefcakes who pump iron."

"Who are they, then?"

"All types. Attorneys, doctors, dentists, financial advisers, businessmen."

"I see," Milo answered skeptically.

"You don't seem convinced."

"Well, I know some of the groups you mention, and I've never met anyone who uses steroids," he answered.

She took another sip, and looked around demonstratively.

"You have to take the search for perfection as a starting point. You're probably familiar with that. And so surely you're familiar with how willing people are to use any means to reach their goals?"

She talked with engagement, and a lock of hair fell down on her forehead. She stroked her hand through her hair and fastened it behind one ear.

"I've probably come in contact with a few examples of that, sure," Milo answered.

"It's no different where the body is concerned. The search for perfection and the lack of barriers in the means employed," she began.

She talked about how the limits for what is morally defensible are constantly in motion. How what was considered too far over the line ten years ago, might be just fine today for most people.

"Morality is not anything absolute," she said.

"Isn't it? I thought that's exactly what it was," answered Milo. She shook her head.

"For the vast majority the boundaries are fluid and in motion. Viewed that way you're an uncommon guy if you operate with absolute morality."

"Absolute morality is perhaps taking it a bit far. But give me some examples."

"Okay, take medications as an example, then. Twenty years ago we took one Dispril a year. Today we swallow pain relievers at the first opportunity. As an extreme example."

"Is that morally objectionable?"

"No, but the boundary for what is acceptable shifts. Do you race in the Birkebeiner?"

He smiled scornfully.

"No."

"I didn't think so. But there are thousands who do."

"Is *that* morally objectionable, then?" Milo repeated.

She laughed out loud. A short, rippling laugh that tickled him in his belly and raised smiles at the next table.

"No, of course not. But I promise you that there the boundaries are shifting."

"How, then?"

She told about how for a long time she had tried to conduct doping tests in the popular skiing competitions and cycle races, but was stopped by the organizers. For that reason she shifted to interviewing selected participants. Over a hundred personal interviews, and under the promise of anonymity they had confirmed her assumptions.

"There are people who spend thousands of kroner on a gram of miracle powder to put under their skis. They are equipment fanatics. And don't shun ingesting performance-enhancing substances."

"Such as?"

"Tablets for joint pain. Capsules for better heart rhythm. Ampoules for increased muscle mass."

He rotated what was left of the wine in his glass.

"Interesting. So the Birkebeiners are actually a gang of drug addicts?" he asked.

Once again the contagious laughter.

"Not exactly drug addicts. No, I'm only saying that among all these superficially healthy men—because of course it's mostly men who are involved in such things—a lot of illegal preparations are used."

They were about to finish their wine, and Milo asked if she would like another glass. She said "gladly" with a smile, and he went over to the bar. While the bartender poured two fresh glasses, he observed Anja Nyhagen.

She was sitting with her back to him and one leg over the other. A man at the next table tried to catch her eye—without success.

"Here you go," said Milo when he returned to the table and set the glass in front of her.

"Thanks. Is this the same? It was tasty."

He nodded, and they toasted before Milo continued with his questions.

"But how do these products get into the country? And is it true that they are produced by major, recognized pharmaceutical companies?"

She put her glass aside and put her hands in her lap.

"They come into the country the same way as other illegal substances. Smuggling over the border. And yes, quite a few are produced by recognized pharmaceutical companies."

"But isn't that illegal?"

"Yes and no. Steroids are, in principle, a completely legal product. There are patient groups who need them," she explained.

Just as the directors at Forum Healthcare had argued that it was completely normal to produce and sell these types of medications, she went through all the various patient groups who might need growth hormones or steroids to get healthy. Milo drank from his wineglass impatiently, and had to concentrate not to interrupt her.

When she paused to sip her wine, he leaned over the table.

"That's good enough. I understand that there is a legitimate market for this, but there is a 'but' here, isn't there? There is a 'but' in the air?"

She smiled and leaned across the table too, and gave the back of his hand a little pat with one hand. Milo felt the warmth as a shudder.

"Quite correct, Milo. There is a 'but.' I'm getting to that now. Because far more steroids are produced in the world than the relevant patient groups need. The pharmaceutical company factories churn out millions of doses more than the legal market requires. And obviously they aren't doing that for the fun of it. They do it because there is a market for it. A different market than the legal one," Anja explained.

"The juicers," said Milo.

"And other exercise fanatics in search of the perfect body, and who have money and want results. But who lack time."

He nodded thoughtfully.

"How big is this market actually?"

"Hard to say. But I would guess that ninety percent of the steroid use in Norway is illegal."

Milo raised one eyebrow.

"The legal market is only ten percent?"

She shrugged her shoulders.

"I don't know. The only thing I'm quite sure of is that the legal market is marginal compared to the illegal one."

"But the pharmaceutical manufacturers maintain that it's completely legal to produce this," said Milo.

He thought about the Forum directors who quite openly defended themselves when he asked questions about their production.

"This is produced in countries like India and Pakistan. All the major pharmaceutical companies have factories there. Or they own companies which, in turn, own factories," Anja explained.

"Pakistan? Are a lot of steroids and growth hormones produced there?"

She nodded while she took a handful of the peanuts Milo had set on the table. He took a couple of nuts too, and noticed how impatient he was to understand this market better.

Anja took a sip of wine and continued.

"In these countries you can just walk right into a pharmacy and buy as many ampoules as you want. You don't need a medical certificate or a documented medical need. Then the products are taken to Europe."

Milo made a mental note that he should check the travel activity of Banno and others in the circle around the Downtown Gang. There was no doubt that they used and sold dope. But were they also behind the import itself of dope to Norway? From Pakistan?

Anja explained further about smuggling over the borders.

"Probably the customs officials are bribed pretty generously, so that the goods get into the country."

"Is that something you believe or that you know?"

Once again there was a shrug of the shoulders.

"I'm only stating that the ampoules come into the country. And it's not exactly one by one. We're talking about large consignments—"

"—which selected customs agents are paid to let pass?"

"Or which can be dropped from airplanes. I've heard about that too. Sometimes raw materials are smuggled in that are refined into finished products."

"So that production itself happens here in Norway?"

"Yes. But then the quality is much lower. What comes from the factories in India and Pakistan is, after all, produced by recognized companies. The production in Norway probably goes on in some out-of-the-way warehouse or farm, and you can imagine how impure such products can be," she explained.

Her wineglass was now almost half-empty, and she pointed at the glass.

"This was really good. Almost dangerously good."

"Dangerous?"

"Temptations wherever I turn," she said, holding his eyes.

Milo noticed that there was no longer any doubt what she was up to. And he noticed that he didn't have anything against it.

"Your husband is on a trip?"

"Yes, he travels a good deal for work."

"What does he do?"

"Security expert at Telenor."

"Good man?"

"Very good man."

The sentence was full of affection. But void of passion.

Milo thought a moment about Theresa and her ultimatum,

which she had maintained was not one. And he felt that right now he was unable to relate to it. He found his topcoat and put the case with his credit cards in the inside pocket.

"Shall we go to my place, then?" he said.

"Yes, let's do that," she answered.

They took a taxi, let themselves in and undressed each other.

FRIDAY

24

"Bless me, Father, for I have sinned. It's been three days since my last confession."

"God have mercy on you so you can repent your sins and believe in His mercy."

"Hello again."

"Twice in one week. Well, I never. Have you had some sort of religious awakening?"

"No, relax. More like a need to confess. Maybe not that either, but a little breathing room to talk in."

"Fire away. What's bothering you?"

"Well, right now it's more that I'm not bothered."

"Should you be worried that you don't have anything to worry about? That sounds almost Protestant."

"Yesterday I was unfaithful to my girlfriend."

"I see."

"With a married woman."

"Hmm."

"And it's been a long time since I felt so well. I almost didn't sleep, but even so it's like I've gotten a vitamin injection. I slept maybe a couple of hours. Or not even that, before she left—"

"Thanks, spare me the details."

" . . . at four o'clock in the morning. And I ought to feel miserable. I ought to have a guilty conscience about my girlfriend, but the fact is that I don't in the slightest. Just a feeling that I ought to."

"Hmm. But you need to understand that your actions involve a double betrayal."

"In what way?"

"You betray your girlfriend. And you are involved in betraying the husband of the woman you were with. A third betrayal is if they have children together."

"Theresa and I don't have such a defined relationship that I would call it a betrayal—"

"You were the one who used the word 'unfaithful' first. Besides, even if she knows that you have a, what shall I say, looser relationship, then it's not necessarily the case that she likes that. Didn't she try to put her foot down? It seems to me as if she has gone along with the way things are simply because she is afraid that otherwise she will lose you."

"You're pretty smart, Father."

"Thanks."

(Pause.)

"You say I am betraying the husband of the woman I was with. That's going too far, I think."

"Why is that?"

"Because I can't be responsible for her actions. She's the one who's married to him, and she's the one who chooses to be unfaithful."

"So you don't have a responsibility? What if this leads to them separating? In that case, doesn't that have something to do with you? If you are a passenger in a car and you get the driver to keep going faster and suddenly she runs someone down, aren't you then also responsible?"

"You used the word 'betrayal.' That I am betraying him. I don't agree with that. Obviously I am responsible for my actions, but I'm not responsible for his happiness. If he isn't able to keep his own wife happy and satisfied, then he has responsibility too, damn it!"

"Watch your language, please."

"Sorry."

"The point, my son, is that your actions have ripple effects. Whether you want them to or not."

(Pause.)

" 'What therefore God hath joined together, let not man put asunder.' Have you heard the words of Mark before?"

"Yes, Father."

(Pause.)

"Do you know what is one of the biggest problems with you young people today?"

"No. But I have a feeling I'm going to find out now."

"Your boundless selfishness."

"If you say so."

"The other major problem with you young people today . . . or not only the young, but almost all of us . . . is the desire for immediate gratification of needs."

"What do you mean?"

"Any need we have, we can, no, we *demand*, to have satisfied immediately."

"I understand what you mean, but aren't you being overly

pessimistic? Are things really so bad with us humans? You're not turning into a doomsday prophet, are you, Father?"

"I'll give you doomsday prophecies, if that's what you want. 'This know also, that in the last days perilous times shall come. For men shall be lovers of their own selves, covetous, boasters, proud, blasphemers, disobedient to parents, unthankful, unholy, without natural affection, trucebreakers, false accusers, incontinent, fierce, despisers of those that are good, traitors, heady, highminded, lovers of pleasures more than lovers of God.' Paul's second epistle to Timothy, chapter three."

"If you say so."

"What do you think when you hear that?"

"Well, that it certainly may describe our times somewhat. But that it just as easily fits the Roman Empire. That, basically, that's how we humans are."

"Perhaps you're right. That was a digression, in any event. Where was I?"

"You were talking about selfishness and about gratification of needs."

"Exactly. Because when you start to 'use' people, things can get really bad. When you combine this demand for immediate gratification of needs with boundless selfishness. It's as if you young people no longer have time to get properly acquainted. Everything has to work out from the very start, and if it doesn't, then it's just a matter of jumping ahead to someone who seems more perfect and that you think suits you better."

"I understand what you mean, but to be honest, I don't feel that I'm quite there."

"I know that, my son. I know that. You're a good person, but you are also marked by your background."

"My background? What do you mean?"

"Your mother. Whom we have talked about. Whom you lost. Don't you think that affects how you relate to women today?"

"I think this is getting very pseudopsychological."

"I mean your background may explain your behavior. But not excuse it. What you have done when you are involved in committing adultery is to work against God's will. And I know that in principle you don't think this is a big deal, but it is my duty to tell you that this is not something the Church turns a blind eye to."

"With all due respect, Father, aren't you exaggerating now? This happens every single day, everywhere in the world. Also among members of our church."

"Of course this happens every day! Because we humans are weak. But that doesn't prevent ideals from standing firm. Or are you so pragmatic that you think morality should be adaptable? Are you really one of those who thinks the Church must adapt itself to people's changed moral standards? Shall we be like the Protestants, then, and adapt the Liturgy and modernize the Mass so people think they're going to a concert instead? Shall I stand there like a hip young priest and sound as if Jesus and the Church no longer make demands on people, in a desperate attempt to attract the masses? No, thanks, let the state church be like that. It's so afraid of pushing people away that it no longer knows what it stands for. And so it forgets that it is in people's spines to despise those who only ingratiate themselves, those who adapt, those who don't stand for anything."

"I didn't mean to provoke you."

"Sorry, my son. I shouldn't have let myself get carried away. Perhaps I get even more provoked when a talented person like you appears to live so on the surface. I want you to think about something."

"What is that?"

"Are you able to keep from giving in to your desires?"

"Of course."

"Try it, then. Try to set your own needs aside next time. See yourself in a greater context."

"I'll try."

(Pause.)

"I should say that you were able to pull me back down to earth again, Father."

"That won't do you any harm."

"Maybe not."

"Remember that you are a leader. You're the type of person who brings people with you. And that means stricter demands are automatically placed on you."

"I'm just me. I'm no leader."

"You influence people. People reach out to you. I know the type. And that means you have to take care that you don't use them. That you don't abuse the trust others show you. Do you understand what I'm saying?"

"I hear you. And understand you. But I can't say I like it."

25

The sun was trying to come out, but it blinded instead of warmed. Milo buttoned up his topcoat on the steps outside St. Olav church and took out his sunglasses.

He looked at his watch. Almost nine. He hadn't been able to sleep after Anja left, so he got up at seven. An hour later he entered the confessional. He thought it would be a fine way to clear his head before diving into the investigation, but now he was not so sure.

So it worked out well that he had one more stop to make,

giving him time to think. But first he had to go by Sunniva's, because he had promised to take her along with him.

They parked by Haslum church, taking the stairs down to the cemetery and following the gravel path farther and farther away from the parking lot.

"Thanks for letting me come along," said Sunniva.

She was walking beside him, dressed in a military green parka, knit mittens, and a beret pulled down over her ears.

"No problem," Milo replied.

He was still not used to the thought of having a sister. That the girl, or young woman, by his side had the same father as him. And so the conversation they both tried to have in the car on the way over felt a little strange.

She tried to catch his eye without succeeding.

"You seem a little . . . down. Is it because of me? Or this place?"

"A little from being here. A little from work. A little from you. A few other things."

"Girlfriend problems?"

"That too."

"I understand."

They left the path and walked between the gravestones until they were standing in front of the right grave.

"Here it is," he said quietly, looking down at the stone with his mother's name.

He still did not understand why Sunniva wanted to see her grave.

They stood in silence a few minutes, and the only sound was the gusts of wind that bent the birch branches.

"It hurts to lose someone," she said.

He could have reacted to the obviously naïve statement, but it seemed sincere from her side.

"Do you miss her?" she continued.

He swallowed.

"It doesn't go away, no. Doesn't let go," he said.

And perhaps it was the case that *he* hadn't let go either. He liked coming out here. Liked the peacefulness in the cemetery and recalling memories. Not from the end, when she was sick and completely beside herself. But memories from before. From the trips, from everyday things, from dinners. Her smile. The hugs. The wet kisses on the cheek that embarrassed him so, but that he almost missed more than anything else. The affectionate nicknames. *Amore*. Beloved. *Caro*. Dear. *La luce mia*. My light.

"I know what you mean. I lost my grandmother a few years ago. I was with my grandparents a lot when I was growing up. On summer vacations. You know, when Mom worked, and Dad couldn't . . . well, you know. When the situation was as it was. Grandmother was like a second mother. And when I think about her now, it's like"—she turned toward him—"like it tickles my stomach."

Milo nodded in recognition.

"But not in a good way," he said.

"Exactly. Like a bad tickle, you know."

"I know. And you never know when it will strike," he said as he started to feel what they were talking about.

"Exactly," Sunniva almost whispered.

"But sometimes it's not a tickle either. But more like a kind of itch," said Milo.

She let out a little snort of laughter, and he looked at her in surprise.

"It itches because it's healing," she said.

"I see."

"That was just something my mother used to say. I always ran around with boys, and came home with scratches and bruises. And when there were scabs, I sat and picked at them. 'Don't scratch!' Mom always said. 'But it itches so much!' 'It itches because it's healing, Sunniva!'"

He smiled and she smiled back.

"Everything that heals, itches, Milo," she said.

"Okay, I'll remember that." He looked at her sympathetically. "When did your grandmother die?"

"Two and a half years."

"What happened? If you want to talk about it, that is."

"It's fine. She got sick. Alzheimer's."

Milo looked at her.

"Were you with her when she died?"

She shook her head slightly.

"No, but my mother and aunt were there. We took turns sitting with her. But a couple of days before she died, when I was there and she was basically somewhere else the whole time and had completely lost the ability to talk, it was like she woke up, and then she fixed her eyes on me, and then . . ."

Milo could hear her take a deep breath down into her stomach before she continued.

". . . then suddenly she smiled at me. Before that some tears ran down her cheek . . . as if she was saying 'I am so fond of you, my girl. And I'm so sorry about all this.'"

Sunniva took a breath, and he could hear her sobbing. He put his arm around her shoulder and stroked her consolingly across her back. He didn't know what to say, so he didn't say anything.

"And do you know what I thought more than once while we were waiting for her to let go, Milo?"

"No. What?"

"That I really wanted to talk with you. My big brother, you know," she said, turning toward him and putting her head against his chest.

He held her and stroked her calmly across her back, incapable of saying anything. She cried quietly. After a while she straightened up, trying to dry her tears with the wool mittens while she looked at him apologetically.

"Sorry! That wasn't the idea. But the tears were just there, right under the surface, I guess. And when I pick at it, then—"

"It's fine. Relax," said Milo. He held her around her shoulders and looked at her encouragingly. "It's fine," he repeated.

She nodded and turned toward the gravestone again. They remained standing shoulder to shoulder.

"You know, I remember very clearly that I was at your house once," she said.

"You were at our house? When?"

"I must have been eight or so. It was December. I remember that Mom had fallen and had to go to the hospital. She must have called Dad out of desperation."

"And he brought you home? While Mama was there?"

Sunniva nodded and smiled.

"She was very nice to me. We sat in your kitchen. I remember that she smelled so nice. And then I remember that I got to try a kind of big Christmas cake. I never had anything like it before. Probably something Italian, you know, about so high."

She indicated with her hands.

"*Panettone*," he said.

"Yes!"

He thought about what might have happened if he had come

home while Sunniva was there. Probably nothing. They probably would have just explained that she was the daughter of a friend. And he certainly would have believed them.

"Do you think they're better off now? Your mother and my grandmother?"

He nodded.

"No one is unhappy in heaven?"

"No one is unhappy in heaven, Sunniva."

26

On their way back to the car he turned the sound on his phone back on, and saw that several new e-mails had arrived.

Most of them were unimportant, but the one from the legal director at Forum Healthcare Norway caught his interest.

From: Tangvald, Truls
Subject: Response from Forum Healthcare Corp.
To: Cavalli, Milo

I refer to previous conversations and correspondence with our main office in New York. We promised to get back to you before the weekend.

It is important for us to express our support for the investigation that is now going on, and our desire to contribute to a reasonable degree.

At the same time our company is subject to financial legislation in both the USA and Norway, which places strict limitations on what kind of information we can give out. Our legal department in New York is working with the case, but has made it clear that the Norwegian legal entity cannot release information about what projects Ingrid Tollefsen worked on and details about them. Only the parent company in the USA has the authority to do this.

In the course of the next two weeks however Bradley Finch, Head of Legal Affairs, will go to Oslo, and he has asked me to set up a meeting with you, so that he can turn over as much information as possible.

I hope you can confirm the desire for such a meeting, so that I can take care of the practical details.

With kind regards

Truls Tangvald

SVP Legal

Forum Healthcare Norway AS

Milo cursed to himself. It was obvious that Forum was delaying the request for access, and it was not timely to wait for two weeks for an American executive who in any event would answer that *this is confidential information, I am unfortunately unable to give you any details* to almost every single question.

He mostly wanted to fire off a furious e-mail in reply, but knew that, regardless, it was wise to wait until his initial irritation had subsided.

They got in the car and he took out his headset.

"I just have to make a quick call," he said to Sunniva, entering Sørensen's number.

He failed to mention that he had hired Lehman as the attorney for Oriana—he would have to shoulder that alone—and instead told him about the e-mail from Forum.

"I see. So the big boys in New York are making trouble for us? But if I know you, you haven't thought about giving up," the chief inspector replied.

"Absolutely not. It turns out that I have to travel over there on some personal business," Milo answered.

"Personal business? In New York?"

"Family affairs, you might say. Besides, the last time I talked with Benedetti, it didn't seem like he'd gotten a green light to go over to question the professor that Ingrid saw there. We need to know what they talked about, but he's sweating the resources," Milo said.

"I understand. But we have budgets to stick to ourselves for that matter."

"Fuck the budgets, Sørensen! I have my own budget. The clock is ticking, and I can leave now."

"Now?"

"Yes, now."

"It's Friday. You won't get there—"

"It's Thursday night over there. The flight takes seven hours. I'll arrive in the afternoon and have time to talk with the Forum gang before they leave for the weekend."

"If you get to meet with them then."

"Believe me, I'll get a meeting with them."

Sørensen thought a moment.

"Okay. I'll continue here at home. The steroid lead is still our best option. And then you'll check Ingrid's movements in New York and pester the Forum lawyers for all it's worth."

"Good. We'll talk on the phone over the weekend," Milo replied and hung up.

Sunniva looked at him with curiosity.

"Are you going on another trip?"

"Yes. I have some running around to do, so I'll have to drop you off at home."

"That's fine. Where are you going?"

"New York."

"Oh, cool!"

"That remains to be seen."

• • •

He stopped outside the building she lived in, and got a big hug from her. On his way home he called SAS, entered his gold card number and got through in just a few minutes. There was a flight at one thirty that would arrive in New York in the afternoon. He ordered a business-class ticket before dashing into the apartment to pick up his passport and a small bag.

In the kitchen he found his iPad. First he booked a room at the Waldorf Astoria. Then he sent off a reply to the legal director at Forum.

From: Cavalli, Milo
Subject: Re: Response from Forum Healthcare Corp.
To: Tangvald, Truls

Thanks for the e-mail.
We appreciate that your legal director wants to cooperate fully with us, and look forward to meeting him.

To make the process as efficient as possible, I am taking a flight from Oslo at 1:30 today.

I will go directly to your main office on Madison Avenue, and will be ready for a meeting as of about 4:00 local time.

I will count on you taking care of the practical details because I will be sitting on the plane most of the day.

I also expect that company management will make the right persons available for the meeting in New York, and that we do not need to involve American police authorities.

Regards

M Cavalli

He smiled as he sent it.

Two minutes later he took off.

In ten hours he would be in New York. To force the bosses at Forum Healthcare to talk. To meet the professor who had been Ingrid Tollefsen's adviser several years ago in Rome, and whom she had traveled to visit right before she was killed.

And to find out what was in the will of the deceased lady friend of his grandfather Antonio Cavalli.

27

He was one of the last to board the flight. Business class was about half-full, and he found his seat alongside a light-haired thirty-year-old woman who reeked of finance.

A sand-colored trench coat lay nonchalantly in her lap, and Milo caught a glimpse of the label: Aquascutum. On the floor was her Prada bag, and around her wrist he saw a light-brown strap and a square watch face framed in gold. It resembled a Cartier. Milo sensed Stockholm girl from far off, and stole yet another look as she moved her phone to her other hand and let her left hand rest in her lap a few seconds. That was all he needed to determine that the watch was a Jaeger-LeCoultre Reverso.

He looked automatically at his own Panerai—which he had inherited from his grandfather—and noted that he had made the flight with seven minutes to spare.

While the flight attendant gave him a choice between a glass of juice or champagne and he checked his latest e-mails, he overheard the woman beside him get a little more work done before going off-line for the next seven hours. She spoke English—almost fluently—but with a Swedish accent.

"They are absolutely interested, so I am leaving to meet the executive group and the majority owners in Hoffman now. I expect a quick meeting in the afternoon in New York, and then I'm guessing that Monday will be included too. Back at the office on Tuesday afternoon," he heard her say.

After the call she tapped on her BlackBerry, while Milo finished the juice and thought about how good it was to no longer be part of the finance merry-go-round. He felt more like a speck of dust in the carousel machinery, a role he was more comfortable with.

The flight began to taxi out, and the woman beside him was in a hurry to gather things into her bag. Milo got up and opened the overhead compartment.

"I can put that up for you," he said, holding out his arm.

"Thanks," she said with a stressed smile.

He closed the bin and sat down again. From the corner of his eye he noticed that she was studying him.

"Are you ready for New York?" she asked.

The question surprised him. Snobs from Stockholm did not usually talk with strangers, especially not Norwegians.

"Yes, but I'm not sure whether New York is ready for me," he answered.

"Kathrin," she said, giving him her hand.

"Milo," he said, squeezing it gently.

Fifteen minutes later they were in the air, and the flight attendant came with snacks and beverages before dinner. Both took sodas.

"I'd rather have a glass of wine with the meal," said Kathrin.

Her voice was melodious, and the aroma of her springlike perfume made its way to his nose.

The flight had taken off in a southerly direction and passed Oslo before the captain turned the nose westward. Kathrin had been looking out the window the whole time. Now she leaned back in her seat while she brought up the footrest and found a comfortable position.

"Oslo is just so nice," she said.

She said it with longing in her voice, not the way an Oslo resident would have said it. Someone who lived in Oslo would have had their eyes firmly fixed on her destination.

"It is a nice city. You're from Stockholm, right?" he asked.

She smiled.

"Is it that obvious?"

He picked up her cashmere scarf, which had slid down on the floor.

"Yes, I'm afraid so," he answered.

"Damn it! You, then? You sound completely Norwegian, but you don't look like it. And Milo is not exactly typically Norwegian."

"Norwegian-Italian. Emil in Norwegian. Emilio in Italian. Milo among friends."

"Ah, now I understand. Where in Italy is your family from? I really love going there."

They chatted about places they had been and meals they had eaten. And when the flight attendants came with food, they both selected beef and the Italian red wine.

"But what kind of work do you do, Milo?"

"I'm a policeman."

Her fork stopped midway to her mouth, and she leaned away from him to get a better view.

"I see. My father was a policeman too. He's retired now. I don't think he ever traveled in business class," she said.

"But I do," he answered.

Now he understood why she was so accommodating and had taken the initiative to talk with him. She did not come from old money. She was a Stockholm girl who'd grown up in a working-class family, and the expensive clothes and bag she had paid for herself.

What he had overheard of both content and tone of voice in the phone call before departure revealed a number of years working in England.

"And you're an investment banker?" he asked, emptying his wineglass.

A flight attendant was quickly on the spot with a refill.

"Is that obvious too?" she asked.

He met her gaze.

"If I were to guess, you work in mergers and acquisitions for one of the big investment banks, and with your background you probably have the Nordic countries as your area of responsibility. Now you've been in Norway to sell a project. You probably met with a potential buyer, and the industry where there is plenty of money in Norway is oil. And the dominant company there is of course Statoil. Now you're on your way to New York to meet the potential acquisition candidate. Probably a medium-size gas company. Shale gas, maybe. And since you have access to the decision makers in Statoil, you either work for Silverman or USB."

Her eyes were now void of self-confidence, and her chin had fallen half a centimeter lower. He smiled at her, and continued.

"But as a policeman's daughter with both feet planted on the ground, you're not a Silverman lady. You don't let yourself be charmed by smooth-talking, greedy Americans. No, you're probably from USB. Union Swiss Broker. If I'm not mistaken, you are one of the heads of their M and A department in London."

He sipped the wine, and suppressed a smile.

"I manage Nordic M and A in USB," she said flatly.

She took a breath and was about to say more, but stopped herself.

Milo sat quietly and relaxed.

She sighed, confused.

"Didn't you say you were a policeman?"

"Yes. But not quite an ordinary policeman."

"No, I'll be damned if you are! What are you, then? Some kind of bloody Sherlock Holmes?"

He could not help laughing.

"Well, this is not a Sherlock Holmes thing. To be completely honest, I overheard you mention Hoffman."

"Yes, and so?"

"They're big in shale gas."

"Yes, but what the hell, there aren't many policemen who know about such things and based on that can work out that I've been at Statoil and work for USB!"

Her tone of voice revealed frustration and fascination.

"I work in Financial Crimes," Milo began, briefly explaining his background.

About his studies at the Norwegian School of Economics in Bergen and Bocconi in Milan. And about his years as a stock analyst.

She looked at him without blinking.

"Milo, I can't recall the last time I was knocked off my perch like that. I . . . I want to hit you," she said.

But her eyes were warm.

"I understand that. But just so you're warned. If you attack a Norwegian official, you have to be neutralized," he replied.

She looked at him, and her face broke into a smile.

•   •   •

They went their separate ways at immigration control at Newark, and he saw her stride off with her bag over her shoulder and a little black wheeled suitcase, while he stopped to give a digital fingerprint in front of a serious immigration officer.

Two minutes later he was through and could check the e-mail on his phone as he passed baggage claim and continued through customs.

In one e-mail the legal director at Forum Healthcare Norway confirmed that he had set up a meeting with their head of legal and several other managers "after they have rearranged their schedules to accommodate you on short notice."

Milo snorted as he read it; the aversion was obvious. But they were evidently afraid to provoke him in such a way that he would bring in American police authorities.

The watch on his wrist showed nine o'clock in the evening Norwegian time, but his phone had reset itself to three o'clock local time. That worked out fine. Manhattan was about an hour's taxi ride away, depending on traffic, and he could easily make the four o'clock meeting.

He walked into the arrival hall and followed the sign to the taxis. On the way he had to go through a wall of private chauffeurs standing with small placards with the names of those they were picking up.

Suddenly he caught sight of his own name in the crowd.

An Asian man, a head shorter than Milo, was standing with a sheet of paper that said CAVALLI in big, bold letters. Behind him stood another Asian man, a head taller and twice as broad.

They looked Chinese, and for a fraction of a second Milo automatically slowed down while he tried to recall whether the Forum director had mentioned anything about being picked up at the airport. He was sure that it was more likely he would have been asked to take a taxi to the main office, and for that reason he kept walking.

Instinct told him it was best not to stop by the two Chinese.

He passed them at a distance of a few meters and went straight toward the exit and the short taxi line. He avoided looking over his shoulder, but as he gave the address to the attendant taking orders at the head of the line, he saw the two come out.

The short Chinese man barked curtly to the bigger man, and both scanned the area around the taxi line.

Milo got the receipt from the taxi attendant with the agreed price into Manhattan, looked over his shoulder toward the two Chinese and met the eyes of the larger one. He exclaimed something, and pointed at Milo.

Milo turned around and went quickly toward the available taxi. The driver opened the trunk, but Milo shook his head. He had only the little travel bag.

Behind him he heard someone call.

"Mister Cavalli!"

Milo ignored them and opened the door of the taxi, and over the roof said the address to the driver, who was about to get back in.

"The MetLife Building, please."

He tossed his bag into the backseat.

"Mister Cavalli. Please wait!"

The short Chinese was now standing right behind him, and his more muscular companion put his hand heavily on the car door and closed it again.

"I think you've made a mistake," said Milo, trying to open the door.

It did not move, because now the burly, crew-cut Chinese man stood with his weight on the door and blocked it effectively.

The short one took care of the talking.

"Mister Cavalli, we must speak together. I represent Jianyu Wong-Dah, who would very much like to meet you."

"I don't know Wong-Dah. And I'm late for a meeting."

But the short man did not listen.

"Please. We have a car, we can drive you to your meeting. Then we can talk in the car," he said.

He smiled as he talked, and clenched a folder in his hands.

His big companion did not smile.

"You're confusing me with someone else," Milo responded, trying again to open the door.

The two gave him a cold feeling, and he was prepared to use his physique to get away from them. At the same time he was not sure how smart it would be to start a fistfight right outside the airport. He imagined how security guards and police would throw themselves over them, and the next few days would be spent talking his way out of the situation.

He looked at the hand that rested heavily on the door. If he were to do anything, the most effective would probably be to grab it, and bend one or two fingers backward.

While he stood there assessing the situation, the driver came to his rescue.

"What the fuck! Are we going or not?"

"We'll leave as soon as these two let me," Milo replied.

"Should I get a security guard?" the driver asked eagerly.

Milo looked inquisitively at the pair.

"Mister Cavalli. *Please*," the shorter one said pleadingly, taking a step away from the car.

Milo fixed his eyes on the big one, who now followed the short man's example. Reluctantly he took a step back.

"Thanks," Milo said, jumping into the backseat.

In the window he saw the two run off, probably to the car to follow him.

"What the hell was that all about?" the driver asked.

"No idea. Just get me to the MetLife Building, and don't let those boys catch up with us."

"No problem," the driver answered, stepping on the gas.

A few minutes later they were swallowed up by the traffic. Milo looked out the back window, but saw no sign of the two.

With that he turned around, took out his cell phone and googled Jianyu Wong-Dah.

28

He was met by a secretary in the oversize reception area and taken up to the thirty-seventh floor. The entire floor consisted of conference rooms, and Milo was shown into the largest one.

There was an enormous table in the middle of the room, and around it were twenty leather chairs with high backs.

"The others will be coming in a few minutes. Would you like something to drink in the meantime?" the secretary asked, bringing his attention to a counter along one wall with various beverages and coffeepots.

"Black coffee and a glass of juice, please," said Milo, going over to the window.

Park Avenue stretched a kilometer or so down Manhattan, before it divided into Broadway and Fourth Avenue. To the right he saw the Empire State Building, and several kilometers away, almost at the tip of the peninsula, loomed the new tower at

Ground Zero. They weren't finished yet, but the buildings were already impressive, and left no doubt about the capacity of New York and the U.S. to rise up after having been brought to their knees.

The secretary handed him the cup and glass and left the room, and Milo sat down at the table. He sat in the middle on one side, and took out the case folder and his notebook. Then he leaned back in the comfortable leather chair, feeling that his body was definitely on Norwegian time.

The Google search on Wong-Dah had not given him any revelations, but instead a heap of new questions. Jianyu Wong-Dah appeared to be some kind of tech mogul who owned companies in China, the U.S. and India. He was on the list of the world's five hundred wealthiest persons, and in the top three of the world's richest under age forty.

Milo had only vaguely heard of any of the companies he owned, and sat now wondering why two of his associates had tried to make contact with him. And not least, how they knew that he had come to New York on that flight.

A peep from the phone distracted him. The text message was from Kathrin.

CALL OR TEXT ME IF YOU HAVE TIME AND INTEREST IN A DRINK, COFFEE OR BITE TO EAT OVER THE WEEKEND. KATHRIN.

He was considering how to respond when he heard voices out in the corridor, and then a small delegation entered the room.

"Mr. Cavalli, sorry to have kept you waiting."

He turned around, and a gray-haired man in a dark suit came toward him with an outstretched hand and introduced himself as Bradley Finch, head of legal.

After him they came one by one and bombarded Milo with name, title and business card before they all found their seats.

Milo remained sitting alone on one side of the table, flanked by empty chairs. The Forum group filled up the other side. They did not appear to see the humor in that.

He set all the business cards in a fan formation in front of him on the shiny tabletop, looking at them and then at the faces.

"I'll have to see if I can keep track of who you are," he said, and the whole row in front of him showed their whitened teeth.

Right across from him sat Finch, with two attorneys on either side from a law firm whose name took up the whole width of the business card. In addition there were two information directors, a marketing executive, a research director and in the far corner sat Oliver Trimonti. His title was no less than senior vice president business operations. A kind of vice managing director, in other words. Milo glanced at him and calculated that in reality Oliver was number two in the corporate group, the man after the CEO himself who had the most influence. But there was little to suggest that he desired active participation in this meeting.

Because it was the attorneys who took the lead.

"First of all, Cavalli, it would be nice to establish a mutual understanding of what kind of meeting this really is," Finch began while he took out pen and notepad.

Milo nodded.

"Absolutely, and thanks for being able to appear on such short notice. But as you understand, we are running a homicide investigation and the time aspect is extremely critical to us," he answered.

"We understand that. But this is an ordinary meeting, and not a hearing in the formal sense, in that you come alone and not in the company of American officials. Have I understood that correctly?"

"You have. I want to know as much as possible about Ingrid

Tollefsen's work, and because this is not something the Oslo office can say anything about, I am coming to you."

"I understand. And obviously we want to help to as great an extent as possible. The loss of Ingrid . . . is terrible."

The use of her first name sounded odd. Milo was certain that Bradley Finch had never met Ingrid Tollefsen, but that did not prevent the head of legal from talking as if she had been a close acquaintance. At the same time he noticed his clear reservation: "help to as great an extent as possible."

Milo guessed that in the next hour he would be presented with a series of formulations and clauses that would make it difficult for the company to give him very much information.

"It is important for us to get as clear a picture as possible of what Ingrid Tollefsen worked with. All information is of interest," said Milo.

Finch straightened up and folded his hands on the table in front of him.

"We have no reason to believe that Ingrid's death has anything to do with her job," he said.

"But it's actually the case that we, and not you, are the ones investigating the killing."

"I'm aware of that, but we must also weigh this against other considerations. We are a company listed on the stock exchange, in razor-sharp competition with other large companies. And giving out anything that might resemble company secrets is not only difficult, but may even be illegal," said Finch. He nonchalantly picked up a sheet of paper he had in front of him. "And I understand that your background means that you . . . have a certain understanding of this," he continued.

He's playing the buddy card, thought Milo. He had encountered this many times before, the hints that "you're really one of us, Cavalli." The truth was that he did not belong to anyone. Not the police, not the financial industry.

He took a deep breath.

"I got the definite impression from your Norwegian colleagues that you wanted to cooperate. And a few minutes ago you repeated that here in this conference room."

"And we really want to. But you must be clear about what restrictions we are operating under."

There was silence.

Milo met the gaze of Finch and at the same time registered that none of the others moved. Their gazes were directed at him.

Slowly Finch picked up a sheet of paper and pushed it across the table.

"I had hoped we could hold this meeting in a constructive tone," he said.

"That's completely up to you," said Milo.

He felt the flight in his body. It was ten thirty at home in Oslo, and his fuse was getting shorter with each passing minute. In the back of his head was a nagging thought that this was a waste of time. Even if Ingrid Tollefsen had been unhappy in her job at Forum, that did not automatically have a connection with her murder. And at home in Oslo, Sørensen was chasing the steroid lead, which had become steadily stronger.

He cast a glance at the paper.

"What is this?" he asked.

"It is a list of the projects Ingrid worked with. I ask you with the utmost seriousness to treat this information with the greatest care."

Milo took a quick glance at the contents.

It was a plain sheet of paper, stripped of logo and anything else, which contained a list with a dozen bullet points.

- Preparation of clinical testing of potential new product
- Result measurements of new version of product
- Basic research

And so it continued.

The paper was completely worthless to Milo. He knew it. They knew it. They knew that he knew it.

Nonetheless, this predictable legal farce was going on. Where the script said that Milo should sigh in discontent, ask a follow-up question, and then finish by saying that he would study the information carefully and get back with any new questions.

But Milo was not good at sticking to the script.

He stood up and the chair rolled back until it stopped at the table by the wall, so that the coffee cups and glasses rattled.

"You're right about one thing, Finch. Namely, that I understand your situation, given my background. And that means I understand something else too."

He made a short pause before he let his gaze glide from the communications director at the far right and over to the vice managing director at the far left.

"I understand that you are doing what you are paid to do. Saying what you are paid to say. And that it's someone else altogether who decides," Milo continued.

He picked up his papers and went all the way to the end of the table, where he sat down right across from Trimonti.

"I think you misunderstand. It seems as if you think this is about you. About your company secrets. About your shareholders," he said while maintaining eye contact with the vice managing director.

Calmly he shoved a document folder across the table, turned it toward him and opened it.

The Forum director automatically looked down at the pictures of Ingrid Tollefsen.

Milo had deliberately placed the picture from the autopsy room on top, and the director raised his head quickly again and looked at him with an angry and confused expression. Then he looked over at his colleagues.

"This is what this is really about," said Milo, leaning across the table and spreading out the pictures.

"This picture is from the hotel, and this was how she was found. Strangled and left on the bed. Here she is from another angle, while the three pictures here are from the autopsy room. I was the one who went to Rome to get the body released and made sure that her father could bring her casket home," he continued.

His index finger made a dull sound every time he pounded it on the table.

Finch cleared his throat at his end of the table.

"Cavalli, I think that—"

"Here are copies for you too," said Milo, sending them down the table. The whole time he was speaking he kept his eyes on Trimonti.

"She was drugged and killed. And she was your colleague. Should you really let your lawyers delay the investigation?" Milo said to him.

"We've given you a list of the projects," said Finch.

Milo ignored him, and spoke directly to the man in front of him, who was becoming increasingly uncomfortable.

"I want to see the reports she wrote, the e-mails, the research results, her travel receipts, meeting minutes and anything else that might tell something about what she was doing at work."

"Cavalli, I think—"

"I want to know everything she was doing," he said firmly, starting to pack up the papers and put them in his bag.

"I didn't fly for seven hours to sit and listen to bullshit from a lawyer."

Finch had also stood up by now, while the others remained seated.

"Now I'm going to the hotel. You can think through how you want it. I must have access to the information I'm requesting. Whether that happens with or without help from the American police is not important to me."

"But there are certain regulations we all have to comply with," said Finch.

He was clearly irritated.

"I'm not so occupied by legal niceties," said Milo, feeling the vein in his neck pound against his shirt collar.

"With all due respect, Cavalli, you're a policeman, aren't you?"

"I'm more interested in results," Milo concluded, leaving the room.

On his way to a meeting with yet another attorney.

29

He found the entrance between the sushi restaurant Wild Fish and the pet accessories boutique Doggy Style.

The low-rises and independent shops south of Union Square were a short taxi ride from the skyscrapers and brand-name stores in Midtown.

The attorney he was going to meet had his office on the border to SoHo, and the narrow staircase was in sharp contrast to the monumental marble reception at Forum Healthcare.

He tried to shake off his anger at the previous meeting, but the thought that now he had to go through the American police authorities irritated him. That would take time.

The stairs led up to the second floor, where Milo had the option of going to the dentist or the lawyer.

"Not a simple choice," he mumbled.

He opened the door to the law office of Leary Patmunster Joyce and entered a waiting room where the secretary had already left for the day, but an Asian man in a suit sat waiting with a briefcase in his lap.

Milo immediately recognized him as the Chinese man who had tried to pick him up at the airport. His large companion was not in sight.

"Mister Cavalli!"

The Chinese man jumped up, and his face cracked a nicotine-stained smile.

Milo remained standing in the doorway, ready to turn around, but did not have time to say anything before the door behind the empty desk opened. Out came a man in his mid-fifties dressed in a double-breasted suit that went out of style sometime in the early nineties.

"You must be Emilio Cavalli," he said.

The voice was powerful and deep. Much like the greenish color of the suit.

Milo nodded in confirmation.

"I'm Oscar Patmunster. Please, come in."

He made a hand movement toward the open office door before he turned toward the Chinese man.

"I thought I made it clear that I would contact you later, and that I don't want you hanging around the office."

"But Mr. Wong-Dah—"

"—will get an answer later."

The attorney went over to him and put an arm around his shoulders. Calmly he guided him to the exit.

"Now I'm going to talk with Mr. Cavalli, and then we'll all take off for the weekend and enjoy it before we talk next week," he said.

As if it was a child he was escorting out.

"But—"

"Next week!"

Milo sat down in a vacant chair, while Oscar Patmunster came grumbling back.

"Who was that, and what was that about?" asked Milo.

"A somewhat aggressive buyer."

"Buyer?"

"I'll explain in a bit. Let's take things in the right order first. So you are Emilio, son of Maria Cavalli, and the grandchild of Antonio Cavalli?"

"That's right. Your e-mail was forwarded to me by my cousin, Corrado Cavalli, and we decided that I could drop in on you since I was in town anyway."

"I understand. May I see an ID?"

Milo gave him his passport, and Patmunster studied it carefully and made a notation on a sheet of paper in front of him. Then he took out a set of documents, which he handed to Milo.

"This is the will of Brenda O'Quigly, and I will now read through it before I explain the contents," said Patmunster in a businesslike manner before he looked up and added in a more personal tone, "And then I'll try to answer all the questions you must have as a result of this."

Milo skimmed the document quickly while the attorney read. Five minutes later he set the document down on the desk.

"I must ask you: Have you understood the contents, Cavalli?"

"Well, I understand that this Brenda O'Quigly has left an apartment that we are now inheriting. Or rather, are getting back. Is that the understanding?"

Patmunster nodded seriously.

"In addition to some personal effects that are in the apartment."

"Yes, I see that. But . . . why? And who is, who was this woman?"

"Your grandfather bought the apartment in 1962, but the ownership was placed in a trust and the usage rights transferred to O'Quigly. And she would have that right until her death."

"I see."

"Both the documents of the trust and her will dictate that ownership of the apartment goes to the Cavalli family after she's deceased. The trust is now being liquidated."

"I didn't know my grandfather had an apartment here in New York."

Patmunster cleared his throat cautiously.

"No, I can imagine that not too many knew about the apartment . . . or Miss O'Quigly, for that matter."

"You mean the relationship between her and my grandfather?"

The lawyer nodded.

"And what kind of relationship are we talking about here?"

Once again a cautious throat clearing.

"In the apartment there are a number of personal effects that could probably explain a great deal."

"I see. And when can I see this apartment?"

"Whenever you want. Here are two sets of keys," said Patmunster, removing two key rings from a light-brown envelope.

Milo took them and studied them. As if they could give him answers to all the questions he was burning with inside. What had his grandfather been up to in New York? And what was his relationship with the deceased woman? That his grandfather might have had mistresses throughout his long life was not an impossible thought. But buying an apartment in New York for her?

"What about the children of this woman? Can't they make any claims on the apartment?"

"She had no children. No heirs. She had only . . . your grandfather." Patmunster awkwardly looked down at the papers again. "I would recommend you see the apartment in daylight. Do it tomorrow. It's late at night Norwegian time now, so I'm sure you're exhausted."

Milo looked at his watch, which showed midnight at home in Norway.

"I'm starting to feel it, and I need to check in at the hotel. But one more question."

"Fire away."

"The Chinese guy?"

"Ah, I'd almost forgotten that. The man out in the waiting room represents a Chinese businessman who wants to buy the apartment."

"Buy it? But how did he know about it?"

"Well, have you looked more closely at the address?"

Milo looked down and read, "Seventy Central Park West."

"Exactly. The penthouse apartment. Those only come up for sale once every ten years. If that."

"So it's that much in demand," said Milo.

"It sure is. The record price in New York so far is an apartment a little farther down the street from this one. Sixteen Central Park West. The daughter of a Russian industrial magnate paid eighty-eight million dollars for an apartment of just over six hundred square meters."

"Eighty-eight million dollars?!"

Milo quickly calculated in his head and arrived at a price of five hundred million Norwegian kroner. Half a billion.

"Now, to be sure, your apartment is not as large. It's only a little over three hundred square meters," Patmunster explained.

Milo was at a loss for words.

His thoughts ran from his grandfather to his mother to the family in Italy and back to the question of who this Brenda O'Quigly was.

Patmunster completed the line of reasoning.

"So, on today's market, it would probably have a value of around fifty million dollars. And that's a lot of money too."

The Waldorf Astoria, on Park Avenue between Forty-ninth and Fiftieth Streets, was the hotel where Milo stayed whenever he was in New York.

As he passed through the swinging doors from Park Avenue, up the steps and into view of the enormous chandelier hanging above the mosaic-covered floor, and continued in toward the enormous reception area, it felt as if he was coming closer to a previous age of greatness.

The carpets were soft, the elevator doors were engraved, and the atmosphere was marked by subdued talk.

He noted that nothing had changed since the last time he was there, and found an available receptionist who checked him in and gave him a room on the twenty-sixth floor.

"With a nice view of Park Avenue. I hope you'll like it."

"It sounds fine."

"Do you need help with your luggage?"

"No, thanks, I just have this bag," said Milo.

He went over to the elevators, and studied the custom-made silver doors while he waited. There was a muffled *peep* when one of them arrived, and he entered it and pressed twenty-six.

The elevator was carpeted too, and the walls and ceiling were covered in dark mahogany that shone after one of the employees presumably polished the woodwork every night.

The hotel room was about twenty square meters and dominated by an enormous double bed. Milo went over to the windows and checked the view. Right below, he saw the roof of a small church, and on Park Avenue yellow taxis glided from intersection to intersection like little toy cars.

He glanced at his watch, which showed quarter past one Norwegian time. Quarter past seven local time. His body was worn-out, but his head was busy processing the last few hours. He was still irritated after the meeting at Forum Healthcare and the pompous head of legal, but at the same time not surprised that the meeting had gone so badly. And now the irritation had subsided and made room for increasing wonder about what his grandfather had done in New York since the early 1960s.

It was too early to go to bed. He had to adjust to American time so that he did not wake up in the middle of the night. He needed a shower, but then remembered that he had not had time to answer the text from Kathrin.

DONE WITH MEETINGS NOW. WILL HAPPILY HAVE A DRINK OR BITE TO EAT IF YOU HAVE TIME. MILO.

The response came quickly.

HAVE TO GO OUT WITH A COUPLE COLLEAGUES, MANDATORY

DINNER, BUT COULD YOU JOIN US? THAT WOULD BE REALLY NICE.
WE'RE GOING TO BALTHAZAR ON SPRING STREET. BE THERE AT 8:30.
WILL YOU COME?

He responded that he would, undressed and got into the
shower. He stayed there a long time, feeling the hard shower
stream hammer against his chest.

Balthazar in New York has only the name in common with Balta-
zar in Oslo. The Oslo restaurant serves innovative Italian dishes,
while its namesake in New York is a classic French bistro.

The place was packed when Milo arrived at quarter to nine
and started looking for her. Waiters in white shirts and black
vests scurried between the tables, where New Yorkers of all ages
put the workweek behind them.

The sound level was loud, as it should be in Manhattan, and
the atmosphere was animated.

She was sitting on a barstool, sipping a glass of white wine,
and on either side of her was a suit-wearing American shorter
than her.

She caught his eye, smiled and waved him toward her.

"So nice that you could make it."

He kissed her on the cheek, and greeted the other two. They
introduced themselves as Eric and Tim, neither of whom was
particularly happy to get a competitor.

"We're just on our way to the table now," she said, taking
hold of Milo's arm and letting him accompany her over to the
four-person table along the mirror-covered long wall.

Tim saw his chance to slip down on the sofa beside her,
while Eric and Milo were referred to the chairs across from them.

They ordered, and Tim and Eric took turns talking. About
work. About "done deals." About bonuses. About who had done

and said what. About who had exploded in meetings. About who had told off clients. And about who had screwed clients.

The whole time Kathrin and Milo listened politely while they sent each other an occasional understanding smile across the tablecloth.

As Tim ended a story with his own roar of laughter, Kathrin saw her chance to change the subject.

"So, how did your meetings go?"

Milo felt her knee next to his.

"One went to hell. It's too soon to conclude whether the other one was good or bad."

"What kind of work do you do?" asked Eric.

"I'm a policeman."

"Police?"

"Milo investigates financial crimes," Kathrin explained.

The two others glanced at each other, and Milo could actually see how they rewound in their heads to remember if they had said anything wrong.

"That's right. I'm a kind of financial policeman. So this entire conversation is being recorded," he said.

For a second Eric and Tim gaped at him before Kathrin burst into laughter.

"My God, you should have seen your faces now!"

Like most other financiers, Eric and Tim lacked self-irony, and the damage was irreparable. After this the conversation across the table was almost divided in two. The two Americans drank more and talked between themselves, while Milo and Kathrin were finally speaking Norwegian and Swedish across the table.

"Tell me, Emil, Emilio, Milo. Half Italian, half Norwegian. Those are actually two quite different cultures. Is that right?"

He looked at her.

"Yes, I suppose."

"I'm thinking about behavior. Italians and Norwegians. Or Scandinavians, for that matter."

"The difference can probably be summed up with the word 'full,'" he said.

"How is that?"

She looked inquisitively at him.

"In Norwegian, or in Swedish, 'full' refers to too much drink."

"And in Italian?"

"Then it refers to having eaten too much. To be stuffed." He took a sip of wine. "And there really you have the whole difference. In Norway it's about drinking. In Italy it's about eating," he concluded.

She shook her head slightly.

"And where do you fit in best?"

He shrugged his shoulders.

"It depends, but I'm probably more of a food guy."

After dessert Eric impatiently drummed his fingers while he waited for Kathrin to finish telling a story about a Midsummer celebration a few years ago.

"Tim and I were thinking maybe we should move on. Have a drink somewhere else. Do you want to come along?"

"I would actually prefer a cup of coffee and a bit more wine," said Milo, looking at Kathrin, who nodded.

"I think I'd like that too, but we'll see each other on Monday, boys. Thanks for everything today," she said.

The two men had just been summarily dismissed, and they understood it. Tim calmly took out his wallet and retrieved a few bills, but Milo stopped him.

"Relax, I'll get this."

Eric and Tim looked questioningly at him.

"But—"

"You'll get a chance to pay when I fine you," said Milo.

The two snorted a kind of smile in return and mumbled something about getting the check next time, before they disappeared.

Milo looked at Kathrin.

"I got the definite impression that they didn't really like me," he said.

"Definitely. You were impudent and rude."

She sent him a red-wine smile.

"Too bad, because I really liked them. I'm sorry if I chased away your colleagues," he said drily.

"No, you're not sorry."

Milo took the last drops of wine in his glass.

"No, I guess I'm really not," he said.

"Me neither."

They ordered coffee and more wine, and after she had told him about her family, Milo told her about his mother. And she sat quietly and listened.

"What about your father?" she asked when he was finished. "How has he coped with this?"

He considered telling her for a moment. About the years they almost weren't on speaking terms. About how he had just found out that he had a half sister. About how he felt that he really didn't know his own father as well as he should.

But suddenly his phone vibrated, and Lehman's name lit up on the display. Milo looked quickly at his watch, which showed seven o'clock at home in Oslo. They had been sitting in the restaurant for almost three hours.

"I just have to take this," he said.

It must have been important if the attorney was calling on Saturday morning.

"Of course. I'll visit the restroom in the meantime," she said, getting up.

"Hi, it's Milo."

"Oh, hi, are you awake? I actually only meant to leave a message."

Lehman sounded confused.

"I'm in New York."

"Oh, I understand."

"But what are you doing up so early?" Milo asked.

"I always get up at six o'clock. Regardless. And start the workday at seven o'clock. So I thought I should update you on the case with the asylum seeker."

"Oriana."

"Exactly."

"Tell me," said Milo.

"Well, I'm afraid I have bad news."

Milo leaned back in the chair. He did not need more setbacks in the investigation now.

"Tell me."

"Well, I've had all the papers from UNE sent over and reviewed them. And the case processing is scandalous. With all due respect, Cavalli, it's not exactly the sharpest knives in the drawer who work in the public sector," Lehman began.

Milo recognized the condescending tone from the courtroom when Lehman worked to tear apart every single submission of evidence to Financial Crimes and as far as possible discredit all the investigators who testified.

"The problem is simply that this girl is an undocumented asylum seeker. Do you know what that means?"

"In practice, yes, but not legally."

"That her appeal possibilities are used up, so to speak."

"All of them?"

"The way the case process works is that UDI makes a decision, which can then be appealed to UNE. The Immigration Appeals Board, that is, which is under the Ministry of Justice."

"And that's already been done?"

"Yes, the girl was assigned a public defender, poor thing. And he didn't follow up very well. Forgot to point out case-processing errors, hasn't observed deadlines, and so on. He gets paid the same however the case goes. If the girl gets to stay or is deported."

"You mentioned case-processing errors?"

"Yes, it took us ten minutes to see that."

"But isn't it just a matter of appealing again?"

"No. She has no more appeal opportunities with UNE."

Lehman fell silent, and Milo emptied the half-full wineglass in two big gulps.

"Damn it! It must be possible to appeal this higher up in the system? You did say they've made a mistake. That she has the right to residency. But isn't there any other way to get her to stay?"

"Not unless you want to sue the Norwegian government, so I suggest you let the case be and simply—"

"Wait a minute! What did you say?"

"I said I think you should let the case be. You've done what you—"

"No, before that. You said 'sue.'"

"No, I mean, since the appeal opportunities are used up, there is a theoretical opening to sue the government, through UNE."

"On what grounds?"

"Primarily three: case-processing errors, strong humanitarian considerations, and that the decision was very unreasonable."

"And how does Oriana's case fit in?" asked Milo.

"Probably she satisfies all three. Even I can be moved in a weak moment by what she and her family have been through. But I would mostly advocate taking them on the formal aspects. On the case processing. Not on nonsense like human consideration."

"And you can do that?"

Lehman snorted into the phone.

"I can take them with both arms tied behind my back and a blindfold on."

"Do it!"

Milo felt his heart beginning to pound harder. He did not know if it was the wine, the irritation at the Forum directors, the many setbacks in the investigation or simply the testosterone that had been released by having met Kathrin.

"Listen here, Cavalli. I understand that this is important to you, but not really why. I went along with helping you, but are you aware of what a lawsuit against the government will mean? Are you aware of what it will cost?"

"Are you aware of how much money I have?"

He heard Lehman sigh.

"You're serious, then?"

"Yes, I'm serious. And I will repeat what I said to you at the office. No one can find out that I'm financing this, but I'll set aside what's necessary. How much should I set aside so that you'll be satisfied? Two million kroner? Three million?"

"Start with one million, then we'll take it from there."

"Okay. What is the process going forward now?"

"Well, a lawsuit will take at least a year, but we'll get started and ask for a preliminary injunction, so that the deportation decision is frozen and she can stay in the country throughout the entire process."

"Good! I'll call her in a few hours and explain, and then we'll deal with the rest when I'm back in Oslo."

"That's great," Lehman replied, taking a brief dramatic pause. "You're out of your mind, Cavalli."

"You may be right," Milo answered, ending the call.

A few minutes later Kathrin was back.

"Did something happen? You look so thoughtful," she said.

"I've just decided to sue the Norwegian government," he replied.

SATURDAY

30

He woke up early and stayed in bed listening to the sounds of the city: the cars honking twenty-six stories below. A truck gunning its enormous diesel engine. A siren not that far away.

His head was heavy. Due to poor sleep and good wine. Even so he felt good. Somehow or other he was satisfied with waking up alone. Satisfied that they had been content to share a taxi. Satisfied that he had simply followed her into the reception at Lotte New York Palace, kissed her and strolled through the New York night the short block from her hotel on Madison to the Waldorf on Park Avenue.

Was it his confessor's words that had sunk in? About resisting temptation and not betraying others? It couldn't be that, he thought. He felt no regret about the night he had spent with Anja in Oslo, and not for the hours flirting with Kathrin either. It was more a feeling that he didn't need more last night. He knew that, in any event, he would see her again.

He swung his legs out of the bed and onto the soft carpet. The phone was on the table, and he looked up Oriana's number.

"Hello," she answered cautiously.

"Hi, it's Milo."

"Oh, hi."

He told her about the conversation with Lehman and about the problems with the appeal.

"I know that. There aren't any more possibilities left in the system."

"There's one more possibility," said Milo.

Briefly he went through the plan to sue UNE, and that he had set Lehman in motion to get a preliminary injunction.

"We'll get your rights back, Oriana. They won't be able to throw you out as long as the case is being processed. And when you win, you can do what you want."

She did not reply.

"Are you there?" he asked.

"Yes."

"Fine. This is going to take time, but I promise you that we will complete the whole process. But then I have to ask you for something too."

He heard her breathing.

"You have to tell what you saw that evening two years ago. We have to find that out, and you have to testify," he insisted.

"I don't really know—"

"And you have to do it now."

"I won't do it on the phone anyway. And I'm not talking with that Sørensen."

"I'll be back in Oslo early in the week. We'll do it then. Okay?"

"But . . ."

She fell silent again.

"But what is it?" asked Milo.

"Even if you manage to get a temporary injunction, I don't have money for . . . a legal case can take years, and in the meantime . . ."

"I'm going to set aside some funds in a separate trust for the sole purpose of financing your legal case. You don't need to worry about that. You will get to see all the papers before you give the testimony."

"But that's a lot of money, for sure, and I don't know—"

"What, Oriana? What don't you know?"

Milo pressured her; he had no intention of letting her slip away this time. But he could hear that she was uncomfortable.

"I don't like being in debt to a . . . man . . . who perhaps expects something in return."

She sounded like a person who was familiar with the problem of being in a debt of gratitude. Milo thought about how dependent she had been the last few years on help from others. Help to escape, help to hide, help with papers, help with housing and jobs. And in the long series of persons there was probably someone who liked to remind her of what they had done for her.

"Oriana, I'm not going to ask for anything other than your testimony in return."

"But why are you doing this, then?"

"Because it's the right thing. Period."

"Okay."

"So do we have an agreement?"

"Yes."

He felt relief when she said that. A feeling that the pieces were going to fall into place. In the end anyway. Then he remembered her little sister.

"Is there anything new about your sister?"

"Anything new? No, what would that be?"

"I was only wondering if you'd thought of anything else in connection with her disappearance. If I can, I'd like to help you find out what happened then."

"Thanks. But there's nothing new," Oriana said.

The breakfast restaurant was half full of other jet-lagged guests, and he was shown to a table by the windows facing Lexington Avenue. A pot of coffee and a glass of fresh-squeezed orange juice came to the table while he visited the buffet and picked up a bowl of fresh fruit, an omelet and some slices of toast.

He browsed a little in *The New York Times*, and thought through the day's tasks. First item on the program was to check his grandfather's apartment by Central Park. Then he had arranged to meet the professor who had been a kind of mentor for Ingrid Tollefsen, and whom she had visited only a few days before she was killed.

Breakfast did him good, and his head felt better. There was still a hint of pounding in the back of his head, and he decided to walk it off when he was through with breakfast. His body said three o'clock Norwegian time; his phone only showed nine. In other words, he was in no rush to get to the apartment, and followed Park Avenue up to Fifty-ninth Street before he turned left and found the way to the southeast entrance of Central Park.

At a leisurely pace he strolled through the park and cut across toward the Upper West Side. Around him couples and singles were walking, families with and without strollers. And both bicyclists and joggers of all shapes and sizes trying to get rid of as many calories as possible.

He thought back on his first trip to New York, with his mother and father. He must have been twelve or thirteen, and he still remembered the strange feeling of both familiarity and strangeness. The feeling in the taxi to Manhattan of coming to something known. As if he'd been there before. Simply because he had seen dozens of movies from the city, and thereby immediately recognized buildings in the skyline. At the same time the city was foreign because he knew he had only barely scratched the surface of it.

He approached the exit on the west side of the park and saw the row of high-rise buildings in front of him, excited about what was waiting in one of them.

At the exit to Central Park West he stopped and checked the GPS on his phone. Five minutes later he was standing in front of the building and had no time to inspect it more closely before the doorman opened and scrutinized him.

"Mr. Cavalli, I presume," he said.

"That's right."

"I'm Mike. I assumed you would come today. Patmunster called yesterday. I'll take you up to the apartment," he said, going in ahead of him.

The floor was marble, and in one corner a security guard was sitting behind a kind of reception counter, with a row of small TV screens in front of him.

Mike showed him into the elevator, and on the way up to the twentieth floor he told him briefly about the building and discreetly about who lived there. There was old money on every floor.

The elevator stopped gently, and they came out into a corridor with a tiled floor and soft runner.

"There are only two apartments on this floor," said Mike, going over to a door without a nameplate. He took out his bunch of keys and unlocked it. "So. I'll let you look around in peace. But if there's anything, just press 0 on the house phone."

"Thanks, Mike."

Milo went in and closed the door behind him. He felt his heart pounding. What was he going to find out about grandfather Antonio?

He went down a broad hallway and looked into bedrooms and guestrooms on both sides before he came into a large kitchen. Milo immediately recognized the Italian furnishings. He went farther into the living room with sliding doors out to an imposing terrace. His gaze glided from the massive dining table to the walls that were covered with paintings and graphic prints.

He went over to the glass door and opened it. The terrace floor had the same tiles as the house on Sardinia, and it struck Milo how familiar and foreign the whole thing seemed at once. Just like New York itself. He had no problems picturing his grandfather padding about in this apartment. Impeccably dressed in a classic suit, lamb's wool sweater and tie.

Milo went over to the edge of the veranda and looked down at Central Park.

"I'll be damned!" he exclaimed.

The view was magnificent. The park was stretched out below, and he could see the lakes and over to the Central Park Zoo and the Metropolitan Museum.

He went in again, past dining rooms and a library.

It was in the last bedroom he found what he was looking for.

On the nightstand was a framed photograph of his grandfather. On the wall a crucifix was hanging, and on the bed was a shoebox with a pair of worn, ankle-length boots on top.

He looked at the picture of his grandfather, which must have been taken sometime in the 1970s.

Solemnly he picked up the boots and studied them. They were black, worn, and very old. The soles were completely worn-out, and in several places they had come loose from the uppers. The tag that indicated the size had been scraped away long ago, and the laces were broken. But it was easy to see that they had belonged to a man.

Milo immediately understood that they had once been his grandfather's, but wondered why in the world they were here, in an enormous apartment on the finest street in New York?

At the same time there was something familiar about them. As if he had seen them before. Or was it something his grandfather had said once?

He set them on the floor and opened the lid of the shoebox. It contained postcards and pictures. He picked up a postcard from Rome, with a picture of St. Peter's Square.

He recognized his grandfather's handwriting, but not his language. The text was in simple English. A language he did not know his grandfather had mastered.

Rome, 3/7 1963

Cara Brenda,
We made a choice, and I stand by it. But my feelings are not gone. They are strong.

Antonio

Another postcard was from Sardinia.

Sardinia, 7/31 1975

Cara Brenda,
I miss us.
    I'm coming in September.

    Antonio

And so it continued. Sporadic cards with simple declarations of love. No exaggerated use of adjectives, simply a statement of facts. And Milo could imagine his grandfather writing them with a concentrated expression and slow hand movements.

    But had he really done that while his family was around? After grandmother Francesca had made dinner, after the conversation around the table, perhaps he had quarreled with Maria, or they had laughed. And afterward had he gone up to his office and written to a woman on the other side of the Atlantic?

    Milo continued browsing through the bundle, and spread out a handwritten letter. The content gave Milo the shivers.

Milan, September 2, 1977

Cara Brenda
I still can't come this month. You have perhaps heard about the national tragedy that has struck us here in Italy. So many dead young men. So meaningless.

    But when this military vessel sank earlier in the spring, it would turn out that our family is affected in a very special way. This means that I cannot leave here before this particular situation is under control.

The rest of the letter was about how he missed her and hoped to see her soon.

Milo read the first part over again. The year made him certain that this referred to the same shipwreck that both Benedetti and Sunniva had talked so vaguely about.

But how had this affected the Cavalli family? What kind of family secret had Milo so obviously been shielded from all these years?

He decided to ask Corrado, but his eyes were drawn to the shoebox, where he saw more photographs. On one of them he saw his grandfather together with Brenda, with the Statue of Liberty in the background. Probably taken on the boat on its way out to Ellis Island.

He remembered how respectfully his grandfather talked about the many people who had emigrated to the United States.

"They went from the known to the unknown, and never looked back. That takes courage!"

Milo caught sight of an old black-and-white photo he recognized. He had seen the same one on his grandfather's writing desk.

The picture showed three boys smiling at the camera with their arms around each other's shoulders. All had dark pants folded up at the ankles, and you could see that the belts were tightened to the innermost hole to get them to stay up. The shirts were off-white, the sleeves rolled up.

These were clothes to grow into, and the boys radiated poverty. But their laughter and smiles radiated energy.

He knew it was his grandfather standing in the middle, and that he was eleven or twelve years old when it was taken. That is, sometime in the 1920s.

The place was Sicily, and suddenly Milo recognized the

footwear. His grandfather had on the same boots that were now on the floor in the apartment.

Milo picked up the boots again.

They were unmistakably adult size, and on the photograph he saw how the skinny legs of his grandfather disappeared down into them and that they were many sizes too big.

"All I have on in that picture, I inherited from my uncle," he remembered his grandfather having said once.

Milo paid no attention to it then, but now he understood. The alternative to the oversize clothing and shoes had been to run around bare-legged in worn-out shorts and undershirts. And now he also understood why the three boys were smiling like that toward the camera.

With the adult clothes on they felt like men. No longer boys.

He picked up another postcard. Sent from Milan not many years before his grandfather died.

Milan, 5/5 1985

Cara Brenda

Only you with your background in Ireland can really understand how poor it is possible to be. How poor I have been. That is our bond. From one poor person to another. That is why it is so strong.

Antonio

And Milo remembered an incident in a shoe store. He and his grandfather had been shopping. Both had found shoes that fit perfectly, but then his grandfather gave them back to the clerk and said, "I'll take these, but one size larger."

Both the clerk and Milo had looked uncomprehendingly at his grandfather, who explained.

"I've never been able to walk in shoes that fit."

Milo told his mother, who had shrugged, and the incident disappeared into oblivion.

Until now, when he suddenly felt that he understood.

Milo left the shoes and box where they were, and went back to the living room. He looked around for a place to sit down, and went out on the terrace. He tried to call Corrado to tell him about the apartment and what he had found out about their grandfather, but his cousin did not answer.

There was still some time before he would meet Ingrid Tollefsen's adviser, Chiara Salvatore, down at New York University, and he remained standing with the phone in his hand. He felt like talking with someone, and called Sørensen.

The chief inspector answered quickly.

"Milo! How'd it go yesterday?"

Milo told him about the meeting with Forum, and that it would probably take longer to get access to Ingrid Tollefsen's work with the pharmaceutical giant.

"Not surprising. And when are you meeting the professor she visited over there?"

"Soon. In an hour," Milo replied.

"You sound a little down."

"Just a bit thoughtful."

"Okay. Where you are now?"

"I'm in an apartment in Manhattan."

"Apartment? I thought you were staying at a hotel."

"Yes, I am. I'm just clearing something up."

"Family business?" Sørensen asked, and Milo could hear him blowing cigarette smoke past his phone.

"Yes, you can safely say that. Family business."

31

Professor Chiara Salvatore was a thin, short woman with a large nose, and immediately reminded Milo of a bird, which the piercing voice underscored.

She was dressed in a black pantsuit and beige blouse that revealed two pointed breasts that matched her nose. Milo estimated her age at between forty-five and fifty.

He sat down in a small love seat in her office; the professor herself sat at the desk. After some introductory courtesies he began.

"The murder of Ingrid Tollefsen is being investigated both by the Italian and the Norwegian police, and I'm here because you are one of the last persons she had contact with."

Chiara Salvatore nodded seriously while she stroked imaginary crumbs away from the razor-sharp crease in her pants.

"It's really awful to hear that she was killed. I've known her a few years now, and we sat right here and talked together only a couple of weeks ago."

She shook her head as if to underscore how incomprehensible it was.

"What was it that was so important that made her come all the way here just to talk to you?" asked Milo.

Salvatore straightened up in the chair.

"That's what's a little strange. In the e-mail it sounded so urgent. But when she came here, it was actually just some of the same worries and problems as before. I didn't think that much about it then, just thought it was a little odd, but now I'm really surprised by it," she answered.

"You have to explain that."

"To be honest I don't know whether she was in crisis

mode about the usual things, or if perhaps she'd changed her mind. Perhaps she didn't say what she really had on her mind after all."

Milo slid forward to the edge of the sofa and tried to find a sitting position where he could note down the key words from the conversation.

"What do you mean by the usual things she had problems with?"

"Both personally and at work. I'm sure you know the story of her brother who was killed? About how he got on the wrong track?"

Milo nodded.

"I guess she never stopped blaming herself. She lived in Italy for several years, and probably thought she should have been closer to him." The professor suddenly smiled mournfully. "My tiny baby brother, she used to call him."

Milo nodded.

"But what kind of work problems did she mention?"

Salvatore reached her hand out for a tin, supplied herself with a lozenge and sucked meditatively on it.

"It is true that for a capable and honest student like Ingrid, who was really more of a research type, it was a tough transition to go to a commercial pharmaceutical company. An American one on the stock exchange."

"Tough? In what way?"

"You know. Demands for profitability in the projects. Bosses who nag, colleagues with sharper elbows than her, but not an equally sharp brain. It was a bit of a culture clash, you might say. I always thought she should have stayed in academia."

"Did she mention any particular colleagues?"

Salvatore thought about it.

"I don't remember a name, but I gathered that she did not get along too well with her boss."

"The research director in Oslo?"

The professor nodded and put her hair into place behind her ears. Milo took notes while he tried to reconstruct the conversations he'd had in Oslo. The bosses of Ingrid Tollefsen had been full of praise for her. Had that only been a bluff? Was that why the company had denied him access to the projects she had worked on?

"Did she say anything concrete about what she was dissatisfied about? Were there any projects she worked on where there was conflict with her superiors?" he asked.

Chiara Salvatore shook her head.

"I don't really know if I can shed any light on this," she said.

"We have reason to believe that she came to New York to talk with you about something in particular. She asked you to use her personal e-mail address. And then you say that you only had a kind of friendly chat?"

"Yes. But I'm also saying that it was odd. When I think about it now anyway. She couldn't have come here just to talk with me. Or else, as I said earlier, she pulled back." Salvatore straightened a bundle of papers on the desk and put a ballpoint pen into a mug with other pens and pencils.

"How did she seem?" asked Milo.

The professor thought for a long time.

"Was she afraid? Stressed? Angry?" he continued.

"Nervous," Salvatore answered at last.

"Nervous? How?"

"Well, just the way she conducted herself. The way she checked her cell phone all the time. Her eyes. I don't know. But when you ask me to think back now, I would say nervous. Or uncomfortable. I thought perhaps it was man trouble. You know, a quarrel with her boyfriend or something like that."

"Do you know if she had a boyfriend?"

Salvatore shrugged her shoulders and smiled at him.

"A beautiful girl like Ingrid? There must have been men in her life. She had a boyfriend in Rome anyway when she lived there."

Milo wrote that down in his notebook and browsed a little in it.

"Did she mention anything about steroids?"

"Steroids? No, why should she have?"

"Think carefully, Professor. If not steroids, perhaps growth hormones?"

She shook her head, and Milo set aside his notebook.

They continued talking about the time in Rome. About how Salvatore and Tollefsen had met each other and what they had worked on. Even if they never developed a friendship, it was clear that there was respect between them. A mentor and her protégé.

"Who is Lucca, by the way?" Milo asked suddenly.

Professor Salvatore looked at him with surprise.

"My husband is named Lucca. *Dottore* Lucca Salvatore. Why are you wondering about—"

"You wrote in the e-mail that Lucca had asked about her. And then you suggested dinner."

She swallowed almost imperceptibly.

"Nothing ever came of it," she said.

"But those two knew each other?"

"Of course. She met my husband on a couple of occasions in Rome."

"But did they also meet when you weren't around?"

Milo held her gaze. He was incapable of pretending to be tactful.

"What is it you're actually suggesting?" she asked.

"Nothing. I'm just wondering how well they knew each other."

"Well enough that we could have gone out and had dinner together, the three of us. Not well enough that they've seen each other alone," she answered readily.

Her irritation filled the small office.

"And what does your husband do?" he asked politely.

"He runs a research company."

"And what kind of research are we talking about?"

"Medical research. They specialize in clinical trials for the pharmaceutical industry," Salvatore explained.

Milo was startled.

"Don't the companies do that themselves?"

The Italian professor sighed in disbelief at what she saw as a silly question.

"In the pharmaceutical industry, as in all other industries, it's about specialization. It's more cost-effective to have large units that do many tests. At the same time, using a third party ensures independence."

Milo nodded in understanding.

"I see, but we don't need to go into detail about that now. It was actually the conversation between you and Ingrid I was wondering about. The whole thing seems so strange. Traveling all the way to New York just to talk about general dissatisfaction with her boss and her job?"

"Absolutely. But as I said, it could be that she changed her mind, that she had more on her mind."

"Or else you weren't the one she really came to see," Milo concluded.

It was the picture of his grandfather and Brenda with the Statue of Liberty in the background that started him thinking. And Kathrin was not hard to persuade.

He met her at the ferry pier, and together they took the boat, first to Liberty Island and then to Ellis Island, through which all the immigrants had been channeled—or rejected—on their way to the New World.

"It's really unbelievable. I've been in New York so many times, but I've never taken the time for this. I've just rushed from meetings to dinners, and barely had time for any gallery visits. I should have done this a long time ago," Kathrin said contentedly.

They stood at the back of the ferry, observing the Manhattan skyline grow steadily smaller.

"I was here when I was little, but I don't remember much of it. My grandfather often spoke about his admiration for those who left. They had no idea what they were coming to. Perhaps they'd gotten a letter from a relative who said there were opportunities here, and then they were on their way," said Milo.

They walked along the railing, and looked toward the Statue of Liberty as it came steadily closer, becoming more and more monumental.

"Imagine the feeling of seeing her after weeks at sea," said Kathrin.

He looked at the enormous landmark and tried to imagine what it must have been like. Leaving everything familiar and arriving in the harbor in New York. Seeing the Statue of Liberty coming closer and closer, with the skyscrapers in the background.

That was what grandfather Antonio also must have thought when he'd visited New York for the first time. Milo recalled the photograph of him and Brenda, taken on the boat on its way out to Ellis Island. While it all had seemed unreal yesterday, it slowly occurred to him that this had really happened. Antonio Cavalli loved his wife and his children and grandchildren, but his entire adult life he had also loved another. An Irish immigrant, or daughter of Irish immigrants who had lived here in New York, and whom he had visited at regular intervals over a period of over thirty years. And who now was gone, and had taken their story with her to the grave.

"What are you thinking about?" Kathrin asked.

"My grandfather."

"Did he live here?"

"No. Well, he did have an apartment here—"

"Jeepers, he owned an apartment here in New York?"

"It's a long story. I'm not even sure I know all of it yet," Milo replied.

They landed at Ellis Island, and as they went through the door to the redbrick building, Kathrin grasped his hand. It was as if they were both filled with a kind of solemnity.

Because the immigration control on Ellis Island was the story about the large numbers. Over five thousand people squeezed through every day in the big arrival hall. Twelve million people who today had over a hundred million descendants in the United States.

But behind the big numbers there were small, heartrending stories. And while they quietly strolled from room to room and looked at pictures and texts, they were captivated by the story of the little family from Ukraine. With their tuberculotic two-year-old son who had to be quarantined, and whom the parents could only visit for a few minutes every Sunday. And who died after eight weeks and never joined the rest of the family on their new start in the United States.

And there were stories about the courage to press forward. About the Polish girl who got so irritated that the men were tested on whether they could solve simple arithmetic problems, while she got questions about how you washed stairs: from above and down, or from below and up? "I didn't come to America to wash stairs," she said to the immigration officer who responded by stamping "approved" on her papers.

And at last they stopped at the enormous black-and-white picture of an overfilled rowboat, taken in a Norwegian fjord in 1906. "The beginning of the emigrants' journey," it said, and Milo began to understand what courage really was.

"That was powerful," said Kathrin, as they left the building and went back to the ferry pier.

"Yes," answered Milo.

On the ferry back to Manhattan they were both thoughtful.

"Now I really don't feel like heading out to a customer event this evening, but I have to," said Kathrin.

"If you have to, then you have to."

"What will you be doing this evening, Milo?"

"I feel a little worn-out. So I think I'll order room service and relax in front of the TV."

"Ah, that sounds nice. By the way, what sort of thing are you really working on? If you can talk about it, that is?"

He told her in brief terms about the murder of Ingrid Tollefsen, and that a few years earlier she had lost her brother.

Kathrin got a worried wrinkle on her forehead, and he spared her the details of the killings. He did not go into the theories about organized crime and steroids either, and how these were produced legitimately by the major pharmaceutical companies in developing countries before they were smuggled to the West.

"So both she and her brother were killed?"

He nodded.

"That's terrible! And I thought you worked on less dangerous things, like financial crime and people who manipulate the stock market."

"I do that too. But who said that financial crime isn't dangerous?" he said.

"You know what I mean. It's one thing to be greedy and to be involved in rate manipulation, for example. But it's another thing altogether to kill people."

Milo breathed in the sea air and looked at her.

"Greed is a strong motivating force," he said.

"But greed doesn't kill people."

"Doesn't it?"

"No. I've never been around anything like that anyway, and I probably work in the world's greediest industry," she said.

He did not reply.

"I thought it was affect that was the main reason for most murders. You know, passion, love, hate," she said.

"That, and economic motives. I've worked in the same industry as you, and if you think about it, you know it can also be marked by a certain type of passion."

"What kind of passion?"

"The passion to accumulate. The passion to maximize. It's naïve to think that it doesn't affect some. Or anyone," he said.

"Sheesh, I didn't think you were so liberal."

"I'm not. I'm a realist."

SUNDAY

32

He woke up early and gave up on trying to sleep longer. Instead he realized that his body was unlikely to adjust to American time, so he put on his workout clothes and found a treadmill in the hotel's exercise room.

He had slept restlessly and tried to reconstruct parts of an unpleasant dream. He was lying on a gravel track, and felt the small stones poking into his skin. He was shot, and heard voices, and when he rolled over on his back he saw that he was lying on the gravel track at Ingieråsen School. People were standing closely packed around him. His gaze glided from Sørensen's pale face over to Ingrid Tollefsen, who was standing silently beside him, and on to Oriana, Oliver Trimoni from Forum, Sunniva and Theresa. And he broke into a cold sweat when he saw that each of them was holding a pistol.

But then he heard a loud voice, and Banno pushed his way forward between Sunniva and Theresa, not with a pistol but a sturdy syringe. And suddenly he saw that all the others also had enormous syringes instead of pistols. Banno leaned down toward him, showing teeth, and Milo was completely paralyzed and unable to keep him from putting the needle right into his throat. The image turned fuzzy, and he heard Banno whisper, "Sleep well, boss."

And then he woke up.

After forty-five minutes on the treadmill he showered, then indulged in a long breakfast while he read the thick Sunday edition of *The New York Times* before going to St. Patrick's Cathedral for morning Mass.

The cathedral towered in relation to Norwegian churches, but not compared with the largest in Italy. The rows of pews were filled with people of all types and ages, and he found a place on the dark wooden pew alongside a Latin American couple.

The liturgy was exactly the same as during Mass in Italy and in St. Olav parish in Oslo, and gave him a strong feeling of belonging. The only difference was that the language was English.

He wondered if it was also this church his grandfather had visited when he was in New York. If it was here that he and Brenda went to seek forgiveness for their unseemly behavior. To pray. To confess.

After Mass he remained seated a few minutes in silence before he walked the few blocks back to the hotel.

He was sitting on his bed with the iPad studying the Forum Healthcare Web site and what was written about their research when Corrado called.

"*Ciao cugino*! Hi, cousin!"

"*Ciao*, Corrado."

"Sorry I didn't answer when you called yesterday, but it's been a steady stream of preparations for a fashion festival, you understand. Did you see the lawyer about the will?"

Milo told him about the meeting with Patmunster and about the apartment, and finally about what he had found, the correspondence between their grandfather and Brenda, the pictures, the shoes.

"So that was what our grandfather Antonio's secret was?"

"What do you mean? Did you know he had a secret?"

"All men carry a secret, Milo. One they don't dare share with anyone. One they carry alone. That's the way it is."

"I see."

"Of course it's that way."

"So what are your secrets, Corrado?"

He got a roar of laughter in response.

"I tell you almost everything, Milo, but only almost. The last five percent is for me alone to carry."

"Maybe you're right. That we are all harboring something."

"Of course I'm right," Corrado answered sincerely.

"It's just that I'm starting to get a little tired of these family secrets."

Milo told about the encounter with Sunniva at home with his father.

"There, you see! Even Uncle Endre has had his worries. So, Aunt Maria knew about that?" asked Corrado.

"Yes."

"And what's she like? Your sister, that is?"

"She seems . . . quite all right."

"So what's the problem?"

"I don't like being deceived."

"Listen, Milo. Listen to your wise cousin now. If your mother forgave him, and if this Sunniva is cool, then you don't need to complicate things even more."

"Oh well. But speaking of family secrets, Corrado. What do you know about a shipwreck in Italy in 1977? A military vessel."

Corrado remained silent on the other end.

"Why do you ask?" he asked at last.

Milo told him about what Sunniva had said, and about the letter from their grandfather to Brenda. He omitted mentioning Benedetti, who had lost his brother in the shipwreck.

"I've heard about it, but actually not that much," said Corrado.

"But what do you know?"

"Milo, listen here. I think this is something you have to talk about with your father. I don't know the difference between what I know and what I'm making up," he answered cryptically.

Milo paced back and forth in the hotel room and felt a rising frustration over the evasive answers.

"Can't you just tell me?"

"Can't you just talk with your father?"

Milo realized that he was at the end of the road where Corrado and this topic were concerned, and Corrado used the chance to change the subject back to the apartment they had inherited.

"That's quite a location! Grandfather knew what he was doing."

"Yes, the apartment is really incredible. Prospective buyers have already come forward, and the lawyer estimated a price of around fifty million dollars."

"That's not bad. But I don't need money right now. Do you, Milo?"

"No, I have enough to get by."

"Then let's keep it, for the time being," Corrado concluded.

• • •

He was lying on the bed, surfing between TV channels, but finally nodded off. An hour later he woke up. His head was heavy, and he only wanted to keep on sleeping, but forced himself up. He did not want to risk staying on Norwegian time, and wake up in the middle of the night.

He took a refreshing shower, and came back to two text messages. One from Sørensen and one from Temoor. Both contained only two words: "Call me." The only thing that set them apart was Sørensen's exclamation point.

He hoped Temoor had something good for him, so that he was not completely empty-handed when he called the chief inspector afterward.

The computer specialist answered on the first ring.

"How's New York?"

"How'd you know I was here?"

"I keep tabs on you. I can see your cell phone on the screen here."

"I ought to report you to the police."

"You don't dare. Got too much on you, you know."

"Tell me, are you at work now? Thought you were at home with Grete, baking rolls."

"Shut your mouth!"

"Relax. It was nice to visit you. I mean it."

He heard Temoor exhale dejectedly into the receiver.

"Do you know what she said the other day? 'Shouldn't we invite Milo and his girlfriend to dinner sometime?'"

Milo had to smile.

"That was nice."

"Do you know what I said? 'I think we'll let Milo and his girlfriend be. We don't have room for his harem here in this little apartment.' Ha!"

"Is it that bad?"

"Bad? Damn it, you're like a parody of James Bond!"

"And right there I feel we're through with the small talk. What do you have for me?"

"Does 'chief compliance officer' say anything to you?"

"Yes. It's a title. A position in big companies. The person who ensures that the company complies with all regulations and conducts itself in an ethically responsible manner, you might say."

"Total bullshit, of course. But now it turns out that Ingrid Tollefsen contacted the man who is chief compliance officer at Forum Healthcare."

Bingo! Milo felt his pulse pounding.

"When was this?" he asked.

"A week before she was killed."

"Do you have the e-mail?"

"Yes, I'm sending it over to you now. There are two e-mails. One was sent via a sort of 'ethics hotline.' Then this compliance officer replied, and they arranged a meeting."

"So he was the one she was going to meet in New York?" said Milo.

"In New York, no. They were going to meet in Rome," Temoor answered.

"In Rome? She was going to meet the compliance director in Rome?"

"It says so in the e-mails. But there was someone else she had contact with in New York, it appears," said Temoor.

"Yes, a Professor Salvatore. We've just spoken with her."

"Her? I have an e-mail that she sent to a *dottore*—not professor—Salvatore."

"*Dottore* Lucca Salvatore?"

"That's right."

Ten minutes later he had everything sent over from Temoor. The e-mail correspondence between Ingrid and the compliance director at Forum Healthcare was short and concise. She wanted to talk about what she called "irregularities in research," but did not specify what. At the same time she asked that the inquiry be treated confidentially.

From: Anderton, Greg
Subject: Conversation
To: Tollefsen, Ingrid

Ingrid,

Your inquiry will be treated confidentially, and as of today I am the only one who knows that you have made contact.

I am going to Europe next week, both to Paris and Rome.

Would one of those places work for a meeting?

An alternative is that I come to Oslo, but perhaps it would be nice for you if we met someplace other than your workplace?

Sincerely

Greg

Ingrid then replied briefly that Rome worked well because she was going to a conference there. She had suggested a meeting early on Tuesday morning.

The day after she was killed, thought Milo.

He proceeded to look at the other e-mail Temoor had found. The one to Lucca Salvatore, the husband of Chiara Salvatore.

From: Tollefsen, Ingrid

Subject:

To: Dottore Salvatore, Lucca

I need to tell your wife.

My conscience does not allow me to remain silent any longer.

Ingrid

Now this is starting to resemble something, thought Milo.

Chiara Salvatore had obviously been uncomfortable when they'd talked about Ingrid and her husband, and flatly denied that they'd had contact without her. But this e-mail confirmed the opposite, namely that there was something between them. And that Ingrid threatened to tell his wife about it.

Then we've established a motive, in any event, thought Milo.

It would not be the first time a man took the life of a mistress to protect himself. Or a scorned wife took the life of a mistress to get her husband back.

He grabbed a beer from the minibar while he returned to the e-mail exchange with the ethics director in Forum.

So Ingrid Tollefsen had sounded a warning internally about irregularities in the company through their ethics director, and thereby she must have been seen as a whistle-blower. But before she was able to tell what was going on, she was killed.

With that we also have a motive that points toward the employer, in addition to the motive that points toward affect or jealousy, he summarized to himself.

He sent a quick text message to Benedetti and asked him to find out all they could about *Dottore* Lucca Salvatore, and then forwarded the e-mail Ingrid had sent, where she'd threatened to inform his wife.

With a healthy portion of self-confidence he finally called Sørensen. He briefly recounted the developments.

"If you say so. Two more motives, that is. A few things have happened here at home too."

"What?"

"I just had it confirmed that Farak and Mohammat Ambhal-ajad were in Rome at the same time as Ingrid Tollefsen. You know who they are?"

"The twins. In the Downtown Gang."

"Exactly. They came from Islamabad a few days earlier, and stayed at a hotel only a kilometer or so from her hotel. That means we have established both motive and occasion," said Sørensen.

"And the motive is?"

"Her private investigation of the killing of her little brother."

"So now we're up to three motives, right? This is spreading in quite a few directions," said Milo.

He heard the sound of a lighter on the other end, inhalation and puffing out that could be heard like a sigh.

"I can buy the jealousy motive. But the part with Forum I'm unsure about. Don't misunderstand me, because I think the folks there are some smooth eels in buckets of slime. But a company doesn't go and kill troublesome employees."

Milo agreed that it sounded farfetched, but did not say any-thing. Sørensen continued.

"I think the killings of Tormod and Ingrid are connected, and I think the solution is in the steroid-smuggling Pakistanis in the Downtown Gang. We'll wait for a court order and take ac-tion this week. So if you want to be part of that, you have to make it back by Wednesday afternoon. But at the same time you should check as much as you can on what you're sitting on now. Especially that Salvatore couple."

"That's fine. I have something I have to do tomorrow, but I'll take a flight Tuesday evening and be back on Wednesday morning," Milo answered.

After they hung up, he googled Lucca Salvatore. He found a newspaper article where, in part, it said that he alternated between living in Rome and New York. Furthermore, the company he was co-owner of was mentioned. It was called Medical Research and based in New Jersey.

It was time to talk with someone who could tell him more about Medical Research—and about the industry it was part of.

MONDAY

33

It was Anja Nyhagen who had given him the name. After some introductory courtesies where they avoided any direct reference to the night they had spent together, he asked her for advice.

"You have to talk with Alex Marcody. I met him at a conference in Boston, but he's affiliated with New York University. Brilliant guy," she had said.

Marcody was a former doctor, but now he was a professor of medical ethics who had written several books about the pharmaceutical industry. She retrieved his business card, and a few minutes later Milo reached him on his cell phone.

"Norwegian police?" he answered with a trace of skepticism.

Milo explained that he had gotten the number from Anja, and then briefly what he was working on. With that, the skepticism disappeared.

"I'll be more than happy to speak with a policeman about what goes on in the pharmaceutical industry," Marcody replied.

They agreed to meet in his apartment in Tribeca at the

lower end of Manhattan, after he was done with classes at the university.

Alex Marcody was a tall, dark-haired man in his late forties with an alert gaze and energetic handshake.

"Thanks for seeing me on such short notice," said Milo as they sat down at the dining table. Marcody cleared away some papers.

The apartment was small, and the table obviously served both as a place to eat and to work.

"From what I understand, you need a kind of crash course in the pharmaceutical industry?"

Milo nodded.

"Quite specifically about research and development. And then I have some questions about a couple of companies, in case you're familiar with them," he said.

"Before we start: coffee?"

"Please," Milo replied, and Marcody disappeared into the kitchen.

A few minutes later he was back with two espressos, and got right to the point.

"Are you investigating any specific companies in the industry?" he asked with curiosity.

Milo set aside the coffee cup.

"Let me put it this way: I'm extremely interested in understanding the mentality in the industry and how these companies operate," he answered diplomatically.

Marcody smiled.

"Yes, I can tell you something about that. I've experienced the industry both as a doctor and a researcher. Okay, let's cover a few basics first. There are a great many myths about the pharmaceutical industry. And they're hard to dispel," he said, emptying his cup in one gulp.

"What myths are you thinking about?"

"Well, for example, that they spend so much money on research and development. Exactly the area you're interested in. Next that the industry is so innovative and constantly comes out with new products."

"They don't do that, you think?"

"It's not something I *think*. These are facts. I'll get to that. First of all, just so we have a couple of things clear to us. This is one of the world's most lucrative industries. We're talking about a global market of eight hundred fifty billion dollars."

Milo calculated quickly in his head. About five trillion kroner.

Marcody continued.

"I don't have such fresh numbers on the profitability right here, but if you go back a decade, the combined profits for the ten largest pharmaceutical companies on the Fortune 500 list were greater than the profits for the other four hundred ninety companies combined."

Alex Marcody spoke of an industry whose purpose in principle was curing and relieving people's illnesses, but which to an ever-greater degree since the mid-1980s had focused on earning the most money possible. Maximization of shareholder value was the mantra, which Milo was quite familiar with from his time as a stock analyst.

"And what is most profitable is not necessarily constantly developing new products, but rather making sure to sell as much as possible of what they already have."

Marcody spoke clearly and articulately and kept his eyes on Milo to be sure that his Norwegian guest took in everything he said.

"Today's pharmaceutical companies are run by marketing. Not innovation," he said.

"Well, it's hardly a crime to earn money. If they didn't, there would be zero innovation. And the companies themselves maintain that they spend billions on research, in particular," said Milo.

"Yes, they maintain that. But at the same time they aren't showing all their numbers. Much of what they call research and training is pure marketing. Doctors are invited to conferences and presented with manipulated research results, and that's called continuing education," Marcody said scornfully.

"What do you mean by 'manipulated research results'?" Milo wanted to know. He quickly made a note in his book.

"The most common is that when a new product is going to be tested for its efficacy, it is tested against a placebo, a sugar pill, that is. And not against a product that is already on the market. That way the new product looks better almost regardless, even if it is not necessarily better for patients than what is already on the market. There are many examples of new products that come on the market actually being worse than existing ones, but the companies hammer away with their doubtful research results, which show that the product has 'documented good effect,'" said Marcody, making quotation marks in the air. "And the background for this manipulation is of course being able to market something as new and pioneering, so that the companies can jack the price up further in relation to the older products on the market. Another widespread trick is to test the products on persons younger than the patient group they are actually meant for."

"Why is that?" asked Milo.

"Because younger people experience fewer side effects. And

that way the companies can market the products as both effective and without major side effects," Marcody replied.

He noticed Milo's skeptical expression.

"You can choose to believe me or not. I'm telling you what the industry has become, and then you have to assess whether it's relevant or not. Shall I continue?"

Milo nodded.

Marcody proceeded to show statistics indicating that the greatest innovation within pharmaceuticals occurred through publicly financed research, for example in connection with universities. That was where the truly sensational advances came from.

"And then one pharmaceutical company or another buys the patent, makes a group of university researchers wealthier, markets the new product, and earns billions."

"And what's so wrong about that?"

"The problem, in any event here in the U.S., is that it's the public sector that finances the research, while the companies make money on it and get a patent monopoly, which means that they can dictate the price. In practice the public, that is, the taxpayers, finance the companies' profits. That's what's perverse," Marcody explained.

He stood up and went to get some mineral water in the kitchen.

"Can you say anything about what kind of products the companies are promoting on the market, if it's the case that it's only rarely that we're talking innovative products?"

"The most profitable thing the companies do is to promote so-called 'me too' products, and to put pressure on the authorities to get their patent rights extended."

Marcody explained that "me too" products were simply imitations of existing bestsellers.

"Where the length of patent rights is concerned, that involves billions of dollars, and the companies use an army of lawyers and lobbyists. You can imagine if you earn a billion dollars on a product every year, there's a lot that argues for extending the monopoly as long as possible."

"And they're able to do that?"

"Oh, yes. They are extremely innovative when it comes to convincing politicians. In 1980 a patent lasted an average of eight years. Twenty years later the duration of patents increased to fourteen years."

Milo thought about what Chiara Salvatore had said about Ingrid Tollefsen, that the encounter with a thoroughly commercial American pharmaceutical company did not necessarily go without a hitch for a conscientious, academically inclined Norwegian girl. But commercial prodding was one thing. Homicide was something else again.

"You say that the companies manipulate the research results, but isn't it the case that this is being done more and more by independent companies?" he asked.

Marcody's face broke into a big smile. As if this was a keyword he had been waiting for.

"There is no such thing as independence. The companies that conduct the tests for the big corporations are completely at the mercy of the pharmaceutical giants to get projects. It's not the ones who *do* research who have the control, it's those who *finance* the research who have the upper hand. Previously it was the case that researchers worked completely independently. Today the pharmaceutical companies dictate everything from how many test subjects there should be to their diet during the tests. And they even decide how the results will be published, or if they shouldn't be released at all. In other words, they have full control."

He looked at Milo seriously. The smile was gone.

"Today there is a completely separate business, a major industry, simply to conduct tests for the pharmaceutical companies, and it has become a major problem getting hold of enough test subjects. For that reason the companies pay good money to those who manage to acquire guinea pigs."

"Is it now you're going to say that the pharmaceutical companies exploit the poor in developing countries?" asked Milo.

"No, they don't need to. They can exploit people here in the U.S. There are plenty to choose from."

Marcody went over to some folders he had on the bookshelf, and came back with a copy of an article from the Bloomberg news agency.

"Some years ago, in May 2006, the authorities in Miami decided that a former motel should be demolished. It had been used as the biggest test center in the U.S., with over six hundred beds."

Milo looked at the article. The owner of the hotel was FCB International, which had paid undocumented immigrants to participate in the trials. The conditions at the center were characterized as "ethically doubtful," and a researcher from the University of Miami characterized the place as one big "human bazaar," where as many as seven or eight test participants were stowed into each room in the almost dilapidated building.

"Is this common?" asked Milo.

"It's not uncommon, in any event. *The Wall Street Journal* disclosed how a pharmaceutical giant used homeless alcoholics in Indianapolis in their tests. And you should have heard the company's explanation."

Marcody paused briefly before he continued.

"An executive with the company maintained that the homeless were actually driven by altruism, and deep inside wanted to give something back to society!"

He rolled his eyes and let Milo finish taking notes.

"I'll give one more example since I've gotten started: I don't know what kind of investigation you're involved in, but it may be good to know that sometimes lives have been lost too."

Milo stopped taking notes and looked up at him.

"I can e-mail a *Boston Globe* article to you where they write about a forty-one-year-old woman," Marcody began. "This woman had struggled for years with schizophrenia and suicidal thoughts, but this was kept under control through treatment and medications. Then her doctor convinced her to participate in an experiment with a new antipsychotic drug. The doctor was paid well to find test subjects, and the woman was taken off her usual medication and instead put on various doses of this new product. When she got leave from the experiments, she went right out into the Mississippi and drowned herself. She should have had treatment, not participated in an experiment," said Marcody.

"That sounds crazy, the way you tell it."

"It *is* crazy. And I can send you documentation of all this. The reason that this is not generally known is that the companies are smart enough to see when they have to give in. Settlements are made with the opposing party when the case is in the process of growing out of control, enormous damages are paid, and then they bind the injured parties in legal agreements so that they can never talk publicly about the case again."

Milo turned to a new page, and continued noting key words. The way Marcody described the pharmaceutical industry, it had moved miles away from its original social purpose. That it was about earning the most money possible did not surprise Milo, but that the industry resorted to manipulation and even law-breaking was hard to swallow. He thought about the conversation with Anja Nyhagen about the market for steroids. About how apparently legitimate products were channeled into a black market that was far bigger than the market for patients with medical needs for these types of products.

It was the polished financial powers in symbiosis with smugglers, juicers, and organized crime.

And Forum Healthcare was in the middle of it. Listed on the stock exchange in the U.S., but with steroid ampoules that reached all the way to a fifteen-year-old Norwegian who finally had been summarily executed.

"Do you know a company called Medical Research?" Milo asked after a little while.

Alex Marcody nodded slowly.

"Absolutely. They specialize in conducting tests for pharmaceutical companies. They have offices and test centers in an old motel in New Jersey. A forty-minute drive from here."

"Do you know whether they've been involved in cases like the ones you've just been talking about?" asked Milo.

Marcody shook his head, and Milo wanted to curse.

"Medical Research hasn't been involved in any. Yet. But their predecessor was."

"Predecessor?"

"Yes, Medical Research is not that old. They've probably only been active a little more than two years, as far as I know. But the owners, a couple of Italians and two Americans, previously ran a company called Frontier Research."

"What happened?"

"They tested a new heart medicine for one of the big

companies. It turned out that two dozen persons who were involved in the trial only a few months earlier had been involved in testing another medication under the auspices of Frontier. Some new pill for stomach ulcers. The mixture would turn out to be fatal for several of the test participants."

"Fatal?"

"Five died of heart failure. One of those who died was only seventeen. A boy on the run from child services."

34

Kathrin was delayed.

Milo found a window table, ordered a vodka tonic and googled Medical Research.

The company described itself as a "next-generation research company based on fundamental scientific traditions." But based on the description Marcody had given of the closed motel and the offices in a somewhat run-down part of New Jersey, Milo assumed that behind the antiseptic white Internet images from a sterile laboratory environment, the reality was off-white.

They might very well maintain that they were on "the front line of American scientific medical research," but Milo knew that it was more a matter of being well-located in the backyard of Wall Street.

A new search told him that the company's owners, Lucca Salvatore, Daniel Bergamoro and Thomas Schweibeinder, each had a one-third share. Salvatore had the medical background. Schweibeinder was a former head of research at one of the big pharmaceutical companies, while Bergamoro was described as an investor in technology and health.

Milo checked Frontier Research, the company they had run before Medical Research, and Marcody's story was confirmed.

The company had closed down after the fatal tests a few years earlier, but a short time later they were running again with their new company.

So, one of the owners was Lucca Salvatore. The husband of Chiara Salvatore, Ingrid's mentor. Who had not seemed particularly enthused when Milo asked about how well Ingrid and Lucca knew each other.

He sipped his drink and looked around the place. Kathrin was still not to be seen, and he proceeded to check his e-mail.

One of them was from Lehman. The subject field was blank, and the e-mail contained nothing but a link to an article on *VG Net*.

Lehman Sues the Government

The high-profile attorney Philip Lehman is mad as hell about the treatment of the undocumented asylum seeker "Juliana" who is living in hiding. Now he is suing none other than the Norwegian government.

By Jørn Ekvett and Ola Selsfjord

"The authorities have acted in both an incompetent and inhumane way here. Incompetent because they have committed a number of serious case-processing errors. Inhumane because they completely overlook what happened to the family of the poor girl," Lehman thunders.

He is best known as a defense counsel for businesspeople with doubtful reputations, but is now showing a different side. After becoming aware of the girl's situation, he chose to get involved in her case.

"Does this mean that you are working pro bono for her?"

"A number of us are involved and outraged. She will not have to pay a penny for this. And we are willing to fight all the way through the legal system."

The rest of the article contained a little of the background of the case, and a "no comment" from both UNE and the Ministry of Justice.

Milo noted that the journalists were content that Lehman was fighting gratis for the poor undocumented asylum seeker, and had to praise the attorney for how elegantly he had answered without lying.

"What's making you smile like that?"

Kathrin kissed him lightly on the cheek and sat down at the table. She set her bag on the floor next to her chair and set her cell phone on the table.

"Just an e-mail I got," he replied.

"Okay, then. You seem excited." She looked at him carefully. "Have you had a good day in the pursuit of criminals?" she teased.

"Yes, I'd say so. Not bad at all."

"So who's the villain, then? Is it a sick ax murderer? Or the greedy businessman? Or maybe an hysterical professor?"

He sipped his drink.

"All of them. They're all guilty. We're all guilty."

"Oh, that's deep. Are you in a thoughtful mood?"

"I'm in a thirsty and hungry mood."

She took his hand and squeezed it.

"Me too."

He pulled her to him and kissed her.

Then he stroked her hair.

"Will you order a glass of white wine for me?" she asked, getting up. "I'll be back in a few minutes."

He nodded, and soon made contact with the waiter. Two minutes later a wineglass was on the table.

The taste of her mouth still lingered on his lips until he rinsed it away with the bitter flavor of vodka and tonic.

Her phone, which she had left behind, suddenly vibrated. Without thinking, he glanced down at it and immediately turned cold. He did not recognize the number, but the name that now showed on the display he definitely recognized.

OLIVER TRIMONI.

The second in command at Forum Healthcare. Senior vice president of business operations. Who Milo had forced to look at pictures of the dead Ingrid Tollefsen during the meeting on Friday afternoon.

Was that why Kathrin was slipping in all these questions about his work?

Instinct made him get up, put a fifty-dollar bill on the table and leave the place.

Out on the street he turned left while he discreetly tried to see if anyone was shadowing him.

He continued another block, turned right, then left again and disappeared into a Gap store.

Behind a clothes rack he looked toward the entrance to see if anyone was following, but only saw shoppers with big bags.

For a moment he considered going back. Confronting her. Bawling her out. But he did not want them to know that he knew.

He took out his cell phone and sent a text message.

SORRY. HAD TO RUN. SOMETHING IMPORTANT CAME UP. I'LL CALL LATER.

Then he walked quickly out to the street, hailed a taxi and got in.

TUESDAY

35

He was on the phone the whole hour in the lounge before boarding at the Newark airport.

Benedetti reported that they had been unable to make contact with Lucca Salvatore yet, and that they were considering issuing a search warrant for him. Milo briefly reported on the old case involving Frontier Research, in which research subjects had died.

"Salvatore may definitely have had a motive if Ingrid threatened to destroy his marriage. He is already scandalized, and if Ingrid pressured him, he may have cracked. As far as we know, he also had opportunity. He is supposed to have been in Rome at the relevant time, but we still lack concrete evidence."

"I know," said Milo.

He reported that he was on his way back to Oslo, and had scheduled a new hearing with Oriana.

"Oriana?"

"The asylum seeker. The one who most likely can tell what really happened to Ingrid's brother."

He related what Sørensen had said about the two Pakistani gang members who had also been in Rome when Ingrid was killed.

"You follow that lead, and we'll stick to Salvatore," Benedetti concluded.

After they ended the call, Milo called Sørensen.

"As soon as we have testimony from Oriana that confirms who in the Downtown Gang shot Tormod Tollefsen, we'll take action," said the chief inspector.

"Sounds good. But it still remains to link them to the killing in Rome."

"We're getting there. We're getting there," Sørensen answered.

They ended the call, and Milo looked up his father's phone number. He sat there staring at it. He wanted to know what his father knew about the shipwreck over thirty years ago, but was uncertain whether he had the energy to dig into family secrets now that the investigation had entered an even more intense phase. He decided on an intermediate solution, and wrote a text message instead.

I HAVE TO TALK TO YOU ABOUT A CERTAIN SHIP THAT SANK IN 1977. I'LL CALL YOU WHEN I'M BACK.

He was about to call Oriana when his father phoned.

"Why are you asking about this?" he wanted to know.

"Because this shipwreck has come up in several contexts," Milo replied.

He did not want to tell him what Sunniva had said, but related what he had found out about his grandfather in New York.

"So Antonio had an apartment and a mistress in Manhattan? Well, I'm not surprised," his father said.

He almost sounded pleased.

"And he's not the only one who has mentioned this shipwreck. I would really like to know what happened. What it means," said Milo.

"It doesn't really concern you," his father answered evasively.

"I think it concerns me to the very highest degree. And I want to know."

His father remained silent a moment. When he spoke again, there was a note of resignation in his voice.

"When are you back from America?"

"Tomorrow, but I'm going straight to work."

"What about dinner here on Thursday?"

"Agreed. And then you'll tell me?"

His father sighed.

"I have to think about it, Emil. I have to think about it."

They finished, and Milo had no time to analyze his father's response. He needed to call Oriana before he boarded the flight.

"Hello," she answered in a low voice.

"Hi, it's Milo. I'm on my way back and I'm landing early tomorrow. Will you be ready then?"

She did not have time to answer before she burst into tears.

"Oriana? What is it?"

"Olena . . . I don't know what I should do."

"What about Olena?"

"She's disappeared."

"I know that. She disappeared several years ago."

He heard how she dried her tears and tried to get control of her sobbing.

"No, she's been in Oslo almost the entire time."

"What?"

"But now she's disappeared."

WEDNESDAY

36

"The whole thing was arranged when she disappeared from the refugee camp that time."

Oriana was sitting at the same table in Sørensen's office, with a steaming cup of coffee in front of her. There were black circles under her eyes and her voice was husky. Her clothes were wrinkled, as if she'd been wearing them for days.

Neither Milo nor Sørensen tried to interrupt her, even though they had questions ready.

"We knew we would be deported. Mama was sick. Papa was completely desperate when he thought about what was waiting in Chechnya. We had already made preparations for me to go underground after my degree, when the opportunity suddenly came up."

Through their contacts in the local community a family in Kvinesdal had offered to help. They had a girl a couple years older than Olena, and the family was moving to Oslo. It all happened quickly. Olena was smuggled to Sørlandet, where the cover story was that she was their niece. The family lived in a remote area, and Olena mostly stayed on their property or in a cabin along with the mother in the family. False papers had been arranged, her hair dyed and cut, and Olena turned into "Lillian."

When they moved to Oslo a few months later, it was as a family of four. Mother, father and two daughters.

"The municipalities don't talk with each other, and no one in Oslo questioned whether the youngest girl was really their daughter."

The whole thing had gone without a hitch. The little sister started school in Oslo, made new friends and slipped into the crowd.

Oriana took a sip of coffee while she continued to stare at the tabletop.

"I saw her at regular intervals. It was so good to see that she was doing well. The idea was that I would take over responsibility, but as time passed, we talked about that less and less. I was satisfied that it worked out."

She remained quiet a few minutes.

"What happened?" Milo finally asked.

"On Sunday, when I let myself in to clean at the gym, someone was waiting for me. There were two of them, but fortunately one of them was on dope. He grabbed hold of me, but I bit him as hard as I could on the hand so he had to let go. Then I ran out and hid in the woods."

She stayed there lying on the ground for several hours before she started on her way home to the rented room. She knew that the people she rented from were away that weekend, so she went by way of the neighboring lot and hid behind some bushes for almost half an hour to see if anyone was in the room.

"Finally I went in. There was complete chaos. They had ransacked it. Pulled things out of the cupboards and shelves."

She spent Sunday night in Frogner Park, before she got hold of a girlfriend at Kringsjå where she could sleep on the floor.

"Monday evening the parents called . . . the ones that Olena lives with, that is . . . and said that she hadn't come home from school."

Oriana paused briefly, wiping away a tear with the sleeve of her dirty sweater.

"But I don't think they told the whole story to the police."

Sørensen checked his computer. Entered a few commands.

"Yes, I see the missing persons section has set up a case here. For a Lillian Jacobsen. Monday evening."

Oriana nodded.

"That's her. They've taken her to prevent me from telling what I know."

"How can you be sure of that? Have you heard from them?" asked Milo.

She took her phone out of her pocket and held it up toward him.

"Someone sent me this message: 'You keep your mouth shut and don't say a word to the police. Then she dies. Wait for further instructions.' "

"What number was it sent from?" asked Sørensen.

"It looks like it was sent from a Skype account. It can take a long time to find out. Too long," answered Milo.

Sørensen stood up and came around the desk.

"They're asking you to keep your mouth shut. About the murder of Tormod Tollefsen?" he asked.

"Yes."

"Because you have something to tell, right?" he continued.

"Yes."

"That means you know who kidnapped her?"

"Yes. In any case, who's responsible. But I don't know where they have her."

"Have you heard from them again?"

She shook her head and swallowed heavily.

Milo got a cup of water and emptied it in one gulp.

"There are two things I'm wondering about, Oriana. Why is this happening now? And how did they find you and Olena?" he asked.

"It's happening because you've started rooting in the case again. Asking questions. That makes them uneasy. And then they must have found out that you talked with me. I don't know how. Maybe someone saw us. Or tapped my cell phone."

She met his gaze. There was nothing accusatory in it. It was just a statement of fact.

"And they've found her because they know her identity. The false papers came from somewhere, right? Someone made them, delivered them and got paid."

She slid the fingers on her right hand back and forth across the knuckles on her left hand before she set her eyes on Milo.

"That's how they operate. Offer help with false papers, and make money on it. At the same time they also have something they can use to pressure you later. If anyone they've helped happens to work their way up in life, get a job, or a life, it's just a matter of threatening them, and they're happy to pay to keep their new life. Or else they can threaten you into silence. Like now."

Milo sat down at the table across from her.

"But you're talking with us anyway?"

She looked at him with clear eyes.

"You have to help me. I can't live like this anymore. They always want something from us. They'll always be able to demand things from us. It's an endless threat."

He nodded slowly.

"I didn't come to Norway to clean gyms and live in fear. I could have done that in Chechnya," she continued.

There was a defiant strength in her voice.

Milo thought about the Polish girl who, a century earlier, had said something similar when she was interviewed on Ellis Island. "I didn't come to America to clean stairs," she said, and was welcomed to her new life in the new world.

And Milo understood that Oriana was the toughest person he had ever met.

"Okay, Oriana. We'll help. But then you have to help us," he said.

She nodded firmly.

"Do you have someplace to stay? Can you stay with your friend?"

She shrugged her shoulders, and Milo stood up.

"Sørensen, we have to talk with the missing persons section. Oriana, wait here."

They went into a quiet room to make a call, and put it on speakerphone. A detective named Amundsen answered, and Sørensen explained the situation.

"Okay, I'll make a note of all that here. But we're sitting on a couple of other new missing persons cases too . . ."

"Have you gone through electronic traces? Her cell phone?" Milo interrupted.

"Well, we've gotten a pile of data from the phone companies, but haven't had the capacity to review it yet. But tomorrow we're having two new detectives transferred who—"

"Can you e-mail all of it to us? We have capacity," said Milo.

"Uh . . ."

"Just do it," said Sørensen.

They ended the call and phoned Temoor. Milo briefly summarized the case.

"Okay. Send it over right away," he answered.

"As soon as we've got it from the missing persons group," said Milo.

Suddenly the cell phone rang, and he answered while Temoor was still on the line.

"*Ciao Emilio,* " said Benedetti on the other end.

"*Ciao.* How's it going?"

"We've found Lucca Salvatore. He's in for questioning now, and we're probably going to indict him. He was in Rome, and he was caught on a video camera barely a kilometer away from the hotel."

"Okay."

"The problem is that we haven't managed to clearly link him directly to the hotel yet, but we'll have to see what seven or eight hours in interrogation does for him," said Benedetti.

Milo and Sørensen went back to Oriana, who was still sitting at the table. The coffee cup was no longer steaming, and she stared blankly out the window.

"We've spoken with the department that is investigating the disappearance of your sister," said Sørensen.

"The kidnapping," Oriana answered.

"The kidnapping. And we have also put extra resources on the case. But now you need to tell everything you know, so that we can lock these people up. Do you understand?"

She nodded.

"I understand."

Sørensen turned on the recording equipment and read the time and their names out loud.

"Now, Oriana. Is it the case that you saw what happened, the evening Asgeir Henriksen and Tormod Tollefsen were shot at Ingieråsen School?"

She nodded.

"You have to answer so we get it on tape," said Sørensen as patiently as he could.

"Okay. Yes, I saw what happened."

"And there were several members of the Downtown Gang there, right?"

"Yes."

"Can you tell us what you saw?"

She bit her lip and looked up at Milo, who sent her an encouraging smile.

"Who shot Tormod Tollefsen? Was it Banno?"

"No, it wasn't him."

"Was it one of the twins?"

Sørensen rubbed his palm over his bald pate, as he had a habit of doing when he was stressed.

"Can you just say who shot Tormod?" he asked.

"It was Asgeir Henriksen."

37

"What?!"

Sørensen's chin dropped even further as he stared at her.

"Asgeir Henriksen was shot when he tried to rescue Tormod," he said urgently, as if he was trying to convince himself.

Oriana looked at Milo.

"Now I'm sure you understand why I never contacted the police. The national hero Asgeir Henriksen, the man who cared so much about the students that he sacrificed his life, suddenly sees his name dragged down into the mud by a bloody asylum seeker," she said.

In her eyes was a mixture of annoyance and despair.

"We believe you," said Milo. As much to Sørensen as to her.

The chief inspector took out a pack of cigarettes as he appeared to be trying to think of something encouraging to say to her.

"Sorry. Please tell what you saw," he said.

She looked at him, and he held the cigarette pack out in conciliation. She took one, and Sørensen fired up for both of them.

"Okay," said Oriana.

She had been out running that evening, and was standing at the entrance to her room when she heard loud voices. Automatically she took a few steps toward the road, and realized then that the voices were coming from the athletic field by the school. This was the week before the end of the school year, and it had been a light summer evening.

She positioned herself behind one of the big bushes in the hedgerow in front of the house, and immediately recognized several of the regulars at the gym where she cleaned. Among them was also a young man who looked Norwegian, Asgeir Henriksen.

"It looked like they were arguing. I could see Banno poking his index finger into Henriksen's chest, who was shouting something right in his face," Oriana related.

"What about Tormod? Where was he standing?" asked Sørensen.

"He wasn't there. Yet. He came walking up on the far side of the field, along the fence. He had a gym bag over his shoulder, and appeared to be lost in his own thoughts. He was tossing something up in the air and catching it. At first I thought it was a stone, but later . . . after I found him . . . I realized it must have been the ampoule."

Tormod Tollefsen had come closer, and it was only when he was ten meters away from the others that they noticed each other.

"Banno shouted something to him, so he stopped. Then two of the Pakistanis went over to the fence and said something to him," said Oriana.

She did not hear what they said. Just saw how Tormod took a short step back before they took hold of him and pulled him over the fence and over to Banno, Henriksen and the others.

"I heard Banno scream to him," Oriana told.

Her voice had become gradually steadier as she saw the two policemen were listening attentively to her.

"Did you hear what he said?" asked Sørensen.

"Something about not getting mixed up in their business."

"What did Henriksen do?"

"Nothing. He stood and watched. Until Banno gave him a pistol."

Sørensen scratched his neck and looked inquisitively at her.

"It was Banno who gave it to him?"

"Yes, I just said that."

"Continue."

"Banno called to him."

"To who? Henriksen?"

"Yes. 'Shoot him!' And then something like, 'You have to clean up this damned mess.'"

For a while Asgeir Henriksen stood quietly with the pistol down along his side, which made Banno even more impatient. He looked around to see if anyone was coming down the street, and then went right up to Henriksen.

"I'm not sure, but it looked as if he was holding a knife against his throat."

Slowly Henriksen raised the gun, Tormod Tollefsen turned around, and moved a few meters away before he was shot in the back.

"And you're quite certain that it was Henriksen who fired the shot? There were no others with guns out?"

Sørensen's voice was quite calm, and he spoke slowly, as if to underscore how decisive this was.

"I'm quite certain. He stood there with the gun in his hand. Completely motionless." Oriana met his gaze. "Then Banno quietly took the pistol from him, and shot him in the head."

There was silence. Oriana seemed worn out, but at the same time relieved. As if a weight had been lifted off her. Something that had weighed her down the past two years. Milo stood pensively, trying to sort out the new information. Sørensen took a couple of drags on the cigarette before he tossed it in the coffee cup, which gave off a hissing sound.

"Fuckin' hell!" the chief inspector said quietly, sitting and staring at a point on the wall.

It was as if his brain was winding back two years. To all the interviews, the technical findings. His chest heaved and lowered.

"Shit!" he shouted, striking both palms on the table so that the glass tipped over and Oriana jumped back in her chair.

Sørensen stood up and paced back and forth in the room.

"They said he'd gotten in trouble, and was hard to deal with. I remember they said he'd been in an argument during PE and—"

"And Asgeir Henriksen was his gym teacher," Milo filled in.

He sat down at Sørensen's computer, logged into the system and started searching.

"How well did you actually check Henriksen back then, Sørensen?"

"Obviously not well enough."

"I see he was co-owner of a company with an office address in Hølen. Where the hell is that?" asked Milo.

"Between Vestby and Son. Yes, it was some company or other. I think they imported beauty products, as far as I remember. From Asia."

"Asian Beauty Import," said Milo, letting his eyes glide across the screen after the crucial piece of information.

He found the history of the company. The accounts, change reports to Brønnøysund, auditors' reports.

Suddenly he stopped and leaned back in the office chair. He kept staring at the screen.

"What is it, Milo?" Sørensen asked, coming around the table.

Milo pointed at the screen.

"Today Asian Beauty Import is owned one hundred percent by a Robert Guldbjerg. Two years ago, that is when Tormod was killed, it was owned fifty-fifty by Guldbjerg and Henriksen."

"Yes, and so?"

"But look here. Look at this report to Brønnøysund the year before that. There was a third shareholder in the company three years ago, whom Guldbjerg and Henriksen bought out. Agari AS. And look who's the chairman of the board of that company," said Milo, clicking on the company name with the cursor.

"Reeza Hamid," Sørensen read out loud.

"Who is Reeza Hamid?" Oriana asked from her seat.

"He's known as the finance minister. One of the key persons in the Downtown Gang," Milo replied.

He thought about the well-dressed, robust man he had chased through Oslo and finally arrested a week and a half ago.

He was still in custody and in due time would be confronted with this information.

"So Asgeir Henriksen ran a company along with central people in the Downtown Gang a few years ago—" Sørensen began.

"But they sold their share the year before Tormod Tollefsen was killed. Something or other came up between them," Milo completed.

Sørensen jotted down information on his pad.

"Where is the company located?" he asked.

Milo found the address, entered it in Google Maps and chose the satellite image. He zoomed in.

"It looks like a commercial area," he said.

"And we're going there as soon as hell!" Sørensen exclaimed.

His face was red and he almost had to gasp for breath.

"Do you think they have Olena there?" asked Oriana with hope in her voice.

"No idea, but we have to check," said Sørensen.

Milo scrutinized him.

"But why would they keep her there? They aren't partners anymore. They own dozens of properties in Oslo where they can hide her, and where—"

"Where they don't want us to find her. They don't want to connect her kidnapping directly to them and their companies. I don't know why, but maybe they're calling in a favor, maybe it's off target, but right now it's all we've got," said Sørensen. He tapped his finger on his notepad. "What do we know about this Robert Guldbjerg, who now owns this racket alone?"

Milo made a quick search on the Internet, and clicked on the first result. The link took him to a local newspaper site and the headline FITNESS KING FROM SON. The article was eight years old and illustrated with a picture of a suntanned man with enormous muscles and a minimal bathing suit, flexing his biceps for the photographer.

"I'll bet a year's salary that the beauty products these boys imported from Asia were far from creams and shampoos," said Milo.

38

Oriana was given a cell to rest in while Sørensen and Milo set the paper mill in motion. Arrest orders were issued for the persons named in the Downtown Gang who had been present during the killing of Tormod Tollefsen, in addition to search orders on Asian Beauty Import.

The raid in Hølen and Son would also be coordinated with local police.

It was almost six when everything was ready.

"Now let's go," said Sørensen.

"I'll take my own car. I have to drop Oriana off first," Milo replied.

"Great. See you at the meeting place."

Milo had briefly considered driving her home to his apartment, but realized that might be too risky. Another alternative was to call Sunniva, but there were limits for dramatic debuts as his new half sister. So he ended up booking a room at the Grand Hotel for her.

She was sleeping heavily in a kind of fetal position, but with a facial expression as if she had a stomachache. He tapped her shoulder carefully, and she woke up with a little twitch and looked at him in confusion.

He gave her a few moments before they went down to the car, which was in the basement. Shortly after, they drove out of the police station garage in the direction of central Oslo and the Grand. On the way he called Temoor.

"This is Temoor."

His voice sounded energetic over the speaker in the car.

"It's Milo. I'll be out for a few hours now, but I wondered if you've found anything on the mobile traces around the kidnapping."

"Haven't worked on anything else today. Was actually just about to call you. Hold on a moment while I finish keyboarding."

Milo turned left toward the bus terminal when he came to Grønland, and they heard Temoor tapping in the background. They passed the Postgiro building and continued toward the Vaterland Tunnel.

"There we go," Temoor began.

"What have you got?"

"Well, the girl apparently had the phone on when they picked her up at St. Hanshaugen, and I can follow her from a base station there and over to the Regjering block and further east. The last signal is from the base station right below the Sjømann School. You know, the one that's on the way up toward the Ekeberg restaurant. The main thruway passes right below this base station in and out of Oslo on the east side. Either north toward Gardermoen or south toward Moss. The signal from the phone has come from the same spot for almost a full day."

"They must have taken the phone away from her and discarded it," Milo replied.

Beside him Oriana sat chewing on her knuckles.

"Most likely, yes," Temoor said. "But what I did was to look at the dataset from the telecom companies of which SIM cards were active at the same place. In the same time period."

"There must be thousands?"

"In the ten-minute period I concentrated on there were, let's see, 21,458 active SIM cards there."

"Fuck!"

"Relax. I knew I didn't have time to go over all of them, so I cross-checked against the phone numbers on a number of our usual suspects, you might say. And I found a couple that are extremely interesting. At the same time and place the phones of both Farak and Mohammat Ambhalajad were active."

"The twins," said Milo.

"Exactly. And I can trace both back to St. Hanshaugen, where the signals to the girl's phone started."

"Brilliant, Temoor!"

"Yes, yes, relax, there's more."

"Of course," said Milo.

Because while Olena's phone could be traced no farther than to the foot of Ekebergåsen, you could follow the twins electronically down Mosseveien.

"Toward Son!" Oriana exclaimed.

"Who was that?" asked Temoor.

"Oriana is with me in the car. The big sister," Milo explained.

"I see. But no, not Son. Not that far."

"Where then?" asked Milo.

But he already knew the answer.

For the third time in a week he stopped outside the storage building. The closest streetlamp was out of order, and the nearest source of light was from the windows of the gym a little farther away. But that was not where Milo intended to go.

Two times he had called Sørensen, but came straight to voice mail. Finally he sent a text.

Oriana was still in the passenger seat. She had flatly refused to get off at the Grand when she understood what was going on.

"I'm coming with you," she said, and there was no time to discuss it.

Milo got out of the car and looked around. There were no other cars or people in the vicinity. He walked quickly up to the loading gate and the alarm panel. Through the dirty windows in the gate he could see that the parking area inside was empty.

Quickly in and quickly out, he thought as he entered the simple code he had seen the managing director of Quick Storage use a few days earlier.

The gate opened with the customary metallic creaking and moved slowly upward. Milo jogged back to the car and cast a glance at Oriana.

Fear and expectation were written on her face, and he could see she had her hands folded on her lap. As if in silent prayer.

Deep down Milo was doing the same. As he put the car in gear and they rolled in through the gate, he said an Our Father and a Hail Mary, but did not cross himself to avoid making Oriana even more worried than she already was. She appeared to be stressed to the utmost.

He parked and jumped out of the car.

"We have to be quick," he said to her over the roof of the car, then went behind and opened the trunk.

He tossed aside a bag of empty bottles he had not had time to redeem, in search of a suitable tool. He needed a bolt cutter, but it was at home in his apartment along with the rest of his tools. A hammer was next on his wish list, but he was not in the habit of keeping one in the car either.

He pulled up the floor of the trunk, pulling out warning

triangles and finally found the lug wrench for changing tires. He weighed it in his hand, and felt the cold metal against his skin. It would have to do.

He started almost running toward the corridor and slapped his hand on the switch so that the fluorescent lights started blinking to life. A few days earlier he had passed through the same corridor, along the same orange compartment doors, in the company of Sørensen and the Follo police. Only to find a compartment that had recently been emptied.

He felt his heart pounding over what he expected to find. He was sure that Banno and his people knew they had searched the compartment the week before, and did not expect the police to come back a second time.

This time the compartment won't be empty, he thought.

The question was whether they were too late.

They stopped in front of the compartment, and he immediately saw there was a new padlock in place. He started hammering it loose with the lug wrench.

The sound of metal against metal filled the corridor, and Oriana held her hands to her ears.

The first blows deformed the padlock, but it did not give way. He felt how the blows, combined with the steadily growing sense that every second counted, made him warm and sweaty.

He continued hitting. With each blow he found a rhythm, as he usually did when he hammered away on the boxing bag at home, and he concentrated on hitting as cleanly as possible where the iron loop went into the lock housing.

With a sharp crack it broke, and the pieces fell down on the concrete.

He dropped the lug wrench and took hold of the handle to the door, pushing the lock to one side and opening the compartment door in one quick motion. In the first few seconds his eyes had trouble adjusting to the darkness inside.

An odor of urine, sweat and feces struck them.

"Olena!" Oriana called, forcing herself past him.

She was in the far corner, with duct tape over her mouth and around her hands and feet—lifeless.

"Olena!" Oriana repeated, along with a series of words he did not understand.

She got down on her knees bent over her little sister, crying while she talked. Milo crouched down beside her, and felt for a pulse.

"She's alive," he said to Oriana.

They released her from the tape, and gave her a few light taps on the cheek. Slowly she opened her eyes and stared vacantly at them.

Oriana continued talking to her in their native language while she rocked her in her arms.

Milo looked at his watch. They had been there five minutes, and he wanted to get out as quickly as possible. He tapped Oriana on the shoulder.

"We've got to get out," he said.

She nodded and let him pick up Olena's small body.

She was light, and he jogged down the corridor with her in his arms while Oriana followed behind.

They were approaching the end of the corridor when they heard the sound of the gate opening.

He turned abruptly to the right, into the storage labyrinth to an unlit corridor that also led to the parking area.

With quiet steps he moved along the wall and stopped by the corner, where he set Olena down on the concrete floor. He signaled for them to be quiet, and took a quick look around the corner in the direction of his little Fiat. A truck had just parked farther back, so that it partly blocked the loading gate, and Banno and the twins got out.

He pulled his head back, while he thought through the situation. Less than thirty meters away he could hear Banno's voice.

"Get her quick! I'll watch this little punk car."

Milo quickly looked around the corner again, and saw the twins trotting toward the corridor they had just been in, while Banno remained standing with his arms crossed, leaning against Milo's car.

He knew that in less than two minutes the twins would discover that the compartment was empty. Then it would be too late.

He could not manage all three.

But he could manage Banno.

"Can you carry her?" he whispered to Oriana.

She nodded.

"Give me a few meters head start. Then you follow, and get her in the car as fast as you can."

She nodded again, carefully picking her little sister up from the floor.

Milo took out the car key and held it ready in his hand. He cursed to himself that he had not brought the lug wrench. He would have felt more secure with a club in his hand.

He crossed himself, crouched down and started running quickly toward the Fiat.

Five meters behind Oriana followed with Olena in her arms.

Banno turned around. His surprised expression quickly turned into a smile, and he pushed away from the car.

"I knew we'd meet again," he said, walking toward Milo.

Milo did not answer, but held his gaze. He knew that Banno

would aim right for his body and then squeeze, strike or head-butt the shit out of him. At the same time he was thinking about what his jujitsu instructor had once said about the training:

Everyone has a weak point.

The fact was that juicer boys had two weak points. One was lack of speed. Heavy muscle mass does not move quickly. The other was the joints, which were usually worn after years of heavy strain.

Milo knew he had to fake out Banno. Not too soon, so that he could adjust course. But not too late either, so that he was able to land one of his crushing blows.

He walked quickly toward Banno, who flexed his muscles and rolled his head calmly from side to side. As he raised his arms to a guard, Milo also made himself ready.

There was only one meter between them when he feinted with his upper body to the left. He saw the blow come immediately. With lightning speed Milo changed direction and made a quick side movement to the right, and in the same motion extended a kick with all his strength. As if he was going to kick a ball as far as he could.

He felt Banno's fist miss his eye, but nonetheless streak past his cheek hard enough to scrape the skin from his jaw to his ear.

At the same time Milo located a kick right in his knee, and Banno howled in pain and went down on his knees on the concrete.

Oriana came running behind Milo, and as he pressed on the car key and unlocked it, she tore open the door and started easing Olena into the backseat.

Milo doled out another kick while Banno was still down, before he rounded the hood and heaved himself into the driver's seat and put the car in reverse. He floored it backwards, grazed the truck and thundered into the freight door. It shook on its hinges and in the rearview mirror he saw the window-panes in the gate shatter.

But he did not make it through.

He drove forward again, and Banno came toward him with an iron pipe that he used to strike the window on the passenger side. A shower of glass poured in over Oriana, who threw her-self toward Milo. Milo leaned over the steering wheel and turned away. Then he put the car in reverse and accelerated again.

He felt the car roll over Banno's foot and heard him howl, but kept his eyes fixed on the freight door behind him.

For the second time he backed into it with a crash, and now it was starting to give way.

But he did not get out this time either.

The lowest part of the gate was now bent out, but not enough.

He had to hit the gate one more time, at higher speed. And to do that he had to turn the car to make optimal use of the horsepower.

As he turned his head, the twins came rushing down the stairs, one of them with a handgun pointed toward the car. Glass shattered, and Milo had no more time to think.

He accelerated, and the car spurted forward. He struck a trash can that was thrown to the side, navigated his way into one of the corridors to the left of the one the twins had just come out of, and which they were now blocking.

The car was slightly more than a meter and a half wide, and he sincerely hoped the corridor was no narrower than that.

The Fiat sped up, and as it slipped into the corridor, both side mirrors were torn off and sparks sprayed where the car scraped along the compartment doors.

For a moment he feared they were going to get stuck, but

they moved quickly ahead, and at the end of the long corridor came out onto a larger open area where there were several trailers.

Oriana was clinging to the car door, while Olena was lying in the backseat, weeping.

In four or five seconds he turned the little car with the powerful engine. His left arm worked the steering wheel frantically while he shifted back and forth between reverse and first gear with his right hand.

The car was now turned the right way, and he let the engine idle. At any moment they would come toward him.

He could not count on Sørensen and the cavalry coming to his rescue.

Milo peered toward the corridor, which was lit up by the car lights. Along both walls there were black stripes of metallic paint from the car. The walls and compartment doors had serious dents.

But he saw no one coming on foot.

Quickly he looked around. Could they be coming another way?

He did not like just sitting there in the car. The feeling of standing wide open to attack made his heart pound even harder.

The only thing clear to him was that he only had one try left.

He looked at Oriana, who was shaking beside him.

"Put on the seat belt. And hold on tight."

He turned toward Olena in the backseat. She was in a fetal position and looked at him in terror.

"Lay down on the floor," he ordered her.

Slowly she crept into place behind the front seats.

He put the car in gear and rolled down the corridor. When there was only a meter or two left, he stepped on the gas. A moment later they were out of the corridor, and he saw the almost ruined freight door fifteen meters ahead—partly blocked by the truck.

There the three men had taken position. All with pistols raised.

The speedometer showed almost fifty kilometers per hour, and it was sink or swim. They rounded the truck, and Milo aimed at the area on the freight door where he had already done the most damage, and thundered into it.

With a crash the gate loosened on one side, and the car slipped out while all the lights and remaining glass shattered. A dog owner got the shock of his life and jumped aside as the car swerved out on the road.

Milo found second gear, accelerated and quickly shifted up to third and disappeared from the Unitor building.

"Fuckin' hell!" he said out loud to himself.

The front window was smashed in, and the side mirror was gone. He turned around to see if anyone was following, but behind them there was only darkness.

Beside him Oriana turned toward Olena in the backseat and stroked her arm.

It was only when he felt the chilly evening wind blow through the broken windows that he noticed that he was bleeding from a gunshot wound in the shoulder.

THURSDAY

39

Milo sat twirling an empty snuffbox in one hand as Sørensen came tramping in.

"You almost look worse than your little toy car," he said.

Sørensen's shirt was coming untucked, and he was balancing a coffee cup, two snuffboxes, a pack of cigarettes and a lighter on top of a notebook.

He looked at Milo, who had his left arm in a sling and a compression bandage on his cheek where Banno's fist had torn a gash in his skin.

On the right side of his throat was a bandage where pieces from the smashed car window had peppered his skin.

"Oriana and the little sister?" Sørensen asked as he sat down with a tired groan behind his desk.

"Still at the hospital. For observation. A patrol is keeping an eye out."

Sørensen nodded in acknowledgment and glanced at the clock, which said two in the morning.

"Tell me what happened," he said.

In brief terms Milo went through the sequence of events. The electronic traces Temoor had found. Olena in the compartment in the storage building. The escape in the car.

He did not need to spice up the story. The drama was written in his bandages.

"Good, Milo. Bloody well done."

"And you? How have you been?"

"Good. It was absolutely no wild-goose chase. I'm coming straight from questioning with Guldbjerg now. He put all the cards on the table at once, and we've confiscated evidence in the office space that turned out to be a production site for dope."

"Steroids?"

"Yep. They imported the various ingredients from Asia, and cooked it together themselves."

The first few years they had collaborated with several members of what later became the Downtown Gang. But then the Pakistani partners decided to use their own contacts in India and Pakistan, and smuggle finished products instead.

"The Pakistanis thought it was lower risk because the products are purer, and they agreed to share the market between them," Sørensen continued.

"But something went wrong," said Milo.

"Or someone got greedy. Guldbjerg and Henriksen started supplying parts of the market in Oslo. Undercut the Pakistanis in price. That led to a major confrontation."

"What about Tormod Tollefsen in the middle of all this?"

Sørensen shook his head.

"Poor kid. He was in the wrong place at the wrong time. Guldbjerg remembers that Henriksen 'had problems with a student he had tried to talk into buying steroids,' but that he thought

he had it under control. It seems as if Henriksen found custom-
ers among his middle-school students. Actually, he had to leave
his position at a school in Son because of complaints from parents."

"And yet he got another job at a different school," said Milo.

"Yes. I called the rector at Ingieråsen School just after midnight. She confirmed that they never checked Henriksen's
references properly. She said something like, they had so little
time, and that he could start on short notice."

Milo leaned forward toward Sørensen's cigarette pack
and fired up a smoke. The nicotine made him dizzy, as if his
body were coming in for a landing. But his thoughts were still
whirling.

"The worst thing is that she also confirmed that the school
administration had discussed Henriksen, but that they didn't
get around to doing anything before the killings."

Milo tapped a little ash into an empty coffee cup.

"But they didn't tell you this two years ago?"

Sørensen shook his head.

"They didn't want to malign a dead man, she said."

"Are you fucking kidding me?" Milo said, shaking his head.

"Instead they've maligned a dead boy. I informed her that
we'll investigate her for obstruction of justice."

"Good."

"And in the offices of Guldbjerg's company we found lists
of names of everyone from paid customs officers to middlemen
and users. Droves of people are being hauled in while we're sitting here."

"Very good," said Milo.

He put out the cigarette and got up. His body ached, and the
effect of the pain relievers was starting to wear off.

"Benedetti called a few hours ago," he said.

"Okay, what did he say?"

"Salvatore held out for a few hours and flatly denied it, even if he couldn't come up with a decent alibi. But when they confronted him with the fact that they had found strands of light hair on a suit coat at his home, the same suit coat he had on when he was caught by the video camera a few hours before the murder, he threw in his cards. The strands of hair are now being checked against Ingrid Tollefsen's DNA."

"Very good. In a way it's good it went that way. She was killed in Rome, Italian police arrested the killer, and he'll be tried before an Italian court," said Sørensen.

He stood up too, and held his hand out toward Milo.

"Congratulations. Two homicides cleared up in barely two weeks."

Milo took his hand, but did not say anything.

"You don't seem especially satisfied, Milo."

"I don't know. Banno is still at large. The twins too . . ."

"They won't get far. Believe me. We'll have them soon."

". . . and I'm struggling with the motive for Salvatore."

"What do you mean?"

"Why did he kill Ingrid?"

"Presumably because they had a relationship. Because she threatened to expose him to his wife."

Milo shook his head.

"I can't get that to add up. An affair. He's not the first Italian man with a relationship on the side, and he'll hardly be the last."

Sørensen shrugged his shoulders.

"I'm sure you know that better than me. What we do know is that there was a relationship between them. We know they had contact. We know that Ingrid threatened to tell his wife. And we know that he has confessed."

"But what about the fact that she wanted to talk with the ethics director? It irritates me that we haven't got hold of him. It sounds like he's been moved to a new position in the Forum group, off somewhere in Vietnam."

Sørensen indulged himself in two pouches of snuff.

"Milo, we have two homicides cleared up. Now I'm going home and sleep for a few hours, and you should too."

They separated at the elevator, and Milo took it alone down to the quiet garage. On the way he checked his e-mail, and swallowed when he saw the message from Kathrin.

From: Andersson, Kathrin
Subject: What happened?
To: Cavalli, Milo

Dearest Milo.

I have thought and thought about what really happened when you disappeared from the restaurant in New York, since you don't answer my text messages. I've replayed the conversations, interpreted what you said. But it didn't give me any explanation.

But then suddenly I think I understood. You must have seen my phone ring when I was away. You must have seen the name, and you must have interpreted it all in the worst sense.

I made some discreet inquiries with Forum afterward and realized then that you've been investigating the company.

Regardless of what you think about me, I simply must tell you this:

I liked you very much.

I wanted to get better acquainted with you.

I didn't know that you were investigating Forum.

Your name never came up in conversations with them.

I've worked for them and given advice in connection with a potential acquisition.

I would like to see you again.

And if you have any desire to talk to me or, even better, see me, you know where to reach me.

XOX

Kathrin

He felt that he missed her. As much as he missed Theresa.

And he didn't have the energy to call either of them.

He got into the Alfa Romeo he was now driving after wrecking the Fiat, and after the ambulance had picked up Oriana and her little sister. Her bag was on the passenger seat, which she asked him to take care of as she stepped into the ambulance and sat down by her sister's stretcher.

He threw off his topcoat, and the bag fell down on the floor. The contents spread out, and he cursed. He quickly collected her notebook, a tin of lozenges and a bunch of keys and set them back in the bag. Then he leaned down and picked up her phone, and looked at it.

What was it Oriana had said? That it was Ingrid's old phone and something about her paying for service and any apps for it.

He pressed on it and unlocked the keyboard. It was not password protected, and the menu screen appeared.

Ingrid Tollefsen's old phone.

There were at least thirty apps. A Chechen newspaper and a meditation app were side by side with an app for a medical dictionary.

Did this mean that the phone contained both Ingrid's and Oriana's apps? That Ingrid had not deleted the content before Oriana got the phone?

He scanned further and stopped at the Dropbox icon. He quickly pressed it and came into a folder that contained two documents. One of them had the title "Project Verbacom."

He felt his body quiver and his fingers holding the phone began to shake. His thoughts went to the slip of paper they had found in the pill bottle in Rome. The paper with the illegible letters, apart from v-e-r-b-a.

He clicked into the document and quickly skimmed it. He took out his own phone, made a quick search on Google and then called Sørensen.

"What is it?" the chief inspector asked sleepily.

"I went into Oriana's phone, which is Ingrid's old phone. Ingrid's Dropbox is active," he said.

"Huh?"

"Ingrid's Dropbox. I found—"

"What the hell is a Dropbox?" Sørensen asked.

"It's a folder that means you can store documents externally—with the Dropbox app—and then have access to documents from many different devices. For example, your computer, phone, iPad."

"I see."

"There are two documents in her box."

"Which are?"

Milo explained the content, and Sørensen listened silently. At last he said, "So that was what she meant by the letters on the scrap of paper. Are you quite sure these documents are genuine?"

"Absolutely," Milo replied.

"Well, that does change things a little."

"I just googled him, and saw that he's in Oslo now. He's going to give a lecture at a conference at the School of Economics BI tomorrow. Or today, that is. In a few hours."

"We'll have to talk with the assistant chief of police," said Sørensen.

Agathe Rodin was in civilian clothes and not happy to be wakened in the middle of the night. She sat with her arms crossed without taking off her coat.

When Milo showed her the printout of the two documents he had found in Ingrid Tollefsen's Dropbox folder, she sighed and looked at them with a heavy gaze.

"This is extremely well done," she began.

"But?" asked Sørensen.

"But it won't hold for a conviction."

Milo leaped up from the chair.

"We've established the motive! We have the whole sequence of events!" he shouted.

Rodin did not seem bothered by the outburst, but got up quietly and patted him on his healthy shoulder.

"I know that. But it won't hold up in court," she said, heading for the door.

"But can we bring him in for questioning?" said Milo.

She turned around at the door.

"Bring him in. Make him sweat. But you're not arresting him."

She turned and disappeared, and neither of them said anything before the sound of her high heels had died away.

"If we don't manage to convict him within the legal system, we should make sure he gets his judgment outside it anyway," said Milo doggedly.

He took out his phone and looked up Ada Hauge's number. He had promised to tell the *Klassekampen* journalist if there was any new information.

The murder of Ingrid will be fully explained at ten o'clock this morning. School of Economics BI. The main auditorium, he wrote.

"What do you intend to do?" asked Sørensen.

"I'm going to humiliate him," answered Milo.

"I'll be there. But you understand that there will be disciplinary action against us if you do anything outside regulations?"

"It will be worth it," answered Milo.

40

The auditorium was packed with students and staff.

It was almost ten, and Milo had been there an hour for the final preparations. Sørensen had positioned himself at the far end of the third row.

Milo himself sat in the middle row, toward the center aisle.

The double door to the right of the podium opened up, and a group of five men hurried in. Milo recognized both the communications director for Forum Healthcare and the Norwegian director, Thomas Veivåg.

But it was the man in the middle everyone had come to see and hear. He greeted several of the professors, and one of them took the microphone.

"It's very gratifying to see so many here today. Especially because we have such an important topic on the agenda. Namely, how the forces in the business community join with society in general. And there are few industries in the world where this is clearer than in the pharmaceutical industry. For that reason it is my great pleasure to introduce Kenneth D'Marco, head of one of the world's most innovative companies, Forum Healthcare."

The audience applauded, and D'Marco took the podium smiling. He shook the hand of the professor who had just introduced him again, and on the big screen behind him the PowerPoint presentation came into view:

SHAREHOLDER VALUE—CORPORATE SOCIAL RESPONSIBILITY
HOW BUSINESS CAN MAKE A DIFFERENCE

By Kenneth D'Marco

CEO & PRESIDENT, FORUM HEALTHCARE

BI NORWEGIAN SCHOOL OF ECONOMICS

"Thank you." He held his hands out to the side, almost like a president trying to dampen the applause. "I have truly looked forward to this meeting with you, where I will tell you how at Forum Healthcare we work every single day on projects that have direct impact on people's everyday lives. Not only in the U.S. or here in Norway, but all over the world."

He paused and pressed the wireless remote control, and the screen behind him was filled by a picture of a little boy.

"But first of all I want to share a little story with you. This is Nathan. The cutest little rascal in the world at age five, but with a serious heart defect."

D'Marco took a sip of water before he continued to talk about how Nathan needed medications that stabilized his heart rhythm, even after necessary surgical interventions had been done.

"Nathan needs medicine every single day. Otherwise he will die."

Then there was a stage pause.

"And he gets medicine. The pills he takes are called Betratex and were developed by our researchers twelve years ago. And that is why Nathan is living an almost normal life today."

Behind him the image changed, and the gathering saw Nathan hitting a baseball with his dad, bicycling with friends and cuddling with his little sister.

"And it's stories like this that make me proud of going to work every single day. Yes, we deliver results to our shareholders. But . . . we also help to keep people like little Nathan alive."

Kenneth D'Marco spoke quietly and pounded in the message. Not once did he check the screen behind him. With a self-confidence only American top executives and politicians have, he mixed in personal stories and reinforced the message with images and text on the big screen.

Along the way he took off his jacket, a little later he rolled up his shirtsleeves Obama-style and after forty-five minutes he was done.

The applause was powerful, and D'Marco showed the assembly his broadest smile.

The professor who had introduced him came up to the podium, thanked him and took out a microphone.

"Thanks for an extremely inspiring talk. We have reserved time for questions, so just raise your hands. But please don't ask the question until you've been given the microphone by one of our assistants in the hall. Both the lecture and this question-and-answer session are being sent on webcast, so it will be good if those who are following us online also hear the questions in their entirety."

A woman in the fourth row raised her hand, and got a

microphone. She wanted to know more about the company's social projects and donations, and what D'Marco considered their most important contribution to society: innovation or direct financial support to nonprofit organizations and projects?

The next question was from a young man. He wanted to learn more about the Forum director's predictions for investments in research in the next ten years, and if he thought publicly funded research was obsolete.

D'Marco answered calmly and self-confidently and appeared to enjoy the situation. The next few questions were about geography and future growth areas, and gradually there were fewer who raised their hands and asked to speak.

As the professor down on the podium let his gaze sweep across the assembly again, Milo raised his hand high and caught his attention.

"Yes, we have a question up there in the middle."

Milo got a microphone from the technical staff and stood up. Several in the assembly turned around, D'Marco directed his gaze attentively toward him and noted the arm in a sling and the bandaged neck and chin.

"Goodness, have you been in an accident? I hope you've been given some adequate pain relievers. If not I have some tablets I can recommend," said the American top executive.

The audience chuckled, and Milo smiled back.

"Just a work accident. First of all, thanks for an extremely interesting lecture," he said.

The Forum head nodded contentedly.

"My question concerns the conflict of interest between companies listed on the stock exchange and the society in which the companies operate," Milo began.

"One moment, before you continue: What conflict of interest are you talking about?" D'Marco asked from the podium.

Milo smiled contentedly that the head of Forum had let himself be provoked into asking a counterquestion. He wanted to produce an exchange that made it natural for him to keep the microphone as long as possible.

"I'm thinking about publicly traded companies' goal of maximizing shareholder value, that is, making the greatest possible profit, versus society's need to maximize the benefit and well-being of its inhabitants."

D'Marco shook his head.

"There is no conflict of interest in that."

"Isn't there?"

Milo looked at him with surprise.

"That's exactly what I've been talking about! About the coinciding interests between business and society."

"Yes, I heard that—"

"But you don't believe what I've said?" D'Marco interrupted.

"I don't mean to be rude . . ." said Milo.

"It only appears that way."

For the second time the Forum head interrupted him, and slightly nervous laughter spread in the hall. Several of the students turned around to look at this suit-clad, bandaged man who was making a fool of himself in front of the head of one of the world's biggest companies.

It was time for Milo to tighten his hold.

"If that's so I'm sorry, but a company like Forum doesn't have unlimited resources?"

Milo stopped and waited for a response.

"Of course not," was the answer from the podium.

"And therefore you can't produce all the medicines you want to. You have to prioritize, right?"

Once again, Milo stopped.

D'Marco replied reluctantly, clearly dissatisfied that Milo was controlling the exchange.

"That's correct. We have to prioritize."

"Exactly. And this is my question: What does Forum Healthcare consider important when the company is going to prioritize which medicines you will produce and which you won't produce? Is it the individual product's contribution to profit margin? Or the individual product's contribution to society?"

There was silence. The laughter was gone, and those who were looking at Milo quickly turned their heads toward the podium and Kenneth D'Marco.

And the top executive at Forum waited just a few seconds too long to reply for the answer to sound sufficiently self-confident.

"It would be a combination of both viewpoints. A holistic assessment," he answered.

"Ah, I understand. That sounds reasonable. So when there is a shortage of certain types of child vaccines while at the same time the market is overflowing with potency pills for men, for example, that has nothing to do with the fact that child vaccines are low-margin products, while potency pills on the other hand are among the most lucrative you can produce? You have simply made, what was it you called it, a holistic assessment?"

D'Marco put his hands behind his back and was rocking impatiently on his toes.

"That's a contrived problem. We don't manufacture potency pills," he said.

"But you do produce vaccines?" Milo asked mildly.

The man at the podium sighed in resignation.

"No."

Milo could hear murmuring in the hall, and he saw D'Marco whisper something to the professor, who then raised the microphone to his mouth.

"Now we're not going to have a general debate on pharmaceuticals here, and it's not really right to ask Mr. D'Marco to defend an entire industry. He is here to answer questions about Forum Healthcare and not other companies. So if there is anyone who has a question about—"

"I have a question that is directly about Forum Healthcare. Only one. I promise," Milo said loudly.

They looked at him as if he was the meeting participant from hell, and D'Marco threw his hands out in a gesture of resignation.

"Thanks. I wonder why you stopped Verbacom?"

In the first row he saw the communications director and the Norwegian managing director turn around. And he saw that they recognized him.

"We don't have a product by that name," D'Marco answered.

"No, I know that. I'm not talking about a product by that name. I'm talking about the Verbacom project that was discontinued two months ago."

The Forum head looked at his colleagues in the first row and then at Milo.

"Tell me, who are you really?"

"Oh, sorry, did I forget to introduce myself? I'm Milo Cavalli. From the Norwegian police. I am investigating the murder of one of your employees, Ingrid Tollefsen, who was killed in a hotel room in Rome just over two weeks ago. In the past week I've tried to get information from Forum Healthcare, but your colleagues have effectively refused me that, and they also failed to report that Tollefsen had sounded an internal warning about manipulation of research results."

D'Marco went over and talked with the professor and then turned to Milo.

"It is not appropriate for me to comment on this in public, and I suggest that we discuss this—"

"Let him ask his questions!"

A young girl a few rows ahead of him was standing halfway up in her seat. Her call was followed up by others in the hall, who also wanted to hear more.

"Yes, let's hear what he has to say!"

In the first row the plainclothes policemen got up and went over to the exit doors.

"Those who are now guarding the door are plainclothes police. You will be taken in for questioning immediately after this. But I would like to return to the Verbacom project. And I want to remind you that this entire session is being sent on web-cast. In other words, you're live on the air, D'Marco," said Milo.

He turned toward the rest of the hall and smiled innocently.

"You obviously aren't familiar with the project I'm talking about, but I can say in brief that this was a project in Forum Healthcare's Oslo division, where research was being done on how to repair so-called insulin resistance."

Milo explained briefly that lack of insulin leads to diabetes, but that there was also a group of diabetes patients who were insulin-resistant. At the research department in Oslo a method had been developed that appeared to reverse this.

"You could potentially have a product that cured diabetes for a large group of patients," he said, turning toward the podium again. "The test results from Oslo were extremely positive, and a prototype was developed that would be tested in the U.S. What happened there, D'Marco?"

The top executive threw his arms out again.

"I am not involved in every research project in our company. Hundreds of projects are going on."

"We're talking about a product that potentially can cure those who suffer from insulin resistance! That is groundbreaking! There is Nobel potential in it! Do you really mean you haven't heard about it?"

But D'Marco did not answer.

Milo exhaled dejectedly into the microphone to demonstrate how foolish he thought the man at the podium was.

"Then I'll have to explain what happened. Because isn't it true that the provisional test results in the U.S. were also positive?"

Still no answer.

Milo turned around toward the rest of the assembly.

"Actually, the results were so good that internally in Forum Healthcare an alarm was sounded. The problem was, namely, that the company also produces insulin. Forum has one of the leading insulin brands on the market, which contributes billions in profit every single year. A new product which the Verbacom project was in the process of working out would reduce sales of insulin significantly. And not only that, it would not produce repeat sales. People who are cured buy very little medicine."

He turned toward the podium again.

"Because isn't it so, D'Marco, that the most lucrative thing for a pharmaceutical company is to relieve, not cure?"

Up on the podium the Forum executive had been joined by the communications director, and neither of them answered Milo's rhetorical question.

"Your second in command at Forum ordered those who tested this new product, a company called Medical Research, to come back with poor results. They did that by reducing the dosage for the test subjects, so that the positive effect was absent. Ingrid Tollefsen discovered this and warned the company's ethics director. Two days later he was transferred to Vietnam so that he was unable to meet her. Instead one of the heads of Medical Research marched up to her hotel room in Rome, drugged her and strangled her."

D'Marco shook his head.

"You cannot blame me or Forum for what an insane man has done!" he shouted.

"That will be up to the prosecutors to decide. But what I can do here and now, is to blame you for your values," Milo answered.

"There is nothing wrong with my values."

"No? Do you recall what your answer was when the Forum research director argued for increased financial support for the Verbacom project, while the vice managing director argued to abandon the project?"

There was almost complete silence in the hall. For several seconds the humming of the ventilation system was all that could be heard.

Milo ran his hand through his hair. That was the signal to the technician at the back of the hall. The one who'd had a thousand-kroner bill discreetly slipped into his hand that morning when only he and Milo were there.

On the screen behind D'Marco the PowerPoint presentation was replaced by a screen image showing the e-mail that had been stored in Ingrid Tollefsen's Dropbox. But the Forum head had his eyes fixed on Milo, and did not realize what was happening on the wall behind him.

A few seconds passed, and you could hear a gasp through the assembly.

From: D'Marco, Kenneth
Subject: Project Verbacom
To: Oliver Trimonti, Larry Mortensen

Gentlemen,
I've reviewed the notes from both of you.

Let it be completely clear that we are in the business of relief—not healing. We will leave that to the Church and the healers.

What the Oslo department has produced is impressive, but we must not forget that the patients' pain is our own gain.

Kenneth

" 'The patients' pain is our own gain,' you wrote."

Milo spoke clearly and calmly.

"That's not what I wrote!"

"No?"

The murmur in the assembly increased in strength, and some were pointing at the wall. D'Marco quickly turned around and looked right at his own e-mail, blown up on the white screen.

Milo cleared his throat gently into the microphone.

"What is ironic about this case . . . what is almost grotesque . . . is that Ingrid Tollefsen had diabetes. She was dependent on exactly those tablets you produce, and she worked on the pioneering research project that could have cured her. And the last thing she did, before she was killed, do you know what that was? It was to throw a little bottle of diabetes medicine down into the courtyard at the hotel. That was her signal, her greeting or code, if you will."

He paused for the final question.

"So my question was actually: What kind of holistic assessment—because that was what you called it, right?—was behind the decision not to develop a product that could have cured insulin resistance?"

Not a single breath could be heard in the whole auditorium.

"But something tells me you don't want to answer that," Milo concluded and sat down, knowing full well that the entire session would be on YouTube in less than an hour.

41

Milo had seen his father smoke on only two occasions. The first time was when they celebrated the eightieth birthday of Antonio Cavalli. The grandfather of Milo and father-in-law of Endre Thorkildsen.

The two had sat on the veranda on Sardinia, each sucking on a cigar, each sipping a drink. Milo recalled that he had reacted to that. Not that his father was smoking a cigar, but rather the fellowship between his father and grandfather. He always thought his father was an odd duck in the family gatherings in Italy.

The second time he saw his father smoke was when Milo arrived at the psychiatric clinic after they found his mother dead. His father was standing by the entry sucking doggedly on a cigarette, his face pale.

So on two occasions he had seen his father smoke. One happy and one unhappy occasion. He assumed it was not because his father was in a good mood that he was now inhaling smoke out on the veranda.

When he caught sight of Milo, he flipped the cigarette in an arc toward the bushes and came toward him.

"Emil," he said in a husky voice, pulling his son carefully to him so as not to press on the injured shoulder.

Milo let himself be hugged.

He could not remember the last time his father had held him that way. Two days of beard growth scratched against him.

Slowly Endre Thorkildsen released his hold and pushed Milo away to be able to look at him.

"I saw the video clip from BI. What a case! How's your shoulder doing?"

"It aches, but it's fine," Milo replied.

Endre Thorkildsen led his son into the living room, and they each sat down in an armchair.

"Drink?" his father asked.

Milo shook his head. He was worn out and needed to sleep. But first there were things he wanted to know. He met his father's gaze.

"You have something to tell me, right?"

His father sighed heavily while he wrung his hands. As if he was washing them.

"I promised myself never to talk with you about this," he answered.

Milo did not say anything and his father continued.

"I understand that Sunniva was a surprise to you. Or a shock—"

"It wasn't a shock. Sunniva is great. I like her. But I don't like the way you've behaved. But that's not what I want to talk about. There's this shipwreck that—"

"I can understand your frustration . . ."

"I see."

". . . and I understand that you are still going to judge me harshly if you don't know the whole story."

"The whole story? What do you mean? You betrayed Mother. Had a child out of wedlock. Behind her back. What more do I need to know?"

His father struck his palms against his knees and got up.

"I think I'll have that drink anyway," he said, going over to the liquor cabinet.

He poured gin over ice cubes until the glass was almost half full and topped it with tonic. On his way back to the chair he drank half the glass in one gulp.

"Whether you like it or not, the two of us are connected. I know you had a stronger bond with your mother . . ."

Milo made no sign of protesting.

". . . but it's the two of us who are left. The two of us, and Sunniva."

"Keep her out of this," said Milo, feeling a flush of irritation rise above his shirt collar, toward the roots of his hair.

"Fine. I'll tell you. Because you're the one who's asking. Then we'll see how it works out."

Milo looked at him uncomprehendingly.

"And Emil, I simply want to underscore that every word is true. I have no reason to lie to you."

"But talk then, damn it!"

His father emptied the rest of the drink, set aside the empty glass and resumed his hand-washing movement.

"You've heard the story many times, about how your mother and I met, right?"

Milo nodded.

"You were studying in Rome, but you met in the summer in Sardinia," he answered.

"The summer of 1977. That's right."

His father recounted briefly the story Milo knew so well. About the encounter through a common acquaintance. The first dinner at home with *nonna* and *nonno*, grandmother and grandfather. And about how he and Maria Cavalli had also met in Paris late that summer.

"It happened so fast. A month and a half later she was pregnant, and three months later we were married," his father said.

Milo shrugged his shoulders.

"I know all that," he said.

The room was quiet. They could almost hear the sound of the ice cubes melting in the glass. He could see his father breathing deeply in and out while he stared at a spot on the wall. Then he began to speak.

"That whole summer your mother was grieving, Emil.

"And the grief had started on May twenty-third of that year. It was just past three in the morning, and the Italian military vessel was en route to Sicily. The crew of one hundred seventeen persons, mostly young men, had been in Lebanon, Egypt and Libya in the course of four weeks at sea. Some of them were career military, others were enlisted youths who saw this as their springboard to a better life. Thirty nautical miles off the coast of Sicily the accident occurred. The explosion must have been powerful and no doubt started somewhere in the engine room. Half the port side was blown open, and in a few minutes the meter-high waves must have torn the hull in two," his father said.

He picked up the empty glass, and the ice cubes clinked as he rotated it, and he stared silently down at them before he continued.

"A single SOS signal had been sent out before the Italian young men went to their watery grave on the bed of the Mediterranean. While their families were peacefully asleep on the mainland. And among the hundred seventeen young men there was a young officer, twenty-six years old. The son of a former admiral, who was one of Italy's most decorated. A young officer who actually dreamed of university studies, but who obeyed his father and tried to follow in his footsteps. A young officer by the name of Luigi Benvolesenza."

"Uncle Luigi?!"

The name of his mother's best friend almost revived him. Had Luigi been on board?

Endre Thorkildsen stood up and made two more drinks. On his way back he handed one glass to Milo, who took it without hesitation.

"Uncle Luigi, yes. He had just gone off watch and changed to civilian clothes. He went to the stern of the ship to have a cigarette before going to bed. What exactly happened could not be said with certainty. Other than that it happened quickly. That cigarette saved his life," his father said thoughtfully, sipping his drink.

The pressure wave from the explosion blew him right into the sea and knocked him out. And because Luigi Benvolesenza was a dutiful, orderly young man, he had his life vest on. And that kept his unconscious body floating.

"While his hundred sixteen comrades disappeared to the seabed, Luigi floated in the waves as the only survivor," his father continued.

Milo thought about what Benedetti had said. That there was one survivor, who had been unable to help clarify what happened.

"I remember hearing that Uncle Luigi had cheated death, but never knew the details," said Milo, partly to his father and partly to himself.

He took a solid gulp of the drink while he thought about his mother's friend and the many visits to him in Rome. There was nothing in the apartment that signaled a military background.

"What happened later? And what did this have to do with Mama?"

His father set down the glass and stroked his beard stubble.

"The explosion did not just knock him unconscious, he also lost his memory," he said. "And as fate would have it he was picked up by some fishermen from Tunisia. They took him back to their village at Sfax, more than a day's journey away, where he was cared for. While Italy was in shock and sorrow at the loss of the young men who were serving the fatherland, and specu- lations about sabotage were running high, Luigi was living iso- lated and with amnesia in a village in Tunisia. With compound fractures in his hip and legs and internal bleeding, it took many months before he came to his senses. And even longer before his memory completely returned. But then it was too late," his father said.

"Too late? What do you mean?"

His father sighed and looked up at the portrait of Milo's mother on the wall. Maria looked lovingly down on them both.

"Luigi was Maria's fiancé," said his father.

The information struck Milo with force.

"Fiancé?"

His father nodded.

"But . . ."

Milo's brain was working under pressure. He scanned his memories. The scenes. The talks. The gatherings. The trips to

Rome. The visits in Uncle Luigi's apartment. His mother's good-
night kiss in bed. The door ajar out to the hallway. The strip of
light that kept the darkness away. Sounds from the living room.
The voices of his mother and Luigi. The giggles. The laughter.
The sobbing. The subdued weeping.

And Milo suddenly knew that his father spoke the truth.

Maria Cavalli and Luigi Benvolesenza had loved each other.

"When did you find this out?" he asked his father.

"As soon as Luigi came back."

Endre Thorkildsen had just brought Maria back with him to
Norway, where everyday life was filled with furnishing a new
apartment, a new job, and waiting for the firstborn. The phone
call from Rome turned everything upside down. After months
as a convalescent, one day Luigi got his memory back. He made
his way to the capital city of Tunis and called his father. And
when he arrived in Rome a few days later, he was met by hundreds of journalists and relatives of his dead military comrades.
He was taken straight to the military hospital for observation
and debriefing, and from there he called his fiancée, whom he
had been told had gotten married to a Norwegian.

"It wasn't easy for any of us," said his father.

"What happened?"

"We jumped on the first flight, and drove straight to the hospital."

He swallowed heavily and breathed jaggedly before he continued.

"And there I was standing and watching Maria be reunited
with the one she loved, who she thought she had lost forever."

"But didn't she love you?"

"Well, yes. In a way she did. She liked me. She liked me a

lot. There's no doubt about that. It was love. But she truly loved Luigi, and perhaps even stronger after he had virtually risen from the dead."

The same evening she started talking about divorce, but before they had even discussed it, Milo's grandfather put his foot down.

Antonio Cavalli was strong in his Catholic faith.

"A Cavalli does not get a divorce! Not even for love," he'd said in a raised voice.

Milo thought about his grandfather and Brenda in the U.S. What was it his grandfather had written to her? "We made a choice."

"Did she really want to divorce you?" he asked his father, who shrugged his shoulders.

"She wanted to be with Luigi."

"What about me? Did she ever talk about having an abortion?"

His heart rate suddenly doubled.

His father looked him in the eyes.

"Never! There was never a word about that. The fact is that you made it possible for her to stay."

"I held her back," said Milo.

"She wanted to be with you. And she loved you more than anyone else on this earth. You know that."

Milo nodded.

"But how—"

"Antonio, your grandfather, was a pragmatic SOB. I've realized that even more after what you said about New York," Endre Thorkildsen interrupted his son.

Because even if divorce was ruled out, infidelity was not

forbidden. And so Maria's life had become like that. Loved by two men. Married to Endre in Oslo. With a relationship with Luigi in Rome.

"She saw him as often as it could be arranged. We found a kind of balance in that. In vacations. Scattered weekends. You were along on most of the trips. Didn't you notice anything, Emil?"

He shook his head.

"Good. I always wondered about that. If you knew, and . . . if you lost respect for me because of it," his father said quietly.

Milo shook his head again as he said, "Of course not, Dad. I was more closely connected to Mama because we were always together. You worked, and—"

"I had to live my life, Emil. In order to manage it at all. I couldn't let my life revolve only around her. Them. Wonder when they were going to meet. Or what she felt," he said with a frankness Milo had never heard from him before.

"But how did you manage to accept that she had another?"

His father smiled and looked up at her portrait.

"Because she was incredible. And because I loved her. She was . . . What was it she always told you to be?"

"Pieno di amore."

"Exactly. Full of love. She was full of love, and it was as if the whole situation multiplied her love. And I got to be part of that. If I had denied her that, I would have lost her," his father said.

For that reason he stopped interrogating her about Luigi and simply accepted that he had to share her with him. Which made her even more grateful and fond of him.

"I accepted, and she made it clear that I was also free to meet others."

"So you got yourself a mistress."

His father shook his head.

"No, I worked. Long days. Thought about other things. Tried to control my feelings. The jealousy."

He paused while he scratched the root of his nose.

"And then I thought that finally she would get tired of him. That she would get it out of her system, so to speak."

"But that didn't happen?"

"She never stopped loving him. And then I met Hanne."

"Hanne?"

"The mother of Sunniva."

And Maria Cavalli reacted with relief. As if it reestablished a balance in the relationship between her and her husband. And when she found out about the pregnancy, she had been crystal clear that he should take care of them financially. And after the birth Maria often bought little presents he could give to Sunniva.

Milo emptied the rest of his drink and shook his head in disbelief.

"This is completely unbelievable, damn it. What a bunch of actors you've been! What a fucking chaos. This is—"

"Not completely ordinary, no. I understand your reaction, but we aren't the first who've been unfaithful. And we had good times too. We loved each other. Respected each other."

Milo again thought about his grandfather and the apartment in New York that no one had known about. He thought about Theresa in Italy. And about Kathrin in London.

His father tried to put on a smile before he continued his story.

"We were doing fine for a long time, but then Luigi got sick. Of course you remember that."

"It was terrible. The way he withered up."

Luigi had gone from being a straight-backed, worldly man of about ninety kilograms to shrink down to half of that, barely a shadow of himself.

"Cancer is a terrible thing," his father said.

There was silence between them. Milo knew that his father was making an effort to get out the next words.

"Seeing Luigi die that way . . . seeing the one you love . . . it crushed her. Took away every spark of life. She was never the same again."

Tears began to run quietly down his cheeks, and he made no attempt to wipe them away.

"I tried everything. The psychologist she was already going to. Other psychologists. Medication. Hospitalization. Nothing helped. It was as if she had decided, and I was unable to stop it . . . I couldn't stop it . . . damn it, I couldn't stop it!"

He put his head in his hands while the tears ran freely. Milo's stomach knotted up. Sorrow, which had been as if in hibernation somewhere in his abdominal region, began to be felt. It was the bad tickling he had talked about with Sunniva. The itching.

"It wasn't your fault, Dad. You couldn't have done anything else. She was sick. She had an illness," he said, noticing that for the first time he believed that completely.

And suddenly he also felt relief.

There were a couple of sobs from his father.

"What was my love weighed against the other one's death?" he said quietly, pausing to breathe. "The one she loved from beginning to end."

They sat in silence for several minutes. At last his father stood up, wiped his cheeks with the back of his hand and took out a small box.

"If you want, you can have this."

"What is it?" asked Milo.

"It's some letters that Luigi wrote to Maria. And a report from the psychologist."

"What is it about our family and boxes full of letters and postcards?" Milo muttered.

He had regained control now, even if his eyes were red.

His father stood up and cleared his throat.

"Sunniva is coming later. We thought about having dinner together. Will you stay, Emil?"

"Gladly, Dad."

42

Rome, February 4, 1978

My dearest Maria,

I am gradually starting to return to everyday life, after a few terrible months. The thought of having lost you was too heavy for me to believe I could bear it. Now the thought that I will still get to see you is what keeps me going. You are the dearest I have ever had—and ever will have.

I have finally talked things over with Father, and he has accepted my desire to no longer pursue a military career. That means I will follow the treatment through the end of May, and continue my input to the investigation report, but as of June I'm a free man! I can't say how relieved I am about this. Right now I am contacting various universities thinking about the fall semester. They are all extremely accommodating, and have made it clear that I am welcome as a student regardless of whether all deadlines are long since past. A person should get something in return for being Italy's only war hero in peacetime! So the way it looks now, I will start literature and philosophy studies in the fall.

But most of the time I think about the two of us. About what we had, and what we could have had. My anger is gone now, and I am completely convinced that we should not defy God's plan. But I am just as convinced that I can't manage a life completely without you. If I can get a bit of you at the very least, a taste of you, I will accept that. I know that it is going to hurt me to think that you are with another, but I am increasingly grateful to have been given the gift of life once again. And we will figure things out.

The last few days I have even thought that it is safer for you in Norway. Even if it must be terribly cold there in the north! I don't know if it's the medication or reality, but I don't always feel safe. It's as if someone is following me. It may of course be that the regiment has extra protection for me that I don't know about, but today I even heard voices on the phone for a few seconds. As if I was being wiretapped (don't say this to anyone! If they find out that I hear voices, I will surely be locked up in a psychiatric hospital!!!).

I didn't get to talk with Endre alone when you were here. But he seemed like a good man. The way he tackled an impossible situation testifies to a strong person. I pray to God that he is also good to you.

In a short time you will be a mother, and I weep with joy that we will have an opportunity to celebrate a new life! I am boundlessly happy to see the little one—and of course you. When you come to Italy next time, I will be a free man, and we can be together here in Rome.

I am as always filled with love for you.

Your Luigi

————

Rome, September 23, 1981

My dearest Maria,
You and little Milo (what a cutie!) have just left, and I finally have peace to sit down and write these lines.

After I drove you to the airport—oh, how I hate saying goodbye at airports—I just drove around aimlessly. I had a Prosecco at Bar d'Oro, but without you it had no flavor.

Here at home I go from room to room and try to inhale your aroma, which so far still remains. And I lay on the bed and reexperienced the night. I know I must be content with being able to see you at all, the way the situation is, but the more I get from you, the stronger I want you! I feel whole with you.

Once again I want to ask for forgiveness for my aggressive reaction last evening. But hearing you say that I should see others, be with others, when all I want is to be with you, hurts me so much. I will live with and accept that you are married to another, but then you must accept that I don't go out and get married, but instead live for the times we can see each other.

Write to me soon, my love.

I am as always filled with love for you.

Your Luigi

————

Rome, February 20, 1994

My dearest Maria,

I've been watching TV from the Winter Olympics in Lillehammer, and it struck me that I've never asked if you ski now? In that case it's a sight I would really like to have seen. I am convinced that you would look spectacular in one of those skiing outfits!

I look forward to Easter, when you and Milo are coming here. To be sure, I'm a little worried that now he has gotten so big that we have to be very careful, because I don't know how I will manage keeping the necessary distance to you so as not to arouse his suspicions. I could not live with disturbing his stable upbringing with you and Endre. But hopefully it will all go well, and we'll have some nice weeks together.

Besides we have the days in Sardinia, when he'll be with *nonno* and *nonna*. I've already booked our room at the same hotel as last time.

Oh God, what I wouldn't give to hear your voice now! Or even better, feel your skin, your lips, your breasts, the warmth from you.

Write soon!

I am as always filled with love for you.

Your Luigi

_____

From: Benvolesenza, Luigi
Date: March 3, 2004
Subject:
To: Cavalli, Maria

I was almost unable to hang up when we talked a little while ago.

It was terrible to have to call you with the news, but I couldn't do it in a letter. I had to tell you. Forgive me for having ruined your day.

I will tell you when I know anything more.

But I don't like the darkness in your voice.

More than ever I need your love.

Yours forever,

Luigi

_____

From: Benvolesenza, Luigi
Date: September 28, 2005
Subject:
To: Cavalli, Maria

My very dearest,

This is only getting more and more difficult with every day.

The doctors don't give me much time, and I have started to reconcile myself with the thought.

I can't be anything but grateful for the life I have lived. I have cheated death and experienced a great love. What more can you ask for?

It's strange how the brain and subconscious work. The last few nights I have had a recurring nightmare about the shipwreck in 1977. I hear my comrades calling, and I dream that the waves are pulling me farther and farther away from you, and that I no longer have strength to do anything about it. I always wake up soaked with sweat—confused in my bed.

But the thing is that I never heard my comrades calling, and I don't remember anything from my time in the water. But it's as if my subconscious is asking me to remember.

I've tried not to think too much about what happened, but find myself thinking about it now. About things I think are strange. Such as that the radio telegrapher was not at his post. That Captain Marino, who was never concerned about regulations, came to the bridge wearing the correct life vest. That dinner was postponed for 45 minutes.

But I shouldn't bother you with my mental acrobatics. What means something, and which has always been most important, is that we got an opportunity to love each other after all. Even if it wasn't the way we thought when I proposed to you in Bologna. But maybe then we would have taken everything for granted? For doesn't victory taste sweeter when you have to work for it? Doesn't food taste better when you've worked properly with the raw materials? So isn't love better, if you have to struggle for it?

I look forward to your next visit, even if I fear it will be tough. You must be prepared that my body is in the process of being marked by the disease.

Full of love for you,

Your Luigi

———

From: Benvolesenza, Luigi
Date: April 3, 2006
Subject:
To: Cavalli, Maria

See you again my very dearest Maria.

Forgive me for my weaknesses.

    Remember me as who I was.

    I have always loved you.

    Your Luigi

MONDAY

43

Milo landed at Newark for the second time in just over a week, and less than an hour later he was sitting in a taxi.

He had one matter to finish up before he was ready to reconcile himself with the family history.

The windshield wiper struggled to keep the rain away, and the autumn leaves stuck to the asphalt.

Benedetti was already on the scene at the police station along with a detective Giordano, whom they were told simply to call Mike. He was just as heavy-set and glib as the TV parody of an American police detective dictates.

"Mailo Caveli? Huh? Where you from?"

"Norway and Italy."

"Cool. Ready to go get a bad guy?"

Milo smiled.

"I'm ready."

• • •

They drove in Mike's unmarked car, with two uniformed officers following them in a police car. The drive took less than fifteen minutes, and just before two thirty they parked in front of the Park View Retirement Home.

Mike greeted a man in a white doctor's coat and tie who showed them the way through the corridors. They zigzagged between shuffling elderly men and women, past rooms where the TV was on at maximum volume.

They came into a single room. It was sparsely furnished, with a TV, a bookcase with no books, and a bed made with a white crocheted cover.

At the window stood an elderly man with his hands behind his back.

"I saw you coming," he said without turning around.

"He's all yours," whispered Mike, letting Milo and Benedetti past him.

They introduced themselves, and the old man turned toward them. He was of medium height and slender as an old gym teacher. His beard stubble was gray and matched the cold eyes. He had on a pair of gray pants, checked shirt and wool jacket.

Mario Marino could have walked into any bar in any village whatsoever in Italy, and only drawn welcoming nods.

"What do you want?"

His voice was rough, and he talked with an obvious accent.

"We want to talk about the Corvette F541 that went down between Tunisia and Sicily on May 23, 1977," Milo replied.

The old man did not respond. His mouth was closed, almost clenched, and his eyes revealed no reaction. He was a man who let his face do the talking. Raised eyebrows, rolling eyes, a little smile which in various combinations expressed things like "I don't give a damn about what you're saying," "I don't know what you're talking about," and "you have no idea what you've gotten yourself into."

Milo held his gaze and continued.

"You were the captain on board."

Still no response. This was no surprise to Milo. What he had managed to find out about Mario Marino painted a picture of an unscrupulous, greedy man with a number of lives on his conscience.

"The ship went down between three and four o'clock in the morning, and a short time afterward you were picked up by your friends. Long before the Coast Guard was on the scene with boats and helicopters."

Marino still had his hands behind his back, and stared with contempt at Milo, who didn't care to wait for a comment from him. He felt himself getting furious simply by looking at the old man who stood there in front of him as if he owned the world.

"Two weeks later, on June sixth, you came to New Jersey. You came by sea, and immediately started on your new career. As a reliable employee for Tommy Galvano."

For the first time the eyes of the former military captain revealed uncertainty. Milo was sure that right now he was wondering how the hell this Norwegian policeman had unearthed his story.

It was when he had seen the letters and e-mails from Luigi to his mother and read about the captain that made him decide to dig into the case. First he had done his own research before he called his cousin.

"*Ma Milo, caro cugino.* But Milo, dear cousin. Do you know what you're asking?"

"Yes, and I wouldn't do it if it wasn't important. This captain is alive, I'm sure of it. And one way or another he has a link to the Mafia."

"Do you know how many Mario Marinos there are? There must be thousands. And surely he must have changed his name."

"There must be someone you can ask. This is a guy who must have acquired many enemies in the past thirty years," Milo had replied.

And Corrado delivered the goods. It turned out that Marino kept his name, and only adjusted his first name to the more American-sounding Marty instead of Mario. And Marty Marino had made himself extremely unpopular among several of the other four Mafia families who controlled New York along with the Galvano family. For one thing the Arradondo family was not very pleased with him after he beat up several prostitutes under their protection in the early 1980s, and a few years later he again pushed the limits by expanding the territory for the Galvano family's narcotics sales.

But this was not enough to incite reprisals against him. Instead Carlo Arradondo used the violations in negotiations with Tommy Galvano. In the end this was only about money anyway.

When Corrado via his contacts started requesting information about Marino, it was clear however that some saw their chance to express their gratitude. In less than a day they had the address of the nursing home and a brief history of what the former captain had done after he abandoned his ship and fled to the U.S.

"We have a complete overview of what you've done. There are plenty of people who will inform on you. What we are wondering is why you did it," said Milo.

The other man still said nothing.

"Why did you make sure the ship sank? And let your crew die?" Milo repeated.

But instead of answering, Marino turned toward the window again and stared out at the rain.

"It's fine. I know why," said Milo.

There could only be one answer to the question, and that was that the captain collaborated with the Mafia to let their boats with guns and narcotics pass. He recalled how Luigi referred to the captain as a person with an irresponsible attitude toward regulations. And if you combined that with greed, the path was short to settings where the cash flows were quick and illegal.

"Obviously we know everything about the contraband operation. But why that particular day? What happened?" Milo asked.

"He thinks he's a man of honor. But doesn't know he's a man of dishonor," said Benedetti with contempt in his voice.

They stood silently observing Marino.

"The radio telegrapher," he said suddenly.

Still with the rough voice.

"What do you mean?" asked Milo.

"The radio telegrapher heard a message he shouldn't have heard. About a delivery. I had to react quickly."

Milo thought about what Luigi had written. So he was right that something did not add up when he suddenly recalled that he had not seen the radio telegrapher before the explosion.

"So you killed him?"

But Marino did not answer. It wasn't necessary.

Milo continued. There was one more question he had to have an answer to. A question that was less dangerous for the former captain to answer.

"What did you think when you heard that Luigi Benevolesenza had survived?"

Marino breathed out heavily through his nostrils.

"I remember Benevolesenza. He didn't like me. I didn't like him," he answered.

"You were here in the U.S. when he suddenly came back," said Milo.

Marino nodded.

"That's right. It was too risky for me to go back, but we checked him out."

"Checked him out? What do you mean?"

The old man shrugged his shoulders. Milo thought about what Luigi had written about feeling watched.

"We let him live. His suspicions weren't strong enough. And it wouldn't have looked good if a national hero perished in an accident afterward," said Marino.

"Let him live?!" said Milo contemptuously.

The old captain turned around and stared coldly at Milo.

"Let him live, yes. That's the sort of thing we do. Decide who will live and who will die," he said while his jaw muscles clenched.

Milo had to control himself. He stared at the sinewy old man and understood how close Luigi had been to being liquidated after he came home from Tunisia.

At the same time it was sinking in that if the shipwreck had never happened, Luigi would have come back to Italy and married his mother. And the story of the Cavalli family would have been a different one.

"Cavalli?" said the old captain. It was as if he was savoring the name. "I think I remember a Cavalli from Sicily."

Milo did not answer, but he clenched his fists.

"He was older than me. Hung out with a cou[...]
boys. Errand boys for the bigger boys. Thought they [...]
tough in their big shoes and baggy pants."

Milo still said nothing.

"But then he disappeared."

Marino fixed his eyes on Milo.

"There were rumors that he had come across a cargo.
Which he sold at an unreal profit. And then he disappeared."

They stared at each other.

"Antonio. Antonio Cavalli was his name. Are you in the
family?"

Milo nodded.

"How did things actually work out for him?" asked Marino.

Not out of friendly curiosity, but more as a sadistic attempt
to poke at something sore.

Milo had a desire to raise his voice. Put the old man in his
place, as he tried to pull him—and his grandfather—down to
his level. But he controlled himself.

"Things went extremely well for Antonio Cavalli," he
replied.

Mario Marino straightened up a notch.

"Well then," he said.

Milo took a step backward to make room for Benedetti and
his questions. He had gotten the answers and the confirmation
he needed anyway. Now he knew that Luigi had been right, and
that both he and his mother had balanced on a knife edge.

The Italian policeman cleared his throat and shifted his
weight from one leg to the other.

"There was a Benedetti on board. He was on his last tour
with the Italian Navy before he was going to start his studies.
Vicenzo Benedetti was my brother," he said.

Milo could tell from his voice that he was concentrating on speaking as calmly as he could.

But Marino just stood and looked out the window, and did not turn to face the Italian policeman.

"I don't remember any Benedetti," he said in a tired voice.

Milo could see how the *commissario* clenched his hands, and thought that now it will happen. He'll lose control.

But instead he simply took a step closer, so that his mouth was only a few centimeters from the old man's ear.

"Then I'll make sure that this is a name you remember until the day you die, and still remember while you're burning in hell," he said.

Marino let out a little snort. He still had not understood what was about to happen.

"Mario Marino, you can look forward to a long, difficult public trial in Italy. These nice policemen in the doorway are here to arrest you before you are deported," said Benedetti.

Marino turned around abruptly. His eyes revealed that he had not even considered the possibility of having to stand trial for what he had done, he had gotten off so many times before.

"Arrested?"

Milo took a step toward him.

"Arrested, yes. That's the sort of thing guys like us do. Decide who'll be in prison, and who gets to stay outside the walls."

44

"Forgive me, Father, for I have sinned. It's been three weeks since my last confession."

"God have mercy on you so you can repent your sins and believe in His mercy. What do you want to talk about?"

"Do you think it's possible to love two people at the same time?"

"Love is a strong word. Should I understand it such that you . . . there are two that you . . ."

"I'm not just thinking about me. This is a kind of recurring theme in our family."

"I understand."

"But if love is too strong a word for you, do you think it's possible to feel deeply about two people at the same time?"

"I know it's possible, my son."

"You know? How is that?"

"I haven't always been a priest."

"Uh, but you haven't . . ."

"Do you really think I was firmly convinced about becoming a priest ever since I was sixteen years old?"

"No, but—"

"I was a student, age twenty-one. Studied economics, philosophy and history of religion. Well then, you don't need to say anything. A real mishmash, but that's the way I was at that time."

"I see."

"And I loved a woman. Or girl, if you will. One year younger. She was a charming girl. We met each other through the choir, and before long we were a couple. She studied nursing."

(Pause.)

"What happened?"

"We spent more and more time together. Studied together, ate together, went to the movies."

"And?"

"No, there was no 'and.' That was what we did. It was enough. And we were both believers, so we weren't in a hurry.

But gradually we started talking about a future together. Our families were beside themselves with enthusiasm. I . . ."

(Pause.)

"Yes?"

"I was probably not quite ready for that. I was very fond of her. No doubt about that. But something held me back. The summer I turned twenty-three, I worked at a camp for the disabled. She was going to work as a home-care nurse in her hometown. We would be away from each other for two months."

"Distance is a bitch."

"Amen to that. Well, at this place there was another woman. Not a girl, but a woman. A twenty-seven-year-old psychologist who had recently graduated. I fell hard. I still think I have sore knees. Not because of the fall, but the way she dragged me behind her."

"Ha! Incredible. What happened?"

"I was completely befuddled. I fell in love, and she knew it. And she enjoyed it."

"Of course."

"After two months I was worn out. And when my girlfriend came there, she realized that something was wrong. We talked the whole evening and far into the night. She took it well."

"What did she say?"

"She gave me time to figure things out."

"What about the psychologist?"

"She said she had fallen in love with me."

"So what did you do?"

"I took a time-out. There was a third one I also loved."

"What?! Who?"

"Jesus. The incarnation of God here on earth."

"I see."

"I went to France. My excuse was studies in history of religion, but in reality I was retreating. To a cloister in the south of France."

"And how was that?"

"Like coming home."

"But you loved two women?"

"I felt strong affection for them. But I loved God. That became my path."

"You ran away?"

"Well. The Buddhists put it so nicely when they commit to following their path and faith. They talk about 'seeking refuge.' I don't think I ran away, but it was a form of refuge."

"What did the two women say?"

"The nursing student was very sad, but respected my decision. She's married now with two children, and I baptized the oldest one. The psychologist is divorced for the second time and works as a relationship therapist."

"Of course she does. But how did you know what to choose?"

"I just knew. I had a calling."

"That simple?"

"I wouldn't call it simple. It was the most difficult decision of my life. At the same time as it was almost a given."

"But don't you think it's a bit strange? I mean, if it was God's plan the whole time, why did he let you go through this?"

"To understand. You and others. Understand what you experience and be able to relate to it. I know what love is. I'm familiar with impossible choices."

"And the solution is that I should enter a cloister, Father?"

"Ha, ha!"

"Because I think I'm going to disappoint you. I'm not monk material."

"That's fine. But who are these two girls? Or women?"

"One is a little younger than me. Theresa. She's Italian, charming and somehow or other she's become a part of me. We've grown together. She's loyal and the one person in the world it's most natural for me to be with. There is a feeling of belonging."

"And the other?"

"She's the same age as me. Kathrin. Swedish. An amazing woman. Intelligent and challenging, and completely impossible to stop thinking about. I'm strongly attracted to her."

"Belonging versus attraction, in other words."

"Yes, maybe you can put it like that."

"And what does your heart say?"

"Everything and nothing."

"Exactly. So what will you do?"

"Not what you did, anyway."

"What do you mean?"

"You ran away. Chose neither of them."

"So you will choose one of them."

"So far I'm choosing both."

"That sounds risky, my son."

"With all due respect, Father, no riskier than your choice."

"No, perhaps you have a point. So what will you do now?"

"Go to the airport."

"And where will you go first?"

"I don't know. I haven't bought a ticket yet."

"But you're leaving?"

"I'm leaving."

"And you're coming back?"

"I'm coming back."

"Good, my son. The peace of God."

"The peace of God, Father."

The gray November rain would soon turn into November sleet, but then he wasn't going to be there. The phone had not stopped ringing the past few days, and he had not objected to the imposed leave. Both Norwegian and Italian journalists wanted a piece of him.

He thought about the court session a few days earlier. How attorney Lehman waltzed over UNE in court and had the deportation of Oriana provisionally halted. And he remembered how Oriana, during Lehman's verbal attack on UNE, word by word had straightened her back and dared to meet the eyes of the judges. While the in-house attorney for UNE had become steadily more stoop shouldered, and occupied by the papers on the table in front of him.

Sørensen would be seeing Sigurd Tollefsen later that day. Finally the father would find out what actually happened to his children. His son, who had not fallen into bad company, but who had confronted his teacher and warned the gym that they were being pushed steroids and growth hormones. His daughter, who had uncovered the research manipulations, and been silenced by people who wanted to save their own hides. Ingrid and Tormod Tollefsen both stood up against the injustice they saw, and Milo hoped Sigurd Tollefsen at least found some consolation in that.

Personally, Milo had enough of his own. And his own thoughts.

He wound the scarf well around his neck and buttoned up his topcoat.

On the other side of the street carefree youngsters were running around the school yard at St. Sunniva. Their shouts ricocheted between the walls.

Milo went out on Akersveien. Behind him he heard a door open, and he turned around automatically. The priest came out and lit a cigarette. He caught sight of Milo, and they nodded silently to each other.

Milo could not bear to talk with him about his mother. About the fact that he was a result of a plan that had gone wrong. He could have told the priest that everything felt accidental, that coincidences governed our lives, but he knew that the priest would have responded by talking about God's plan.

There was also another reason he did not drill deeper into that. It was time to let his mother rest. Not everything was appropriate to discuss with strangers. No matter how great an obligation of confidentiality they had.

There was a reason they were called family secrets.

He did not expect anyone else to understand.

It was enough if he did.

He turned left up Akersveien. His car was parked by the St. Olav bookstore, and he got in without starting the engine. The rain was drumming on the roof, and he stared at the slate-gray sky.

He remembered something he had overheard his grandfather say once in Sardinia. Antonio and Maria had been discussing Uncle Marco's indecisiveness in relation to something or other. Maria had been irritated, while his grandfather smiled indulgently.

"*In caso di dubbio, mio caro, non fare nulla.*" When you are in doubt, my dear, do nothing.

It was Leo Tolstoy who put these words in the mouth of

General Kutuzov, during the Napoleonic wars. And his grandfather had taken it as one of his rules of life.

But it was not a war Milo was fighting. He was only faced with a decision.

And regardless he was bad at doing nothing.

He glanced at the backseat to assure himself that his luggage was there. Then he started the engine and let the windshield wipers remove the raindrops.

He used the turn signal and left the parking space, setting a course for the airport at Gardermoen.

He could buy a ticket when he got there.

FOR FURTHER READING

About the pharmaceutical industry

Angell, Marcia. *The Truth About the Drug Companies: How They Deceive Us and What to Do About It* (Random House, 2004)

Elliott, Carl. *White Coat, Black Hat: Adventures on the Dark Side of Medicine* (Beacon Press, 2010)

Hawthorne, Fran. *The Merck Druggernaut: The Inside Story of a Pharmaceutical Giant* (Wiley, 2005)

About economics and finance

Chang, Ha-Joon. *23 Things They Don't Tell You About Capitalism* (Bloomsbury Press, 2010)

Reinert, Erik S. *How Rich Countries Got Rich and Why Poor Countries Stay Poor* (Constable, 2007)

About Catholicism

Pasco, Rowanne. *Svar på 101 spørsmål om den katolske kirkes katekisme* (Answers to 101 Questions about the Catechism of the Catholic Church)